SoWest:
Desert Justice

SoWest: Desert Justice

Twenty original southwestern tales from the
Sisters in Crime Desert Sleuths Chapter

DS Publishing
Scottsdale, Arizona

DEDICATION

To the law enforcers who catch the criminals we love to write about. We honor you.

ACKNOWLEDGMENTS

The Sisters in Crime Desert Sleuths Chapter membership wishes to recognize those individuals whose contributions made this volume a reality. Huge thanks go out to:

Deborah J Ledford, for her tireless efforts as lead editor. Co-editors Nancy McCurry, Susan Budavari, Sally J. Smith and Berkley Bosch for their dedication and hard work, and Virginia Nosky for her line-editing prowess.

Marty Roselius for yet another fantastic cover design, and to Jessica McCown for the generous contribution of the background photograph.

Isabella Maldonado, retired Special Investigation and Forensic Division Commander, Fairfax County Police, and retired Detective Sallie Dillian, Phoenix Police Department, for their insight on law enforcement elements.

Acclaimed authors: Margaret Maron, Kelli Stanley, Libby Fischer Hellman and Jenn McKinlay, for very fine endorsements.

The worldwide network of our Sisters in Crime for their unfailing support.

And to the contributing authors, whose words made this anthology possible.

TABLE OF CONTENTS

TABLE OF CONTENTS

LUCKY ME
SHANNON BAKER

The ledge couldn't have been more than two feet wide.

The mid-morning sun seared the side of the canyon, heating up what little air stirred to a blast furnace of over one hundred degrees. We'd all dipped our shirts and wide-brimmed hats into the river before we started up the trail, but still we couldn't escape the brutal assault.

Everyone except Julie. Her blue cotton shirt, despite multiple dunkings, still looked hanger-fresh even after three days on the river. Her hat shielded her face, which didn't show any flush from the climb or the fierce heat of the Grand Canyon in June. But then, why would it?

Because of her delicate frame and generally weak constitution, I'd been carrying her pack, making our camp, fetching her food and pampering her on this Colorado River trip. Even now, with so much on my mind, my feet throbbed from the hammer toes I'd earned carrying both of our backpacks on the steep six-mile descent of Bright Angel trail to join the boats at the Colorado River. I hoped she'd enjoyed being queen because her reign was about to come to an end.

We shimmied along the ledge, the last in the group of six on our way to experience Thunder River where water gushes from sheer rock several miles up a side canyon. This opportunity was the whole reason I insisted we book this vacation. I told Julie I always wanted to take a rafting trip down the Colorado River through the Grand Canyon but could never afford it. Now we could afford this and so much more.

Julie had resisted, complained about not liking to sleep on the ground, the dirt, the heat, the bugs. In the end, she couldn't deny me this once in a lifetime opportunity and said yes, as she always did.

The river guide, a young buck named Doobie, who also pulled double duty as our hiking leader, slipped around a bend, followed by the others. Perfect.

Julie inched along the ledge, composure cracking and tears glistening in her scared eyes. She turned to me. "I don't think I can do this, Tom."

I gave her that brave, strong, protector face, the one that used to make me feel confident and manly but now burned in my gullet. "You're doing great, Jules. It's just a little farther."

A pebble skittered from under her foot and cascaded down the ledge, careening into razor-sharp rocks until it plopped into the creek bed fifty feet below. Exactly what I had planned for Julie. A tiny squeak of alarm squeezed from her white lips.

"I'm sorry to put you through this," I said in my most sympathetic voice, "but I've read about Thunder River and it's supposed to be amazing. Doobie said this is the worst part of the trail."

She managed a weak smile through trembling lips.

My heart thundered louder than any river rapids as I waited for the perfect moment. "Take my hand, Julie. We'll do it together."

Simple, trusting fool put her little hand into my strong, capable one. A step or two later I stumbled. Sure-footed, athletic, the perfect specimen of a thirty-year-old man, somehow I lost my footing. Accidents happen.

My arm jerked in a reflex to regain my balance, "accidently" shoving Julie at the same time. Helpless Julie. They'd all say she tripped and I tried to save her. They'd say, "She should never have come on this physically challenging trip." And I'd reply, "She only did it to please me." I'd cry and they'd all see how devoted I was to her. Poor Julie. "She was so young and beautiful."

But something backfired. Instead of the scenario playing out with Julie's tragic death as I'd planned, my feet slipped. Her weight against my hand tugged more than I'd bargained for. I tried to let go, but in her panic she held on with a grip far stronger than I'd have thought possible. If it hadn't been for my damaged toes, I might have been able to get my balance but it all worked against me.

Airborne for several seconds, I suddenly landed, smashed my knee on slick rock and wrenched my shoulder on the next bounce. The red walls of the canyon bared their claws and punctured and scraped my skin, tearing at me like a vegetable peeler on a potato. Sixty feet of this would leave me with nothing to soften the blow if I smashed onto the sharp rocks at the bottom.

I managed to grab at a hostile, thorny agave just before tumbling to certain death, the exact fate I planned for Julie. I lay panting on a slim ledge, moaning and wondering how many bones I'd broken.

The others on the trip acted more gracious than I would have expected. They gave up their once in a lifetime chance to see Thunder River to collect me and carry me down to the rafts. Nothing broken, they propped me up and gave me some ibuprofen.

That night Julie set up our camp and brought me dinner. Heat from the rock walls of the canyon pulsed against us as we lay under a sheet dampened in the river.

She kissed my forehead with the softness of a butterfly. It felt more like a fly laying eggs that would turn to maggots. I had to get rid of her. Only a few more days on the river left and here I lay, a pile of bruises and mangled flesh.

Her annoying tears of guilt sparkled in the moonlight. "I'm sorry. I'm such a klutz. You tried to save me and look at you. You're my knight in shining armor."

Julie held my hand in the darkness. "I wish we'd never come on this stupid trip. I can't wait to get home to a bed with clean sheets. I've been thinking about the new house."

The new house. The mansion that eats up five million of the ten we won six months ago in the lottery. The remaining funds will surely disappear in furniture and landscaping. Ten million dollars. Julie's always been lucky. But ten million is taking lucky to a whole new level. Julie wants to spend it all on a house in the swankiest section of Flagstaff. She's picked out the lot, all dotted with pines, nestled among the other multimillion dollar homes. A damned cage.

Ten million dollars should be freedom. That's what it would be for me, once I got rid of Julie.

Two days later, contemplating removing my blackened and throbbing toenails, covered in scabs and grimacing in pain every time I drew a breath, I listened as Doobie explained the technique of riding a rapid. It might seem crazy to dive into a wild river for the thrill of cascading with the waves but this was my aquatic gift. He said we needed to jump behind the raft, let the rapids carry us along and at a certain point, swim with all our strength to shore.

Julie paled. "I'll ride in the raft with Doobie."

"Oh, come on, Jules." I gave her my most boyish grin. "It'll be fun. When are you ever going to ride a rapid like this again?"

"Will you promise to be by my side?" She whined. "You won't let me out of your sight?"

I hugged her tight despite my many injuries. It hurt but what's a little pain compared to ten million clams? "I won't let anything happen to you. I love you."

Pudgy Donna sat across the raft from us. Her last child graduated from high school a month before and was off to some southern university—I knew this and so much more because Julie and Donna clucked back and forth every mile of the river trip. She punched her equally soft husband in the arm. "Let's ride the rapid, Bill."

He might have used English in his reply but all I heard was a growl.

She reacted as if he were a wasp with a nasty sting and exchanged one of those indecipherable looks with Julie. "You're lucky to have Tom. You have so much fun together."

"That's what I love about Jules," I said. "She's always ready for adventure."

Julie forced a brave smile and I kissed her cold lips to seal the deal. We moved to the back of the raft on either side of Doobie, who held fast to the rudder. He grinned a Scooby-doo expression and yelled, "Now!"

I held Julie's hand and we jumped into the icy river together. The water smacked me with surprising force. It felt like hurling into an avalanche thundering down a steep mountainside. Hard, frigid, deadly. A wave crashed over my head, driving me under water. Something sucked at my feet, pulling me deeper. I tilted my head toward the sky but couldn't see daylight. Air pushed from my lungs.

My life jacket managed to buoy me just enough to gasp a mouthful of air. And there was Julie. She screamed, terror laced across her white face and blue lips. She reached for me.

I couldn't let this chance pass by. Despite my own rising panic, I knew I only had to hold her under for a brief time and she'd lose her air. The cold would take hold and Julie—the love of my life, the partner I'd planned on growing old with, the woman who would bear my children and strangle the very life from my body—would meet her tragic and untimely death.

I reached out and she latched onto me. Before I could get another breath or kick to a position of power, her raging hysteria overtook us both. I went down. I kicked and struggled but the current grabbed me. Julie clung to me and in the fight for survival, she somehow loosened my life jacket. The damned thing slipped up under my arms. The neck opened, swallowing my nose and mouth. I couldn't get air!

Julie let go, probably pulled away by the raging current. I kicked but the current at the river bottom sucked my legs and pulled me down. Black dots fuzzed around the edges of my head. My arms and legs grew sluggish with the cold. I...kicked...stroked...saw the fading light of day through two feet of water...

Something clamped onto my jacket and yanked me from the river. A jerk and toss and I landed on the bottom of the raft. Doobie stood above me, dripping, his lean hairy legs balancing him on the rocking boat, his bulging pecs flexed with the effort of yanking me from the river. He grinned. "Welcome back, Tom-tom! We thought you were a goner!"

River guides are pretty good actors. For all their goofiness and laid-back demeanor, they really have to know their stuff to take amateurs on this wild river and keep them alive.

After that, Julie insisted we stay in camp or on the rafts while the others hiked off to see Havasupai Falls and ancient pictographs. Her chatter nearly drove me to drop the pretense and bludgeon her outright. How could anyone talk so much and say so little? She rattled on about her two older sisters and her parents who lived in New York. I'd never met these people. Couldn't be sure they existed except when I paid the cell phone bill.

Why shouldn't she spend hours on the phone though? She didn't work. Hadn't worked since the evening I met her waiting tables in a smelly college bar in downtown Flagstaff. Could that have been only two years ago? She had, and still has, a killer body, with legs that don't quit, and a nice pair of tits, even if they aren't huge. Tight, firm, and ready to play. She told me she'd just moved to town and didn't have any friends or family around. She didn't even finish her shift that night.

I sold insurance and did a pretty good job of it. At first I didn't mind supporting her. But a little help with the expenses wouldn't hurt. She could at least get a part time job. She cooked and cleaned at home, and since she was a tiger between the sheets, I thought maybe she was worth it.

Until her little-girl voice started to rub against my brain like a mental hangnail. She had nothing between her ears. And while what was between her legs once seemed gourmet, even a constant diet of lobster could get old. I was on my way home from the office to break the news I wanted a divorce when she called and said she'd won the lottery.

As a spouse, I'm entitled to half that money. As a widower, I get it all.

We only had two days left on the river. Doobie and the other guides had been scaring us about Lava Falls from the first day of the trip. This gnarly rapid had claimed more than a few lives and even the most seasoned river rats respected its power. The morning briefing included a replica of the rapid built into the river bank sand.

"Whatever you do," Doobie ended with, "stay in the boat. Make sure your feet are secure in the foot straps and brace yourselves. But, dudes, you got to paddle when I say or we'll get caught in an eddy and that'll be all she wrote. Remember, I'll call for one or two strokes on either the right or left. Figure out what side of the boat you're on."

Julie bit her lower lip and trembled.

Doobie maneuvered the rock representing our raft through the hills and troughs he'd built for Lava Falls. "Right here, we're gonna hit the mother of all rapids. See how this wave," his hand cupped over the boat/rock, "will come right over the top. I'm gonna tell you to dive. That means I want you all to get in the bottom of the boat, as close to the middle as possible. And bros and sistas, you gotta dive. We're gonna shoot right through this wave."

Julie gasped.

Doobie grinned. "It's intense. When I yell for a stroke, you got to dig your paddle into the river with everything you got. No time for lilly-dippers, ladies and gents. But dudes, stay in the boat. No matter what. The river does not forgive stupidity, man."

I put my arm around Julie. "This is the last thing. After this, it's smooth water."

She nodded, too terrified to speak.

"You get our life jackets. I'll fill the water bottles." I picked up her pink water bottle, bought specifically for this trip, matching all the other gear she'd purchased. My dented metal bottle had seen its share of outdoor adventures but with any luck, this would be its last.

I got in line with the others and made sure they saw me scoop powdered Gatorade into Julie's bottle and fill it with water.

Donna shook her bottle to dissolve the powder. "You and Julie are a really great couple."

I lowered my head and shrugged as if embarrassed. "She's a terrific woman. I'm really lucky to have her."

I sauntered down the bank as if I needed to pee. Just around the bend I dropped to my knees and packed my own bottle full of sand.

"Tom?" Julie came around the corner just as I twisted the top onto my bottle. "There you are."

I tried to swagger to her, give her that last flash of dashing young husband and protector before she slept with the fishes. But because of the missing toenails, the scoured flesh, and the back that would require traction, my stride was more like limping. "Thanks for coming on the trip. I know roughing it isn't your favorite thing."

She looked into my eyes, her devotion radiating. "It's almost over."

After a couple of hours drifting on quiet water, Doobie stirred. He clamped his dopey beat-up straw hat onto his head with a drawstring. "This is it, dudes."

The roar of Lava Falls sent a shudder through me like the swell of music in a horror film. I bent over to check Julie's feet and make sure they fit securely in the straps at the bottom of the raft. I tightened her life jacket and gave her a lingering kiss.

Donna watched me lavish this care with a wistful glance.

"Two, left!" Doobie's shout above the freight-train of water sent a wave of fear through the small raft.

We plunged our paddles and gave him what he demanded. The water surged around us, buffeting the rubber floor of the raft, rocketing us forward into a gauntlet of sharp rocks, white, frothy mountains of icy river attacking us. A lone body in this would be like a single sock in the devil's washing machine. A lone body would disappear. At the very least, it would turn up with holes ripped through it. Poor Julie.

We rolled and bounced, reacting to orders, adrenaline coursing through us like the river through the narrow canyon.

"Dive!" Doobie screamed. Gone was the pot-headed good time hippy. Doobie was dead serious.

I slid off the side of the raft into the bottom and huddled close to the center loaded with dry bags tied so securely they'd probably come through the Apocalypse intact. As I landed on my knees I reached forward. My fingers closed around Julie's slim ankle.

Water rushed over our heads, drenching everything, blinding us. The roar of the river mixed with shouts and screams created a chaos of confusion.

I jerked Julie's ankle, freeing her foot from the strap at the bottom of the raft. She sailed upward with the buck of the raft as we hit another wave.

I'll never know how I kept my head in the midst of all the lurching, the water and swirl of color and sound. It was the single most focused moment of my life. Freedom, affluent freedom, depended on this last burst of courage. One more foot freed from the straps and she'd fly from the boat. But just in case her luck might help her survive Lava Falls, I had a back-up plan.

I reached her secured foot and yanked it free. At the same time I grabbed the sand-filled water bottle.

Julie probably screamed but all I heard was water crashing against jagged rocks. Rocks that would soon shred my beloved.

She turned and clutched at me, her body flying up from where she'd wedged herself. Her desperate hold on me was the only thing keeping her from the angry torrent of the river.

"Two, left! Dig! Dig!" Doobie screamed.

Julie and I struggled on the right, and everyone else was busy getting up from the dive and back to paddling, so I knew I had no witnesses. I lifted the bottle. A blow to the forehead would look like she crashed headlong into a rock. Which might happen without my help. But I wasn't taking any chances.

I swung the bottle forward but she dropped to the bottom of the boat. Both of my feet jerked from the straps. Julie propelled herself up and into a deadly embrace, lunging at me.

We hit a trough. The boat dropped ten feet and Julie and I, a package of fragile flesh and bones, flipped off the back.

We blasted into the water, diving and tumbling, scraping against something so sharp it felt as if it sheared off my left leg. I fought against Julie but her panic gave her the strength of Schwarzenegger.

I didn't know if I faced up or down. I swirled in water so cold I couldn't breathe. She wouldn't let me go. No air.

Together we bounced from one jagged rock into another. Finally I understood down from up and could make out a glow of light from what must be the sky. We closed in on the surface. My lungs burned.

But my life vest slipped up around my ears. How could that be? I'd tightened it before Lava.

Just before Julie had clutched at me.

We rode a wave down and I pulled my head back, gasping for a taste of air. Julie held me, pushing down on my shoulders and thrusting her head from the water.

In the moment she sucked in a breath, I kicked with all my desire to live. She loosened her grip. With another massive kick I tilted my face and forced my mouth above the water, gulping in as much water as air.

It was enough to allow me to live. If that meant letting Julie live, too, I was willing to do that. I could divorce her, let her keep the money. Just let me out of this river alive.

We careened into another rock, cracking the base of my skull. Of course, as in every situation since we'd been together, I took the shock of the hit and Julie, still clinging to me, floated along for the ride.

The water started to calm. I'd survived. It would be all right. The life jacket made getting breath a struggle but I managed to pull my head up. I looked into Julie's eyes. She really was a beautiful woman. She loved me and made my home a welcoming place. She needed me and made me feel like a man. I could do a lot worse.

This trip and my brush with death was my wake up call to put my life in perspective. I loved Julie.

I almost smiled then.

Right before she brought the water bottle crashing into my skull.

✝   ✝   ✝

From my prone position I can't see the whole room. There aren't many people here, just Julie and what must be her family. She's standing above me, lovely in her classic black dress, despite the faint bruises on her face.

She dabs at her eyes. "He was so handsome and brave."

The other woman—a sister?—gazes down at me. "Too bad he smashed his forehead into a rock."

Julie sniffs and dabs. "What will I do without him?"

The sister shows no sympathy. "It's a tragedy, of course. But why would he go on a trip like this and try to keep up with you?"

Julie pastes on a sad smile. "He was competitive."

The sister shakes her head. "It may have been four years since you last ran the river, but you're still one of the best river guides on the Colorado."

I can't be sure, but just before they close the lid, I swear Julie winks at me.

✝   ✝   ✝

A lover of the West, **SHANNON BAKER** can often be found backpacking, skiing, kayaking, cycling or just playing lizard in the desert. From the Colorado Rockies to the Nebraska Sandhills, the peaks of Flagstaff and the deserts of Tucson, landscapes (and murder) play an important role in her books. Her first thriller, *Ashes of the Red Heifer*, is available in trade paperback and e-books at your favorite online bookseller. The first book in her Nora Abbott mystery series, *Tainted Mountain*, will be available in early 2013 from Midnight Ink.

TOTALED RECALL
SUSAN BUDAVARI

Just as Kenny Connell started down the stairs of his Scottsdale home, the phone rang. His wife, Mara, rushed to answer it. He knew she expected an important call from her doctor and tuned his ears to her conversation.

"Hello. Yes, Dr. Tabor." She listened for a moment, crinkled her brow then sat down on the bottom step. "I understand...Aha, aha." She looked up at Kenny, shook her head and mouthed, "Not good." After several more moments, she said, "Okay, I'll be at your office, eight A.M. tomorrow. Thank you, Doctor."

Mara hung up and covered her eyes with her hands. A few tears dropped down her cheeks.

Kenny hovered near her. His pulse quickened. "What did Tabor say?"

She slowly raised her head. "My MRI and blood tests came back normal, so that rules out the usual things." She took a breath. "I have to face it. I could be in the early stages of Huntington's...what my father had."

"But Tabor's not sure? Just wait until we hear what he says before you assume the worst."

Mara nodded and stood. "You're right. Nothing's certain yet." He hugged her. She broke the embrace. "If things start to go bad, I won't allow myself to go through what my dad did. I'll—"

He raised his hand, urging her to stop. "Let's not go there."

"Agreed. No sense dwelling on this." She picked up her purse, reached in for an envelope and held it up. "Second recall notice on the Mercedes. I better not take chances." She snickered then glanced at her watch. "Have to hurry. I'm due at the car dealership on Camelback."

"I'm going to reschedule. I can take your car in next week."

Mara set her bag on the entry table. "Okay. It's waited this long. Next week will be fine."

"Why don't you call one of your friends and have lunch?

Take your mind off things."

"Nah. I'd rather spend today at home. But thanks for the thought. I feel drained. I'm going to lie down for a while."

When Mara went up to the bedroom, he retreated to his office and closed the door. He punched a number into his cell phone. "There's no way I can tell Mara today. She just got bad news from her doctor. I can't do that to her."

The next morning, when she and Kenny entered Dr. Tabor's office, Mara's hands trembled. The nurse weighed her, took her pulse and blood pressure, then paged the doctor. Mara and Kenny sat in adjacent chairs at the doctor's desk, hands entwined.

Her heart thumped when Dr. Tabor walked into the room holding a thick folder and mumbling something about wonderful April weather in the Valley and the East Coast buried in snow. He shook her hand and Kenny's, then took a seat behind his desk. After flipping through the folder, he put it down and made eye contact with Mara. "How are you doing?"

"Not too bad, under the circumstances."

He brought up Mara's medical record on his computer. "Let me just review a few things then we'll talk." He scrolled down the screen, looking through her test results. "I know you've met with the genetic counselor. What have you decided about getting tested for the Huntington's gene?"

"I've given it a lot of thought." *Especially at night, when I stare out the bedroom window at the desert sky.* "I hadn't wanted to do it earlier, but now that I'm thirty-seven, I guess the time has come."

"Okay, my nurse will draw your blood when we finish up here."

"How long will it take to get the results?"

"A few weeks. We have to send it out to a special lab."

"If I do have this disease, what will my first signs be?" She swallowed. "I can't even remember what my dad was like at the beginning, only how awful things were at the end. Of course, since he was adopted and had no idea about his family medical history, it took a long time for the doctors to figure out what was wrong with him."

Tabor rubbed his chin. "Mara, I want to preface everything by saying we don't even know yet if you carry the gene."

"But if I am a carrier, what do I have to look forward to?" Mara's body slumped. "How much time do I have?" Her thoughts drifted to her father's final days and to the toll it took on her mother.

Tabor moved his glance from Mara to Kenny and then back to her. "Mara, it's impossible to know exactly what symptoms you will have, but generally, people who carry the gene for Huntington's will start having symptoms in their thirties or forties. Usually, behavior changes occur before movement disorders."

"What kind of behavior changes?" She took care to control her voice.

"Well," the doctor began, "in the early stages patients can be moody, irritable, and have memory loss or loss of judgment, and sometimes hallucinations, paranoia or psychosis. Usually movement problems like unsteady gait or falls come later. As the disease progresses, patients can have slow, uncontrolled movements known as 'chorea,' with intermittent quick, jerking of the arms, legs or other body parts. But these changes sometimes happen over a period as long as fifteen years after symptoms first appear."

"My father progressed much more quickly. And I know there is no way to stop Huntington's from getting worse."

Tabor stood and came around the desk. He placed his hand on her arm. "Mara, let's wait for the results of the gene testing. In any event, we'll monitor you closely and take good care of you."

After dropping Mara at the house, Kenny drove to work. When his cell phone rang, he checked the caller ID before answering. "Hi," he said. "I just got back from Mara's doctor. I can't tell her about us right now, not with her being so worried about her health. Baby, I have to be supportive. We'll need to be patient."

"How long did he say she has?"

"He's not sure."

"I see." With measured words, the woman on the other end of the line said, "Tell me a little more about this disease. I've never heard of it."

After Kenny left, Mara changed into sweats and took a long nap in the downstairs guest bedroom. The doorbell chime woke her. She yawned as she walked to the door, then looked out the peephole.

Her friend, Crystal, dressed in a colorful print tunic and white pants, stood on the landing surveying the lush desert landscaping in the front yard. At thirty-eight Crystal worked hard to maintain her slender figure and stay fit. A recent foot injury from a bike accident had her wearing custom-made, laced shoes to avoid limping. Crystal complained daily that the shoes ruined her outfits.

Mara opened the door. Crystal gave her a quick hug then stepped back and gestured toward the yard. "I was admiring your bougainvillea, the gorgeous lantana and the red cactus blooms. It must take a lot of watering to keep them in such grand shape." She wrinkled her nose at Mara's sweats. "Sweetie, don't tell me you're wearing those to the Biltmore."

"Huh? No...What?"

"Better change quickly. Our reservation is in thirty minutes. We've got to boogie."

"What reservation?" Mara rubbed her eyes.

"You're kidding, right? Did you forget? Desert Shrimp Cobb Salad. Champagne. Biltmore terrace." She stopped and took a deep breath. "We set this up a month ago." Crystal folded her arms. "Oh, come on, you're not trying to weasel out of going to lunch, are you?"

Mara realized her mouth was hanging open. She shut it.

Realization dawned on Crystal's face. "You really forgot, didn't you?"

"I'm a bit dazed. Just woke from a nap. Give me five. I'll run and change."

"Oh, poor dear." Then a big smile. "Too much partying last night?"

"I wish."

The lunch with Crystal turned out to be fun although Mara worried about not remembering their plans. She had to admit she hadn't been herself lately with all the uncertainty surrounding her health.

When Kenny arrived home from work, Mara stood at the center island of their alder wood gourmet kitchen slicing tomatoes for dinner. She wiped her hands and hugged him.

"How was your day?"

"Not the best." In a very soft voice he said, "I'm sorry, honey. I'll have to go to Las Vegas on Monday to fill in for Tom. His wife gave birth this morning, two weeks early. The boss wants someone senior to take over Tom's project." He reached for her hand. "Will you be okay?"

"Do you have to go? It's not the best time for me to be alone." With a sigh, she added, "Oh, don't worry, I'll manage."

Kenny's warm brown eyes sparkled. "Come with me. It can be a mini-vacation for us."

She shook her head. "You'll be tied up day and night. I'll hardly see you. If I'm going to be alone, I'd rather be here."

"Call your sister to come out. I'll spring for her airfare."

Mara thought for a minute. "No, it wouldn't be fair to ask her. Not enough notice—her kids, her job. I intend to call her, though. She needs to know what's happening with me." *I want her to have my Medical Power of Attorney.*

Kenny nodded. He grabbed a beer bottle from the refrigerator and took a swallow. "What about Steph, Bebe or Crystal? Couldn't one of them stay with you at night?"

"Let me think about it." She didn't want to deal with their questions about her health, or endure a pity party.

The phone rang while Kenny and Mara watched TV that evening. He jumped up to answer it.

"Hi Kenny. It's Steph. Just calling to razz Mara for not inviting me to the champagne lunch she and Crystal had today."

"Word travels fast." He chuckled. "Yeah, it seems they had a great time. It was good for her."

"I know she's going through a rough period. Is there any way I can help?"

"Funny you should ask." He cupped the phone, lowered his voice and told Mara's friend about his concern over leaving Mara alone while he worked in Vegas.

"Don't say another word," Steph said when he'd finished. "I'll take care of it, and recruit Bebe and Crystal too. Mara won't be alone a single minute you're away."

"Perfect," he said. "Better if you tell Mara. I don't want her to think I'm overly worried about her."

"Leave it to me."

He covered the mouthpiece and called out, "It's Steph."

When Mara hung up, she rejoined Kenny on the sofa. "Did you ask Steph to stay with me next week?"

"Actually, she volunteered when I mentioned I had to go to Vegas."

"Why on earth did you tell her?"

Kenny shrugged. "Dunno. It just slipped out." He put his arm around her shoulders and pulled her to him. "I thought you'd be pleased. Solves the problem of your staying alone."

Mara nodded. "Then you'll be happy. I've accepted her offer."

† † †

In recent weeks, Mara reflected on her life and the people closest to her.

Due to her father's medical history, she and Kenny had decided against having children. She loved kids and her work as an early education specialist kept her around them, but since turning thirty-five two years ago and gaining access to her share of a multi-million dollar trust fund from her mother, she hadn't worked much. She missed it.

None of her best friends held full-time jobs either, but all enjoyed a comfortable lifestyle. Steph and Crystal were divorced; Bebe had never married. Steph shared custody of her seven-year-old son with her ex, a wealthy industrialist who had given her a generous settlement. Crystal avoided talking finances so Mara didn't really know the source of her income. Bebe spent money as though she had plenty but drove a ten-year-old car she pampered. Mara kidded Bebe that if she, Mara, ever got run over by a bus, her Mercedes had better go to Bebe.

On the other hand, Kenny worked long hours as a mid-level computer specialist for a nationwide firm. His salary paid the household expenses. Mara had provided the house, a four-bedroom, two-story Santa Barbara with high ceilings and travertine floors. Situated on over an acre in North Scottsdale, it was surrounded by date palms and extensive desert landscaping.

He and Mara had a prenup, the terms of which became more favorable to Kenny now that they'd been married fifteen years. Mara suspected that he had strayed occasionally, mostly while away on business for extended periods of time, but they were still together as a couple. She marveled that while their relationship might not be as passionate as it once was, Kenny was supportive in ways that mattered. And with his seniority in the firm and web conferencing, he rarely traveled these days. While it would be fun to spend a few days with her girlfriends, she would truly miss her husband.

Sunday evening, Mara and her three friends gathered at her house, sipped wine in the living room and giggled while they planned activities for the following week.

Crystal's face beamed with excitement. "It'll be like high school—party all the time, and sleepovers."

Bebe piped in, "I vote for some culture, like the Hopi Kachina Doll exhibit at the Heard Museum, with lunch in the café, of course. Or that new French film at the Camelview."

After a while, Mara relaxed. Her friends viewed keeping her company while Kenny was away as a fun-filled project. After several glasses of wine, Mara even revealed some details about the illness looming over her and the philosophy she held toward it.

The next day, Steph and Crystal arrived just as Kenny was leaving for Sky Harbor.

"Now ladies, don't have too good a time while I'm stuck in Vegas with a bunch of geeks computerizing a golf course irrigation system." He winked at Steph and Crystal, gave Mara a quick kiss, and then was out the door.

Steph bubbled. "Today, we're off to Kierland Commons for some retail therapy."

Crystal joined in, "We're going to shop 'til we drop," and added a hearty chuckle.

Mara looked around for her keys. "I swear I left them on the entry table. Where are they?"

"No matter," Steph said. "I'll drive."

"But I have to lock up. Give me a minute to find my other set." Mara scowled. "Now where did I put it?" Her friends rolled their eyes, which added to her stress.

Crystal touched Mara's arm. "It's okay. We can go out through the garage and use the keypad to get back in. You can look for them tonight."

Annoyed she couldn't remember moving her keys, Mara grabbed her purse and led the way out.

After they returned from the mall, she found her duplicate house key, but her keychain with her car keys remained missing.

The next morning while Mara was having coffee on the back patio with Steph and Crystal, the doorbell rang. She wondered who it could be so early.

"I can get it," Steph said. When she returned she told Mara, "There's some man here from Speed Plumbing about your leaky bathtub faucet."

Mara raised her eyebrows. "Leaky bathtub faucet? I didn't call anyone." She went to the door. "I'm sorry. You must have the wrong house."

He held up a work order. "It says here that Mara Connell called in a dripping bathtub faucet in the downstairs bathroom. The office confirmed the appointment yesterday." Holding out the paper for Mara to see, he said, "Your name Mara Connell? This your phone number?"

Mara scanned the paper. "Yes, but nothing's wrong with the faucet. I can show you." She led him down the hallway to the bathroom. "See for yourself."

The plumber stood near the tub. "Okay, lady. I see. It's dripping big time."

Mara stared at the dripping faucet then twisted the handle to try to stop the water flow. "I don't understand. This was fine the last time I was in here."

"I'm gonna have to charge you for a service call, anyway. You might as well let me fix it. A few minutes and I'm outta here."

"Okay. Sure. Fix it," Mara said.

Kenny called later that day, and Mara told him what happened. "By any chance, did you have your office assistant request the service call?"

"Nope," Kenny said. "Um. Sorry if I promised you I'd take care of it."

Am I losing my mind? We never talked about a leaky faucet...did we?

After Mara hung up she checked the caller ID history on the phone. A chill ran through her when she spotted yesterday's date next to a call from Speed Plumbing.

At noon the next day, while Mara loaded the breakfast dishes into the dishwasher, she received a text from Bebe saying she was outside ready to drive everyone to the Heard Museum for lunch. Crystal and Steph went to wait with Bebe in the car while Mara finished up.

From the kitchen window Mara saw Steph get into the car while Crystal knelt along the path. *What is she doing? Oh, right, probably tying the laces of those ugly shoes she has to wear.* Crystal stood then, and went to the car, brushing at her wet knees. *Is the irrigation system on? Is that broken too?* Everything seemed to be falling apart lately, not just her.

A few minutes later, a frazzled Mara came out the door, locked it and rushed down the steps. Water everywhere. She slipped and fell on the slick travertine, and screamed. Her three friends raced to her side.

"Are you all right?" Crystal asked. "Can you get up?"

With Bebe holding Mara's right arm and Steph her left, they helped their friend to her feet. When they let go of her, Mara's legs gave out and she slid to the ground.

Steph said, "Someone, call an ambulance." Bebe took out her phone and dialed 911.

Several hours later, Steph and Mara returned to the house, Mara in an ankle cast with crutches, a prescription for painkillers in her purse. After making Mara comfortable in the downstairs guest bedroom, Steph left to fill the prescription for her pain medication.

Around five o'clock Bebe and Crystal returned to Mara's house for a burrito dinner. Afterwards, the four friends agreed Crystal would sleep on a sofa bed in the family room and Bebe and Steph would take the bedrooms upstairs. Mara settled in early for the night and the others said they'd take turns checking on her.

In the middle of the night Mara opened her eyes, loopy from pain medication. In the rays cast by the night-lights in the room she saw a figure hobbling toward her, then a familiar voice whispered, "Time for your pain pills, Mara." Mara propped herself up, popped the pills in her mouth, swallowed some water, then lay back and closed her eyes.

When the first rays of morning sun shone through the window, Steph awoke. Her thoughts turned to Mara. She tiptoed down the stairs and across the travertine floor to the guest bedroom, opened the door and padded up to the side of the bed. Mara lay still. Steph touched her friend's forehead with her fingertips. *Cool. Too cool.* Steph's heart raced. She put her ear to Mara's mouth, then jumped away and shrieked. "Crystal! Bebe! Come quick. Help. Help!"

✝   ✝   ✝

Three weeks after Mara's funeral, Crystal called Kenny who'd been called back to work in Las Vegas. "It's almost a month since we lost Mara. You've been so aloof since she died. What's wrong, sweetie?"

"I need time to grieve."

"I don't understand. Before Mara got sick you were going to tell her about us so we could be together. Now when we can be together, it seems you're avoiding me." She tapped her fingers on the desktop.

"I know but..."

"I miss you so much. I've been thinking of driving up to Vegas to see you. We could have dinner and just talk. Mara was my good friend. We're both hurting."

Fifteen minutes later, Crystal had convinced Kenny they should spend a few days with each other. She said, "I'll need a car and I've always liked Mara's Mercedes—"

"Actually, Mara wanted Bebe to have it. As soon as I finish this assignment and I'm back in Scottsdale, I plan to give it to her."

Crystal took a breath. "Did Mara ever put that in writing?"

"No, I don't believe so. Why are you asking?"

In her most sincere voice she said, "Because...she told me she wanted *me* to have the Mercedes."

"She never mentioned it to me," Kenny said.

"Well, she even gave me the keys a few days before she died. I guess she felt she didn't have much time or—"

"Her death had to have been an accident. Mara never would've taken her own life, no matter what anyone thinks."

"I'm sure you're right, Kenny. I just meant, she often talked about how terrible her father's end was, and so I assumed..."

Before the conversation ended, they'd agreed—rather than

rent a car, Crystal would drive Mara's Mercedes to Las Vegas to visit Kenny.

When she hung up, a broad smile ran across Crystal's face. Everything had worked out just as she'd hoped. The Mercedes was an added bonus. After spending a few days with Kenny, Crystal was confident they would get back together.

She took a taxi to Mara's house, then let herself into the garage with the keypad combination she had seen Mara use.

Crystal got into the Mercedes, and using the keys she'd picked up from the table in the entry two days before Mara's overdose, she turned the ignition and pulled out of the garage.

The telephone rang at Mara's house a short while later. The call went to voice mail.

"Hello, Mrs. Connell, this is Dr. Tabor. I have good news for you. You tested negative for the Huntington's gene. I know how concerned you've been. If you have any questions, please don't hesitate to call."

† † †

Two Arizona Department of Public Safety Highway Patrol officers stood wide-eyed after arriving at the scene of a fatal one-car accident in the desert off I-90, south of Kingman. The seasoned male DPS officer wiped the perspiration from his brow. "Her brakes must've failed as she came around the bend. Had to have been doing eighty-five or ninety."

The younger female officer standing next to him nodded. "Sure was in a hurry to get someplace." She glanced at the victim's driver's license in her hand. "Name's Crystal Brown, resides in Scottsdale."

"This's gonna make the nightly news," he said, lifting his pen from his pad. "Wonder if the brake seal was the problem? That recall's been big news with these pricey cars."

She shrugged. "It's up to the techs to figure that one out." She stared at the clear desert sky for a few moments then said, "The way I look at it, when someone's thrown like this from their car and caught by a clump of ancient saguaros, it's the desert that's claimed them."

† † †

SUSAN BUDAVARI has completed the first two books in a psychological suspense series featuring a Scottsdale P.I. and his physician wife. She has written over 30 mystery/suspense short stories and co-edited and contributed to several award-winning anthologies, including three from Red Coyote Press: *Medley of Murder*, *Map of Murder,* and *Medium of Murder*. Prior to this, Susan was an award-winning scientific writer and encyclopedist. She is currently Vice-President of Sisters in Crime Desert Sleuths Chapter.

FLOATING
LAURIE FAGEN

Floating. Tiny waves ripple at my ears. Sun bathes my face with warmth. Something tickles my hand. The *thu-thump, thu-thump* of my heartbeat fills my head.

"How can you float like that?" my friends would always ask, seeming amazed that I could remain motionless on my back in the water, barely stirring the surface with my hands or feet. *"My feet always sink!"* another would say. *"You're lucky!"*

Sounds of the public swimming pool fill my ears. Children laughing. Water splashing. The thud of the diving board. More splashing. Tweet of the lifeguard's whistle warning someone misbehaving.

The sun is hot, beating down on my face. Too hot. Lips dry. Throat parched. The pool sounds of days gone by fade, replaced by a gentle lapping sound. I blink my eyes open to see a bright blue, cloudless sky. Somewhere a bird cackles.

I lift my head, tucking my legs under to bring myself upright, arms in a slow treading-water figure eight to keep my mouth above the surface. I realize I'm not in my hometown pool. I look around, trying to figure out where I am. Tall, red rock canyon walls surround me and at the base, a small cove. I've floated into tall, thin reeds in one corner that surround, nearly trap me.

"What the...?" I mutter, trying to get my bearings. Frantically I twist around, now treading water madly, pushing away from the grasses, finding myself very much alone. My head starts pounding.

Float. My head drops back into the water, and legs come up into the survival float. The throbbing subsides a bit.

Stay calm. Close your eyes. Big breaths. The *thu-thump, thu-thump* is much faster now. What happened? How did I get here?

I force my breathing into long, steady inhalations as my arms keep me afloat.

Oh, jeez, my head. Make the pounding stop. Relax, Leslie, try to relax.

It seems like I've been floating for hours. When I open my eyes again, the sun is no longer bright yellow, but more orange as it starts its downward trek to the top of the mountain, bathed in hues of deep lavender and peach.

I carefully reach up to feel a lump the size of an orange on my forehead, and something sticky on my face. My fingers are red with blood. I realize something happened. Something bad. But what?

Rob. The boat.

I thrust myself to a sitting position in the water, propelling my arms to the side and pumping my legs in a bicycle kick.

It all comes flooding back. Rob and I, in the small boat. Having a lovely time, rowing across Canyon Lake, into the tiny finger of La Barge Cove. The midday sun had cast shadows over the rock formations as majestic saguaro cacti stood guard. Rob was telling his usual bad jokes. I laughed obligatorily.

Then, as if in slow motion, the oar lifted out of the water, dripping as it rose above the side of the boat, and across the center, connecting with my head. Then nothing.

"Oh, my God, Rob!"

My thoughts race. He must've lost his balance. He's probably in the lake!

I swim out to where the boat was, take a deep breath and dive down below the surface, my arms flailing wildly, reaching, grasping. But it's dark and murky and I feel nothing but cold.

Lungs aching, I claw myself upward and emerge, taking in a cool, deep breath. Water drips down my face, chilled by the dry air. I blink the liquid out of my eyes. My head pounds harder.

I look around. Nothing. No one. Just the occasional bird, gliding gracefully, a silhouette against the setting sun. A dragonfly stops about a foot away from my face, as if looking at me, then darts off.

I resume the survival float, feet up, arms back and forth at my side, balancing. My breathing slows. I remember my childhood swimming classes.

"You could always tread water better than me," my friends would say. *"No fair!"*

Of course, my height had also helped. I was only eleven when I was persuaded to join the synchronized swimming club, but I was as tall as the other high schoolers who frequented the pool. It was one thing to tread water in the five-foot area, where I could touch my toe to the bottom of the pool if I needed. But when the coach's drills took us to the deep end, I would panic, afraid I'd get too tired and slip under and no one would miss me.

The drone of an airplane above startles me. I pull myself up and try to wave, but it's too late. The plane disappears behind the mountain.

Treading water again, I recall Rob's last joke.

"Take my wife...please!" he had deadpanned.

I wondered about the somewhat maniacal look on Rob's face just before the oar smacked my head.

I look around again. This time it's as if the saguaros have doubled in number with their deep, dark shadows cast by the setting sun. I have to get out of here. The shore looks to be about three pool lengths. You can do it. Breast stroke arms. Head above the water. Whip kick. What a time to be thinking about my swimming form. But it helps me focus on getting to that beach.

I drag myself up onto the warm sand. There's the indentation where Rob and I put the rowboat into the water earlier this morning. Two sets of footprints. That was what, seven, eight hours ago?

And there's where the boat had been pulled out of the water. Only two large feet. Rob's.

The sun is warm overhead, drying my clothes. A bead of sweat trickles down, stinging my eye. When I wipe it away, my hand is covered with fresh blood.

Gotta get help.

My head throbs harder as I pull myself up along the rocky shoreline. I trudge cautiously across the uneven stones toward the Apache Trail highway. It's too far. I'll never make it. I almost lose my balance. I stop, steadying myself. Only a little farther. You can do it.

Then the sound. A car. Coming my way.

One hand on my bleeding head, I wave with the other, slowly, then more urgently. The car brakes to a stop.

"Thanks...can I have a ri—?" I start to ask.

"Oh, my gosh, you're the one from the TV!" the young female driver exclaims. "Of course, get in."

She leans across the car's interior and opens the door for me.

I gingerly ease myself into the passenger seat.

"What…TV?" I ask.

"Your picture was on the noon news. This guy said he and his wife were on a bike ride, and…"

"You mean 'boat' ride, right?" I ask.

"No, he definitely said 'bike.' He told the reporter they stopped at a convenience store, he went in to get a couple of sodas, but when he came back out, the woman…I mean you…were gone."

None of this makes any sense. Everything is a blur.

"Can you take me to the nearest hospital?" I close my eyes and lean back.

"Of course," the woman replies.

The car spews rocks from under the tires as it accelerates.

"This is so bizarre," she continues. "On TV, they said your credit card had been used, so they figured you dumped him and took off. Sounded like the cops decided not to go searching for you." She pauses. "But I don't think that's what really happened…right?"

I keep my eyes closed and tell myself it's going to be okay.

"Don't worry. I'll get you there as soon as I can."

The ride gets smoother as we speed down the highway. The motion lulls me half asleep. The breeze from the open window is soft on my face, and the classical music on the radio helps me relax.

It's dark when my Good Samaritan's screeching tires wake me, as we pull into the emergency room lane. Two hospital attendants run out with a gurney.

I made it. I close my eyes again, and my world goes black.

Floating. Tiny waves ripple at my ears. Sun bathes my face with warmth. Birds chirp nearby. The sweet sounds of Native American flute music float through the air. Something tickles my hand. I turn to pet my precious little puppy, who is licking my fingers. I lift my head from an inflatable water lounger, and reach into one of the two beverage holders to press a remote switch. Water gurgles from a large rock formation. From the other holder on the raft, I pick up a frosty glass and take a long sip of an icy, sweet strawberry daiquiri.

I financed the heated pool, Jacuzzi, waterfall, colored lights and even the against-the-current machine—"extravagances" Rob would never allow me to have—after I sold his gas-guzzling, always-in-the-shop Jaguar. I smile, knowing he won't be able to drive again. Not for a long time. Not where he is.

My friends had warned me about him. Thank goodness my pet-sitting neighbor posted my absence on Facebook and called the cops when I didn't pick up the puppy or call. She never trusted Rob either.

But to think he had his girlfriend put on my clothes, my sunglasses and wear my baseball cap with the rhinestones that spelled out SPOILED, then sent her to the ATM to withdraw cash from my personal account.

So much for the man I thought I knew. "Cheers, Rob," I toast with my glass. "Hope you rot in that prison cell."

LAURIE FAGEN is a long-time "writer by habit," and has written for commercial radio, television and cable television news; corporate video, films and documentaries; and magazines and newspapers as an independent writer. She is publisher of the *SanTan Sun News*, a community newspaper in Chandler, AZ, and is a jazz singer as well as a fiber and jewelry artist. She recently won an honorable mention in the *Alfred Hitchcock Mystery Magazine* Mysterious Photograph short story contest. Following a life-long love of reading mysteries, Fagen is making her writing debut in that genre with this anthology short story.

SWEET TASTE OF REVENGE
SUZANNE FLAIG

It's hot. Desert hot. The kind that turns your throat to dust and your lungs to fire. Stella stands at the screen door hoping for a puff of breeze, wiping sweat from beneath her auburn bangs with a sticky potholder. Ten at night and still a hundred degrees. A lizard skitters across the patio and disappears into the vegetable garden.

Tonight she's making prickly pear jelly. This morning she had plucked the fruit from the prickly pear cactus that grows in the back yard, using long-handled tongs to avoid the poisonous thorny spines. After washing and brushing the ruby-red fruit clean, she steamed it until tender, then mashed and strained it.

Now she takes the prickly pear concoction and boils it together with lime juice, pectin and sugar. The timing is important to get the mixture to jell properly. Hot canning jars wait for the jelly to be poured and the lids to be sealed. It's a long process, but well worth the effort. After midnight she finally finishes and turns out the kitchen light.

Exhausted, she moves into the bedroom and peels off her tank top and jeans. They say it's a dry heat, but sweat pastes her underwear against her skin. Naked, she relaxes under a cool shower. Washes away the desert heat. Washes away the day's dust and dirt. Washes away the thick, sweet residue.

In the five years since she moved to this quiet Arizona town, she's gained a reputation for her homemade jams and jellies. The locals, as well as the rare tourist who strays far enough off the beaten path to find his way to her store, buy enough of these sweet treats and her fresh fruits and vegetables to allow her to live comfortably. This place is her sanctuary. She no longer looks over her shoulder at every passing shadow. She's safe here.

He watches. Waits.

She hasn't aged much in five years. She looks even better

now. From his vantage point beyond her window, peering through binoculars, he sees the kitchen light go out and follows her through the field glasses as she enters the bedroom and undresses.

He smiles, remembering their previous encounters. She was good. Real good.

But she turned on him.

She opens the stand early. The women will be here to purchase their fresh produce for the day's meals.

The old woman, Arcelia, shows up first. "Good morning, Stella."

"Good morning. What will you have today? The asparagus is crisp this morning. And I just put up some prickly pear jelly."

"Cabbage, carrots, and I'll take some of that asparagus, too." Arcelia wanders around the store, filling her basket with Stella's fruits and vegetables.

As Arcelia leaves, others arrive. Gloria buys two jars of the prickly pear jelly. Manuel is there for celery and green peppers. Business is brisk throughout the day and finally, about two o'clock, Stella gets a break. Despite the heat, she rests on the wooden bench outside the store drinking a bottle of cold water, her eyes closed against the glare of the afternoon sun.

"Good to see you again, Stella."

That voice. Her eyes snap open. Fear rolls over her like a haboob across the desert, a choking cloud that blinds her and steals the breath from her lungs.

He stands close, feet planted wide, arms folded across his broad chest, crooked smile mocking her.

Stella clenches her fists. "What are you doing here?" She pushes her backbone against the bench, ready to spring, ready to defend what is hers.

"Why do you think?"

She presses her clenched fists onto the wooden slats of the seat. "Get out of here."

He doesn't move, the smile sliding into a smirk.

She holds her breath, unsure of the outcome.

He turns slowly. "I'll be back."

The past roars back at her. Attacks her like a pack of hungry wolves. She slumps down, consumed with hot anger and fear. *It will not happen again. This time he will not win.*

† † †

Five years ago, when she escaped the abuse, she swore to herself she would never be *that* woman again.

"I didn't mean to let the carrots cook too long..." she had said.

His slap had left a handprint.

"The market didn't have this brand of..."

His punch to her stomach sent her to the bathroom, vomiting.

"I'm sorry I folded your shirts the wrong way..."

She wore makeup and sunglasses to cover the black eye.

Her friend, Anne, said, "Why don't you leave that worthless excuse for a man?"

Stella said, "Where would I go? What would I do? I have no money, no family." She stared ahead, at an empty future.

"There are shelters," Anne had said.

"But he loves me. He says he's sorry and it won't happen again."

"But it always does, doesn't it?" Anne left a card on the table with a phone number scrawled in red. Stella scooped it up and hid it in a pocket.

He found the card. Waved it, taunting. "She was here, wasn't she? That meddling witch, Anne. She'll pay, too." The blow came from behind, knocking Stella to the ground.

Stella crawled across the bedroom floor, away from her attacker.

He followed, kicking, each strike punctuated with an expletive. "Bitch!"

Her ribs were on fire, every breath a scream of pain. What had she done this time?

He threw the torn-up card into a metal ashtray he dropped onto the floor. The toe of his boot slid it over to where her face was pressed flat against the carpet. He knelt down beside her.

She watched as the flames from his silver lighter ignited the card, blinding her, the smoky odor mixing with the salty taste of her tears.

The next day, at the supermarket, she pretended not to see Anne and shuffled down a different aisle, eyes focused on the green tile floor. As she reached for a can of peas, wincing in pain, Anne stood before her, hands on hips.

"What happened this time?"

Stella's eyes dropped like stones. "He found the card."

Anne's voice softened. "Come with me."

Stella backed her cart away. "I can't."

"One day he'll kill you," Anne had said.

†   †   †

Stella walks back into her store in the desert, thinking of that day. He hadn't killed her. But she had paid a heavy price to finally get away. Instead he'd killed Anne. And gotten away with it. Now he's found her again. How has he tracked her down?

The door opens and she turns too quickly, knocking a cucumber from its stack.

"I'm sorry, Stella, did I startle you?" It's Karyn, who comes in every day for fresh herbs.

Stella reaches down, picks up the cucumber, smiles too broadly. "No, not at all. What'll you have today?"

"I'm running low on parsley, and I need basil and rosemary." Karyn goes down the aisle, picking up what she needs, then walks over to the counter and hands Stella the bunches of herbs. "Are you all right, Stella?" she asks.

"I'm fine."

"You look a little pale. Maybe you're coming down with something. Brew some tea with lemon and honey. If you don't feel better by tomorrow, I have some homemade remedies to try."

"Thanks, Karyn."

Maybe a homemade remedy is the answer to my problem.

The rest of the day goes by in a blur. Stella thinks of only two things: *When will he return? What will I do when he does?*

He watches her movements from a distance. He knows he made her nervous by showing up and then leaving suddenly. She'll expect him to come back tonight, after the last customer leaves. But he'll leave her in suspense, take her down in the early hours of the morning, just before sunrise.

He thinks about the satisfaction he got following that other one, Stella's friend. *She never saw it coming. But she deserved it. Deserved everything she got. Interfering in our lives.*

He watches Stella shut the doors, turn out the lights, pull

down the blinds. He puts away the binoculars. They'll be of no use tonight. She knows he's there, and will be careful. But no matter. He will get inside. And he'll get his.

After locking the doors and windows and pulling down the blinds, Stella uses what she has on hand to protect herself: plants, food, household products. Brewing a homemade remedy just for him. Setting a trap. Night falls, but she does not turn on the lights. She waits. And she does not sleep.

It's four in the morning when he picks the lock on the side door. He expects her to be asleep in her bedroom, but as he sneaks down the darkened hallway, the blow comes from behind.

She swings the baseball bat across the back of his head, knocking him to the floor, then picks up a pot holding a thorny prickly pear cactus and shoves the spines into his face.

His screams follow her down the hall as she drags him by the feet into the kitchen. He's heavy, and struggling, but she's on a mission and the adrenaline keeps her going. She ties his hands behind his back with twine.

She thought of all the pain he caused in the past. He deserves to know pain. "Hurts, doesn't it?"

One eye swollen shut, spikes still embedded in his skin, he doesn't reply.

"Now you know what it's like to suffer. Like you made me suffer. Like you made Anne suffer."

She opens a jar on the table. The special jelly she prepared last night.

She shoves a spoonful of the poisoned prickly pear jelly into his mouth.

He struggles. His plan for revenge has horribly backfired.

"This is for Anne. You thought you got away with her death. Now you'll know what it's like to die."

Her revenge tasted sweet.

† † †

SUZANNE FLAIG is a freelance writer and editor whose short stories have been published in various anthologies and online. She is currently seeking a publisher for her musical mystery series featuring piano teacher Missy Jenkins. Suzanne has been a member of the Desert Sleuths Sisters in Crime since moving to Arizona from Pennsylvania in 1998. Before she decided to write about murder, Suzanne was a piano and organ teacher, a roller skating coach, and a French teacher. You can learn more about Suzanne and her alter ego, Missy Jenkins, at www.authorsden.com/suzanneflaig.

GOOD NEWS BAD NEWS
ARTHUR KERNS

Betty liked the feel of their new white Buick sedan as they headed north on I-17 toward Sedona. Her husband Ed, sitting next to her had that "tickled pink" look on his face. At first he had objected to buying such an expensive car, but they both knew he didn't mean it. One gets to know their mate after living with them for nigh on fifty-five years.

"Careful now," he cautioned. "This car has a big motor. Don't let it get away from you."

"Been driving for quite a while now, Daddy. Just push that seat back and rest your hip."

"Can't figure out all these knobs down there on the side of this seat," Ed said, fussing with the controls as he raised himself up, then back, then forward.

Her husband had his second hip replaced a month ago and the operation didn't go as well as the first. But then he just turned eighty-one and a person just doesn't heal as quickly as when you were twenty.

"Damn it," he said. "Oh hell. I'll just stay here in this position until we reach Sunset Point."

She let out a deep exaggerated sigh that registered her displeasure with his bad language. Even after all these years, she had to keep a rein on that man.

"Look over there on the left." He pointed. "There's the restaurant where we can buy a good apple pie on the way back home."

"I know that place." She hmmphed, keeping her eyes on the road. They'd stopped there many times. Her pies were much better. She used her mama's recipe. Ed used to rave about them when they lived back on the farm in Iowa.

The traffic thinned as they climbed away from the small settlements dotting both sides of the highway. White bumpy clouds spotted the blue April sky. A nice mid-week morning to take a drive to Sedona, have lunch, then return to their little place in Tempe.

"We'll have to drive to Crown King some day," he said. "Always wondered what was on top of that mountain. Been told there's a small town up there."

"In that case we should've bought one of those SUVs."

Now it was his turn to sigh. She knew what he was thinking. Maybe when their son visited them, he'd take them up there in his jeep to see God knows what. Their son's been promising now for years, but that job of his in Hollywood always keeps him busy.

"We'll be seeing the Bumblebee sign soon." He chuckled. "Always get a kick out of that name."

As Betty slowed for a curve in the road, she saw a lone figure standing on the shoulder. A feeling of unease passed over her like a cloud shadow on a windy day. She pushed her foot down on the accelerator.

"Looky there, sweetie," he said. "That little girl up there looks like she's in trouble."

"No picking up hitchhikers, Ed. Remember what we said!"

The shape grew into a recognizable figure as they approached, a girl in her early twenties wearing torn jeans and a hooded gray sweatshirt. Dirty blonde hair protruded from beneath the hood. She jumped up and down with both arms raised above her head.

"She looks all alone out there. In the middle of nowhere."

Not twenty feet away, Betty got a quick look at the girl's face. Something strange about it that she couldn't put her finger on. Passing by the figure, she knew she shouldn't let up on the gas, but she did. She knew she shouldn't stop, but there she was, bringing the car to a halt on the side of the road. Her finger hit the emergency flashers and she stared into the rearview mirror. The young girl skipped up the grade toward the car.

"We're not letting her in," she said. "Just tell her we'll call the police and have someone pick her up."

Ed wasn't listening. He had already opened the door and with a groan put his leg with the new hip out on the gravel. Before Betty could shout to him to close the door, the rear door opened and the girl jumped in.

"Better get in the car, old man." The stranger's voice was gruff. "We're liable to get creamed sitting here on this highway."

Betty looked over at her husband who had closed the door.

The smile on his face seemed overshadowed by the slight frown. As he turned to speak to their passenger, the girl moved to the center of the backseat and leaned forward. Betty detected strong odors, not all of them from sweat. Her stale breath reeked.

"Let's get going, grandma." The words did not come as a suggestion.

"You looked like you were in trouble, young lady," Ed said, in a formal tone. "How long were you standing there?"

"Forever. My so-called friends dumped me."

Betty eased the car out into the lane and pressed down hard to get the car up to the speed limit. Going up the long grade was a strain on the car, but the motor had sufficient horsepower. This was a big mistake, she knew. They would deposit this person when they reached the Sunset rest stop, which would be none too soon.

"You left your flashers on, grandma," the girl said. "Turn them off, before some cop stops us."

"See here, young lady," Betty said. "Your manners are—"

"Shut up!" the girl yelled. "Or I'll put a slug into pop's head."

Looking sideward, Betty saw the young woman holding an ugly looking small gun next to her husband's ear. With some perverse sense of incongruity, all she could think about was how filthy the girl's hand was.

The girl ordered Betty to turn off onto an exit that led into a rocky canyon. The two-lane blacktop stopped after a mile and became a gravel roadway. The road followed a stream on the left side. Meantime, the girl in the backseat grew anxious. Betty checked the rearview mirror and saw their passenger continually turn and look out the rear window. Finally, she ordered Betty to pull over next to a copse of mesquites backing up to a rocky outcrop.

"Both of you. Out!"

As Betty and Ed got out of the car, the girl ordered them to stand under a twisted mesquite. "Stay there and be quiet."

When the girl pulled down the hood of her sweatshirt, Betty got the first good look at their assailant. Her blonde stringy hair barely matched the darker eyebrows, which were thick and almost touched each other. Betty realized that the girl wasn't so much nervous as jittery. Like what her brother used to call the young colt they had back in Iowa. Jumpy. She elbowed her husband and mouthed the word, "Junkie."

The girl walked a few steps away from them, stopped, and looked up and down the canyon, listening. All Betty could hear were birdcalls, quail and dove. Looking back, the girl waved the small pistol. "Stand there and don't move." She hurried back to the car, yanked open the passenger door, and pulled out Betty's purse and a small travel pack. She emptied the contents on the car's hood.

Betty detected anger building in her husband. In his younger days, if someone pushed him too far, he could be fearsome, but that little tramp was the one with the gun. Just wants money and the credit cards, Betty hoped. "Take whatever you want and take off, young lady. We can find our way back to the road."

"Told you to shut up." The girl's eyes seemed to bounce around. "You old people piss me off." She returned to her newfound treasure, sorting out the wallets, keys, and credit cards. Suddenly, she turned and yelled, "What's this?" She held up a brown medicine bottle.

"My pills," Ed said. "I need them."

Visibly agitated, he began to add something that under the circumstances Betty knew he shouldn't, so she gave him a hard nudge. He looked back and nodded, but she worried about his short fuse.

The girl studied the label for a moment. "What's this for?"

"Pain. Just had a hip replaced."

"Is it strong?"

"Yes," Ed said. "Matter of fact, I could use one now."

"Tough." The girl reached in the car and pulled out a water bottle. They watched her put four to five pills in her palm, toss them in her mouth, and take a long swig from the bottle. She burped.

"You're not going to give me my medicine?" Ed asked.

Betty gave him another nudge.

The girl stared at them, taking deep breaths. "Those bastards dumped me back there on the Seventeen and took my stash. Everything. Uppers. Downers. Floaters." She leaned back on the car fender and jiggled the medicine bottle. "This stuff here will help." Again, the girl scrutinized the canyon, looking up and down and listening. After a few moments, she redirected her attention back to Betty and her husband. "That watch, old lady. Hand it over." She waved the gun. "And the rings."

"Enough, kid!" Ed positioned himself between Betty and the girl. "Take the money and cards over there. Take the car, and just leave."

"Pops I've heard enough from you." The girl's face shone from sweat. She took a step toward him, pointing the gun directly at Ed's midsection.

Betty saw Ed was fuming. She tugged at his suspenders as he pulled away, moved toward the girl, and shook his fist. Then she heard what she feared most. *Crack. Crack.*

Ed stumbled forward, clutching his chest. Turning back to Betty, stunned, he fell to his knees.

Betty let out a scream and dropped down next to him, cradling his head. Blood formed on the upper part of his white shirt. The one she had ironed that morning. The situation seemed unreal. It couldn't be happening. Her heart pounded in her chest. She had to get help. Confused, she got to her feet and headed for the car.

"Forget it, Grandma."

"He'll die," she screamed. "We've got to get help."

"We got to do nothing." The girl smirked and tilted her head to the side. She lunged at Betty, gave her a wicked shove, then walked toward the trees and looked up at the rock ledge.

Betty returned to Ed, who now lay on his side, gasping. She pressed her palm on his wounds. He uttered a moan. She promised help would come. He'd be all right. She kissed him and now began sobbing.

"Cut the crap!"

The girl paced under the trees, pulling at the small leaves. Betty suspected the girl was in deep thought. Perhaps she'd change her mind, let Betty call for help. Meanwhile Ed faded. His eyes shut. His breathing shortened.

"Stay with me sweetheart." Trembling, Betty looked around for something. Anything to help her husband. Not knowing what she was looking for. "Stay awake!" she shouted down to him.

"Oh shut up! He's dead."

Betty stopped crying. She gazed down at the man she loved and with whom she had shared her life since her teens. He was leaving her. The good man, the good husband, the good father, dying like this. On the ground, in the dirt. Because of this little tramp.

Betty felt herself losing control and not wanting to stop the feeling. She wanted to rip the girl's eyes out. Punch her. Do something. Looking on the ground, she spied a jagged rock, the size of softball, like she used to pitch at the ladies league. In one motion she let Ed go, picked up the rock, and got to her feet.

Caught off guard, the girl backed to the outcrop and raised the gun, but not before Betty heaved the rock. It hit the girl's left eye. She screamed and fell to the ground, dropping the gun as she went down. Betty ran up, snatched it, and yelled, "Stay there you bitch. Don't move." Pointing the pistol at the girl, she backed up and hurried to Ed's side.

What to do now? Ed was gone, but still she had to get him away from here, away from this monster. She lifted his head onto her lap and watched the girl leaning back on the rocks, her hand on her eye. Blood flowed down her check as she spewed a stream of profanities.

Then Betty saw it. Next to the girl's head. Something brown and checkered, moving. As she watched, the snake struck, attaching itself to the girl's neck. She screamed and tried to lift herself up from the ground with one hand, while pulling at the snake with the other. Yanking the rattlesnake loose, it dropped to the ground next to her feet. It struck again, at her calf. Yelling, the girl jumped away, one hand holding her neck, the other her eye.

Betty watched. Should she aim at the girl or the snake? Her decision was made for her. The snake disappeared into the rock outcrop. As it did, Betty saw the telltale white bands next to the rattles.

"Get me help!" The girl stumbled forward, gasping.

"Just stay where you are...or I'll shoot."

The girl yelled obscenities, as she lurched toward Betty.

"Stop. I'm warning you, you slag. You junkie. I'm a good shot."

"You old pathetic—"

Betty chose her target, lined up the sights, and fired. The shot echoed down the canyon. The girl fell to the ground. Her energy and fight evaporated. Blood flowed from her eye and from her foot. Looking up, in disbelief, she yelled, "You shot my damn toe off."

"Told you I was a good shot." Without looking at him, Betty stroked Ed's head, thinking how she would no longer give that bald head a goodnight rub before turning over and going to sleep.

"I feel like crap," the girl whimpered.

"Can understand that. That snake was a Mohave rattlesnake." Betty lowered the gun and figured she'd just watch.

"I need...help," the girl said, breathing hard. With a fake smile, she asked, "Will you...?"

"Well, dearie, I have good news for you and some bad news."

"Yeah?"

"The good news is that this shiny car Ed bought has one of those gadgets, where you push a button and you talk to a lady and ask for help. Works anywhere you are. Uses satellites." She pointed the gun skyward. Betty felt a lump in her throat. She didn't know if she was about to weep or shoot this killer on the ground in front of her gasping and clutching her neck.

"Hurry!" The girl began to retch.

Regaining her composure, Betty continued, "So, all I have to do is press a button and say you've got a snake bite from the deadliest snake in the U.S. of A and somebody will come rushing with anti-venom." She paused. "And that's the good news."

The girl closed her eyes, her breathing labored. She rasped, "The bad?"

"No way am I pushing that button."

ARTHUR KERNS retired from the FBI then became a consultant with the Director of Central Intelligence and Department of State. A past president of the Arizona chapter of the Association of Former Intelligence Officers, his award-winning short stories have appeared in a number of anthologies, and he is a two-time winner at the *Cave Creek Film and Arts Festival*. In addition to an espionage thriller set on the French Riviera, he has completed a mystery based on the unsolved 1929 murder of an FBI agent in Phoenix. He is a book reviewer for the *Washington Independent Review of Books*.

CAVE IN
DEBORAH J LEDFORD

A hawk's cry pierced the air as it circled above the three young men who trudged up the path toward a short row of hills. A canned voice announced from a loudspeaker five miles to the east, "Welcome to Kartchner Caverns, the only public caves in Arizona to remain pristine, yet open to the public..." Ringo, Morris and Gee-Lee were always amazed to be able to make out the words so clearly.

The sound that carried in the vast open space of the desert kept Ringo focused on their mission. He moved with speed and purpose, dodging ocotillos that riddled the area along the barely discernable route. Rock pick hammer clutched in his hand, he extended his lead, urging the two stragglers on. "Almost there. Come on, Gee-Lee, move it!"

Gee-Lee cursed under his breath, wishing the Alpha from their pack wouldn't call him by the nickname their foster father had branded him with as a kid. Louis could still hear the man's chiding ring in his ears: *"Louis, hah! More like Louise. Geez, you're such a little girl, Gee-Lee. Move your ass."* Unfortunately the ever-present Ringo had overheard the exchange and the name had stuck. But hey, at least Ringo didn't call him stupid. Most people thought he was. Always quiet, never willing to draw attention to himself, only Morris and an international patent attorney knew the secret Gee-Lee held so confidential—even more cloak-and-dagger than the caves directly beneath where the men trod.

As always, Morris remained with Gee-Lee. Patient and considerate, Morris handed over a bottle of water and worried this would be the day his buddy passed out, right there on the spot, never to pick himself up again.

Jumbo-sized Gee-Lee took a sip, bent over and grabbed his knees with his hands, panting, face nearly as red as the bandana tied around his neck. Morris waited, inhaler at the ready in case Gee-Lee called out for medicinal rescue.

"Not much farther. Hang in there. Slow, deep breaths," Morris said in a voice that always calmed Gee-Lee.

Pissed off from waiting for the other two, anxious to be where he most felt at home, Ringo turned around and met up with the others. "Move your butts, already," he said, reaching behind him and patted his backpack. "I brought champagne to celebrate our anniversary."

"Yeah." Morris sighed. "We've been coming the first Saturday of every month for ten years now. Two hour drive here and back from Tucson, twelve hours in the hole every time. For *ten years*, man. Tammy's gonna think I'm cheating on her if I don't tell—"

Ringo closed the gap to Morris in quick strides. "No one's to know," he said, poking Morris in the chest with his finger. "We agreed."

Gee-Lee cowered, but Morris, held his ground. "I know, I know. This is our secret. And it's been fun, but...I've got responsibilities now. Tammy and I want to start a family right away. And she won't want me out here in the desert where—"

"It's time. We need to protect our find," Ringo interrupted, not even registering Morris's complaint. "I'll start by filing a mining claim with the Bureau of Land Management."

"But it's a cave," Gee-Lee said. "Not a mine."

Ringo rolled his eyes and swung around so fast the collapsible shovel tied to his pack swatted his hip. "We're classifying it as a mine because we don't want the world to know it's actually a cave. Geez Louise, Gee-Lee, use your brain."

"Right. Sorry," Gee-Lee muttered, his cheeks flushing brighter than before.

"It'll only cost sixty-three dollars each," Ringo continued. "Filing a Notice of Intent to Hold can be done now. I can take care of that, too."

Gee-Lee winced, wondering which coveted classic comic book he would need to sell to pay for his part of the expense. "I don't know...sixty-three dollars is—"

"A pittance for what we'll make once people start paying to see this place."

Morris asked, "If you file all the paperwork, doesn't that mean yours will be the only name on the claim?"

"Fine. Do you want to take the time to do it?" Ringo looked back and forth at his companions who lowered their heads to study their hiking boots. "Right. I didn't think so. Morris, you're too busy planning your wedding. Gee-Lee, you're tied up doing…whatever it is you do. That leaves me. To do everything. As usual."

"You really think people will come?" Gee-Lee asked, in an attempt to level out Ringo's annoyance.

"Hell, yeah. Look, the entrance fee to Kartchner Caverns is twenty-three bucks. Even if we charge half that we'll be rich in a year. Do the math. They give over twenty tours a day, fifteen to twenty people per group. For over eleven years. That's…"

"A lot of numbers," Morris said.

"You're making my head hurt," Gee-Lee offered.

"But the Kartchner caves are only a few miles from here," Morris said.

"That's the beauty of it. Kartchner sells out all the time." Ringo's words accelerated along with his steps. "The overflow will come here. Carloads full. We'll sell T-shirts, coffee mugs, caps…" Ringo's voice floated on the still air as he picked up his pace again, leaving a wake of his words.

"What do you think?" Morris asked Gee-Lee after Ringo moved out of hearing range.

"I don't know. I mean, if we can pull this off, won't it take a lot more money to get this thing going? Who's gonna foot the bill to put up a fence around this place?"

"Yeah," Morris said. "And pave a road. Set up a visitor's center. Pay for people to give the tours and sell the stuff Ringo's talking about."

Gee-Lee halted. His head spun as he considered his remaining inventory. He had been saving his choice Golden Age comics. The ones he couldn't live without. The single digit *Batman*'s within the collection he'd never removed from their cellophane wrappers. But if Ringo continued with his plan, Gee-Lee would be left with nothing but the seventeen empty crates that once held his colorful printed treasures, most sold now to help finance their adventure.

"I don't even like coming out here anymore," Gee-Lee said. His stomach churned but he knew he could tell Morris anything without judgment raining down. Ringo—not so much.

"Me neither. This adventure lost its shine for me about three years ago. And I don't just mean the cave hunt." Morris hitched his head toward Ringo's form, now a speck in the distance.

Gee-Lee let out a giggle, his only remaining childish mannerism, one that belied his age and build. Once he recovered he said, "Have you really kept this place secret? Even from Tammy?"

Morris raised his open palm, displaying a ragged scar. The blood promise. Gee-Lee did the same. Ringo also had a matching mark—healed-over gashes intentionally inflicted by a hunting knife ten years ago at this very spot. *"Our secret,"* each had said in unison as they traded each other's blood.

As usual, Gee-Lee's thoughts went to the video game he had been creating the past nine months, so near completion that even away from his computer keyboard his fingertips itched to get back to writing the final lines of code.

Always attuned to Gee-Lee, Morris asked, "How's the game coming along? Ready to submit it to Nintendo yet?"

Gee-Lee couldn't help but smile. "Tonight's the night. A little more tweaking and my patent attorney will run with it."

"That's great. So proud of you, Louis. Not many people know you're a genius."

"Nobody knows," Gee-Lee said.

Morris clapped his friend on the shoulder. "Another one of our secrets. I'll be depending on you to pay for my kids' college. Tammy wants four."

"You got it, bro…but you won't tell Ringo, right? He doesn't know anything about this."

"No way, man. This place is all Ringo has. I'm gonna sign over my share of whatever comes from the caves." Morris tugged the tail of his shirt from the grasp of an ocotillo. "He can have it."

Gee-Lee scanned the remote area. "Yeah, I was thinking the same thing."

"Let's hit it, before Ringo gets more pissy," Morris said, holding out an assisting arm.

Ringo waited at the concealed opening of their find, tapping the toe of his dusty boot as he impatiently waited for Morris and Gee-Lee to join him.

Once they had all grouped together, Ringo said, "Okay, here's the plan. All we need to do is see if this last cave meets up with the other two we've already found. Come on." He raised his outstretched arms to the sky and bobbed up and down on his toes. "This is the day. I can feel it."

They cleared the dirt from a four-foot square of plywood that hid the sinkhole, then they tossed the board aside. Ringo was the first to descend the ladder it had taken an entire Saturday to carry from Ringo's pickup to the cave site eight years ago. Gee-Lee had gained so much weight over the years that the boys had no choice but to install a stable entryway, but now even Ringo was grateful to feel the sturdy aluminum steps meet his insoles.

Darkness enveloped them as they took their first steps on the cave floor. From their packs they each pulled out lights attached to headbands, put them on and continued on the trek that had become familiar after so many years of exploration. Circles of blue-white light bathed the cavernous space. As they dodged puddles of thick bat guano, Palaeozoic rocks came into view. Rust-colored ribbons that resembled crispy bacon hung in strips. Slow constant drips dropped from points of soda straw stalactites into a pool of crystal clear water.

The three were careful to retrace the same line of footprints they first created. Pride welled in Ringo's chest knowing the prints would be there in perpetuity, forever branding the cave as theirs.

After six hours they still hadn't found a passage that would link the single cave to the other two they had discovered. Ringo's hope was that they could claim the site encompassing the total area of all three, but this had been their sixth attempt and they all agreed, their last. As Ringo popped the cork on the bottle of champagne they decided to provide the coordinates of the two linking caves on the claim form and relinquish the smaller cavern to the elements.

The next night, Ringo lay on the twin-size bed of his studio apartment, still wearing his "real work" clothes. He continued to fume about his manager who had chewed him out for belittling an old woman about her lack of computer prowess. Now three A.M. he still hadn't been able to let the confrontation go.

As usual, his attention kept going back to the caves. He took in the topographic maps tacked ceiling to floor along the walls of his apartment. Jagged circles in yellow highlighter marked many of the maps—the area of Ringo's dreams. Evidence that his time hadn't been wasted. He stroked the sharp edge of his rock pick hammer, reimagining the wonders that never seemed to leave his thoughts. Even at his day job, while giving his best pitch to steer customers to the most expensive computer systems, the rust-colored enchantments bewitched him.

He and his foster brothers were twenty-seven years old. He knew they had to get on with the plan while they were still young enough to enjoy all the money they would make from their discovery. Ringo slung his legs over the edge of the mattress, convinced he had to act now. *Right now.*

Rejuvenated by his decision, he crossed the room and took down the maps one by one, rolled them up into one thick bundle and slid a rubber band around the mass. Then he turned his attention to the thousands of index cards that had tracked every finding, every step, every obstacle encountered during the spelunking adventures. He took a body-sized duffel bag from his closet and began to pack everything related to his caves.

Satisfied that the items had been secured in the bag, he went to his wobbly desk, placed the rock pick he considered his talisman on his lap, then booted up his laptop, logged on to the Bureau of Land Management website, and took his first step toward what he was certain would make him rich and famous.

The following Sunday Ringo forged the trail to the third cave. Gee-Lee trudged five paces back, doing his best not to be snagged by a clump of jumping cholla.

"Why are we meeting this week, Ringo? It's not a first Saturday," Gee-Lee said when they reached the sinkhole. Panting, lightheaded and already exhausted, he took his inhaler from his pocket, depressed the plunger and took in a deep breath of the pungent medicine.

Ringo ignored him as he tipped the plywood over and then adjusted his pack, readying to descend the ladder.

"And where is Morris?" Gee-Lee tried again.

"I already told you. Morris was too busy yesterday so we set it up for today instead. And then Tammy made him cancel at the last minute. Said he had to go with her to taste cakes for the wedding reception, or something like that." Ringo poked Gee-Lee's chest with his finger and scowled. "Are you coming, or what?"

"Yeah, yeah," Gee-Lee said, missing his better friend as he followed Ringo down the ladder and into the cave.

"You won't believe what I found yesterday." Ringo turned on his headband light, then waited for Gee-Lee to do the same.

"A new way. This is the path that'll take us to the other two caves."

"Wait a minute. You came here alone? Without Morris and me?"

"Morris backed out and I couldn't get hold of you—you never answer your damn phone!" Ringo took a threatening stride closer to Gee-Lee. "You got a problem?"

Gee-Lee backed up a step and averted his gaze from Ringo's eyes that flashed in the light's glow. "No, no. It's cool. Let's go."

Ringo led Gee-Lee along an unfamiliar path where a ledge had crumbled to the ground. Clumps of wet rubble squashed under Gee-Lee's boots while a sense of foreboding tapped an uneasy rhythm in his chest. Gee-Lee figured the bat population must have been heavier here, their guano so rank he had trouble taking the shallowest of breaths. He pulled the inhaler from his pocket and took another hit.

He picked up his pace to keep up with Ringo. Pulling a flashlight from his pack, he scanned an area of the cave he'd never encountered before, an expanse that resembled a rusty beach. He frowned at lines of footprints stamped in the silt that disappeared into darkness.

"That's weird."

Ringo stopped and turned his head to Gee-Lee. He looked over his shoulder but didn't say a word.

"I see three sets of footprints over there," Gee-Lee said. "Two sets going forward. But only one coming back out."

"Yeah. So?"

"Shouldn't there be four sets?"

After a full minute Ringo pivoted to face Gee-Lee.

Gee-Lee's eyes flicked back and forth, from the footprints to the rock pick hammer in Ringo's fist. "Where's Morris, Ringo?"

Ringo's lips curled up in a garish grin. "Come on. I'll show you."

The deafening screech of hidden bats competed with Gee-Lee's screams.

Ringo's new home he had erected at the hideout campsite near his beloved caves suited him. His one-person tent contained a sleeping bag, the banded topo maps and index cards still concealed in the duffel bag, and supplies to keep him warm, fed and hydrated. He had taken to living in the elements, alone with the desert wilderness, only the occasional canned message over the loudspeaker from Kartchner Caves giving him any sort of "human" contact.

He ran out of provisions after two weeks so he went back to his car parked off the main dirt road, camouflaged now by a covering of dust, as if part of the desertscape. He fired up the engine and took out the cell phone he had stashed in the glove box, then plugged it into the charger attached to the cigarette lighter. His eyes went wide when he saw that he'd missed seventy-six calls and nearly as many voice messages.

The first dozen were from Tammy and he wondered how she could have gotten his phone number. He scrolled down and clicked one at random. A woman's voice blared in his ear: "Ringo, it's me. Tammy. Again. Please tell Morris to call me. *Please?* Tell him I'm not mad. I just need to know—"

Ringo deleted the message.

The next was from his supervisor. He deleted that entry immediately, figuring he didn't want to hear his boss beg him to come back to work. No more hawking computers for him. Ringo smiled, invigorated by returning the snub he'd always had to endure.

After another long list of calls from Tammy, he saw a number that intrigued him. He didn't recognize the area code but tapped the screen to play the message.

"Hello. This is Stanley Templeton, Esquire. I've been trying to reach Louis O'Connell. Louis provided your number as an emergency contact and I hope you can help me out. Nintendo is ready to deal and I must have Louis's approval to proceed. Could you please have him call me right away?"

Ringo frowned at the mobile and wondered what the hell the man was talking about. He deleted that message too. More messages from Tammy, then a few from his foster father—a man he hadn't spoken to in nine years. "Delete," he said, clicking the phone option.

Then, *bingo*, the one he had been waiting for. His finger shook as he hit the play icon.

"Hello, this is Mr. Tate with the Bureau of Land Management for the state of Arizona. I received your claim request and would like to meet you…"

Grateful tears blurred Ringo's vision as he replayed the

message over and over.

Three weeks after establishing his new home, Ringo sat in his tent, the nylon flaps snapping in the creosote-scented breeze. He thought about how things between Morris, Gee-Lee and him had changed nine months ago. They were once inseparable, raised together with the same foster parents until they aged-out of the system. Lucky really, to have had only one home until they were eighteen, then they found apartments in the same complex so they could still remain connected. But then Morris met Tammy and Gee-Lee sequestered himself in his own apartment and neither seemed to have any time for Ringo. Except for their special days in the caves.

Now the first Saturday of the month after ten years had arrived. He saw the date as a good omen. A new beginning. The day Ringo would meet with the BLM man and start a new life.

Feeling reborn, Ringo crawled out of the cramped tent and moved to the sinkhole that led to caves one and two. He glanced at his watch, impatient for Mr. Tate from the Bureau of Land Management to show up for their meeting. Ringo replayed the message in his mind, the man's voice, excited and out of breath, telling Ringo to meet him at the coordinates Ringo had registered—warned him not to tell anyone. Meet him alone. Ringo thought maybe the rep wanted a payoff, to claim the riches Ringo had coveted for so long. No way would Ringo allow that. He tapped the hammer end of his rock pick against his thigh and scowled.

He walked to the top of the bluff and gazed north at the town of Benson fifteen miles away. Then he turned toward where he knew cave three remained hidden. He frowned as he noticed a group of men huddled together, all looking the same in sand-colored shirts and dark brown pants. Ringo knew the plywood that covered the opening must be practically under their feet. In the distance Ringo spotted vehicles, blue and red lights spinning, parked along the two-lane road.

Ringo yelled, "No, no, these are the coordinates. Over here." He waved his hands over his head and jumped up and down. His heartbeat raced as much from the exertion as from the knowledge of what he had "buried" exactly where the authorities had gathered.

A man pointed to Ringo, a glint flashing off something shiny on his chest. Cops, Ringo realized. Armed guards to help him protect his caves from trespassers? Three of the officers ran in Ringo's direction, hands on the butts of their guns.

"That's right! Over here." Ringo continued to wave, a smile so wide his cheek muscles cramped.

When the officers arrived, Ringo clapped the closest one on the shoulder. "When is the BLM man coming? I need to show him where everything is. It's a maze down there, hard to find where the two caves meet…" Ringo's words trailed off when one of the cops ripped his rock pick away and another one pulled out a pair of handcuffs.

"What—what—what? What's going on?" Ringo sputtered. "What're you doing?"

The cop didn't reply, he merely held Ringo's arm as they waited for a white-haired man wearing a suit jacket and sweat pouring down his sideburns to join them.

"Mr. Poplin?" the man asked, taking out a wallet and then exhibiting a gold shield and credentials. "Are you Reginald Poplin?"

Ringo stared at the word DETECTIVE. "Ringo. You can call me Ringo. Where's the BLM man?" He did his best to raise his shackled hands behind his back. "I can't show him the caves if I'm hooked up like this. Too dangerous. It's tricky to get down the hole." He dipped his head toward the group of intruders at the third cave. "There's nothing over there."

"Mr. Poplin, are you aware that Louis O'Connell and Morris Evans have been missing for three weeks? Do you know their whereabouts? Are you involved in something you'd like to confess?"

The detective's words didn't pause long enough for Ringo to respond so he figured he may as well ask his own. "Is the BLM man coming?" he tried again.

The detective shook his head and removed his sunglasses. Eyes blue as the desert sky bored through Ringo. He gave the man a twitchy grin then leaned closer to the lawman and whispered, "It's okay, I get it. I can share. It'll be *our* secret now." He hitched his head toward his campsite. "My caves are this way."

"Actually, Ringo, the coordinates you registered are for the area over there." The detective pointed to where he had come. Where the group of authorities had grown in size within mere minutes.

"But it's a mistake." Ringo trembled as panic overwhelmed him. "I—I must have made a mistake with the coordinates."

"We might've never found you boys if the BLM hadn't recognized your name from the news. They've been reporting missing person's alerts for weeks now. Were you aware of this?"

Ringo made out CORONER printed on a panel van making its way as close to the site as possible. "No...I've been with my caves."

"Well, you won't be visiting your caves anymore. And unfortunately, most likely because of that rock pick of yours, neither will Morris and Louis. We've found their bodies, Mr. Poplin."

"No, no, no," Ringo whimpered, tears coursing muddy tracks down his cheeks. "It's supposed to be a secret."

"Welcome to Kartchner Caverns, the only public caves in Arizona to remain pristine, yet open to the public..." The faint but clear announcement floated on the air as Ringo was led away from his caves.

† † †

DEBORAH J LEDFORD's latest thriller novel, *SNARE,* is The Hillerman Sky Award Finalist. *STACCATO* is book one of her Steven Hawk/Inola Walela series, both released by Second Wind Publishing. She is a three-time nominee for the Pushcart Prize and her award-winning short stories appear in numerous print publications as well as literary and mystery anthologies. Part Eastern Band Cherokee, she spent her summers growing up in western North Carolina where her novels and quite a few short stories are set. She is the current President of the Sisters in Crime Desert Sleuths Chapter. www.DeborahJLedford.com.

FALLING INTO PLACE
Elizabeth R. Marshall

Crazy way to celebrate twenty-seven years of marriage, Paul thought, trying to keep up with his wife on the rocky climb she had chosen. When Kate turned to check on him, he faked a cheerful smile. Her grin in return told him, *You ain't seen nothin' yet, Kiddo.*

The morning was cold, and Paul's breath came out in ragged little clouds—visible reminders of thirty years glued to the seat of an executive desk chair. He was ready to enjoy retirement with his wife, assuming he could convince her to leave her job, but just this morning she had told him she wasn't quite ready yet. Paul tried to remember that Kate was only forty-eight, seven years younger, but damn it, he wanted to travel and play golf with his best friend.

Kate stopped, and Paul caught up with her. "How gorgeous is this?" She gestured around them, arms wide, eyes shining. The ground, sparsely dotted with creosote and brittle bush, palo verde trees and Teddy bear cactus, climbed away to the steep rock slabs of the Phoenix Mountain Preserve, where the mountains gathered around like giant dice players waiting to see the results of a throw.

"Gorgeous," Paul agreed, but he was looking at his wife when he said it, thinking how cute she looked with her dark hair pulled back and hanging from the back of her rhinestone-studded cap.

Kate swatted him. "Pay attention, Honcho." This was short for "Head Honcho," which she had started calling him years ago, when he became CEO of his trucking company.

She went back to hiking, her hips swinging enticingly in front of him, her pale legs moving rhythmically below her shorts. He wondered why she wasn't complaining of the cold, and wished she would; he'd like an excuse to go home and warm her up.

The trail narrowed, with a sharp drop-off to the left and a

steep uphill climb to the right. Paul stopped thinking about sex and focused on putting one foot in front of the other. "You're sure this is the easy part?" he yelled at his wife's back.

And then he saw it. The end of the trail, two hundred yards in front of them—North Mountain, sticking straight up. A paved walk curved around it, very steep and very long, going both down to a parking lot below them and up to the mountaintop. Two people rounded a bend toward the top, and from where he stood they looked like miniatures.

He stifled a groan. "You're kidding, right?"

Kate turned to answer him, but immediately turned back to the mountain as someone screamed, a short, high-pitched sound of female terror.

Paul looked and saw a woman, a third of the way up, glance back as she ran down the path. Up the hill behind her a man hung off the edge of the drop, straining to pull himself back up.

Again the woman turned to check behind her, but she kept moving. From where Paul stood, only the outer edge of the trail was visible, but something must have blocked her way because she suddenly veered onto the shoulder of the path. One foot appeared to strike off center; her ankle twisted, throwing her whole body to the left.

As Paul watched, horrified, the woman went over, sliding and then rolling, picking up speed on the steep incline. She grabbed at a bush, but the branch broke off in her hand. Halfway down the mountain she hit a rock with such force she bounced off it and spun up in the air, limp as a rag doll, before smashing against the ground below. Rocks and dirt flowed over her as she came to a stop on the road a few hundred feet from where they stood.

Or rather, Paul realized, where *he* stood, mouth open, heart pounding. Kate had taken off at a dead run, pulling out her cell phone as she went, barking information and instructions to the person on the other end of the line.

Up the hill, the man had recovered his footing. He yelled down frantically, "Ashley! Ashley! Oh, my God, Ashley!" He disappeared from view.

Kate pushed her badge at the gathering crowd, shouting "Police! Please stay back! Is anyone here a medical professional?" No one came forward. She used the camera on her phone to quickly document the body and the surroundings, then pointed to three of the young men in the group and asked them to remove the dozens of rocks covering the woman who had fallen.

Kate bent to search for a pulse she did not expect to find, but to her surprise the woman moved, slowly and painfully, to curl into a fetal position. A murmur of amazement ran through the crowd. A broken bone protruded through the skin of her upper arm, and the ground beneath her was covered in blood. The woman raised her shaking hands and placed them over her abdomen.

Kate moved closer. "Ma'am, I'm a police detective," she said softly. "Help is on the way. Please try not to move." She squeezed her hand, and felt a faint tightening in return. The woman's right eye looked like it had been punctured. Kate figured that if she survived she would probably lose it. Part of her skull had collapsed. Her mouth was a tight line of pain.

Her face was long, with flat cheekbones and heavy makeup. Kate placed her at late twenties to early thirties. She was thin, almost gaunt, and her nails had been bitten to the quick.

It was a miracle she was moving, and it would be a double miracle if she could speak. "You fell," said Kate. "Can you tell me your name?"

"Ashley," she whispered.

"Do you know what happened?"

"I'm so…" She tried to lick her lips.

Kate hoped she wasn't going to say she was thirsty. She couldn't give her any water without the paramedics' permission, and they were not yet on the scene. She brushed the shoulder-length blonde hair away from the young woman's face and noted that there was a distinct crimp in it, where it had been pulled into a ponytail; the hair tie must have been lost on the way down.

"Let me through!" a man said behind her. "That's my wife."

Kate recognized the man she'd seen hanging off the hilltop as he fell to his knees beside her and tried to hug the injured woman. Instead of reaching for her husband, his wife closed herself up tighter, and said faintly, "Get him away…"

Get him away from me? Kate held out her hand to stop the man, showing him her shield. "I'm sorry, sir. She's badly hurt; it's safer if you don't touch her. Can you tell me her name?"

"Oh, my God, is she still alive? I thought…"

She expected to see relief on the man's face, but Kate saw

wariness, even anger. Kate reached into her fanny pack and took out a small notebook and a pen. "May I have your name, sir?"

"Sam Kingston. That's my wife, Ashley."

Kate said as gently as she could, "I'm sorry, Mr. Kingston, there's very little we can do for her right now. We're waiting for the paramedics."

He touched Ashley's leg before Kate could stop him. "Hang on, baby. We're getting you to a hospital. You'll be okay." His hand came away smeared with blood. He looked at it briefly and pulled a tissue out of his pocket. "Don't try to talk, okay? Don't talk."

Kate kindly, but insistently, got the man to stand up and back away. She understood his need to be with his wife, but after more than twenty years of dealing with things that were not what they seemed, she followed protocol. Kingston stood there, hugging himself, while Kate went back to his wife's side. "Ashley, can you hear me?"

Ashley moaned.

Kate turned back as a second man came through the crowd and touched Kingston's arm. He was a slight man in his forties, dressed in gym clothes, ear buds dangling around his neck. "That was your wife who fell, right?"

Kingston nodded.

"Oh, man, I am so sorry. I didn't see her. I was tying my shoe. I looked up and she was coming at me." He gave Ashley's broken body a quick look and turned away. "I had no time to get out of her way."

"It was an accident," Kingston said. "Not your fault." He brushed the man's shoulder, almost friendly.

Kate took the man's contact info and directed him to stay put and give a statement to the officers when they arrived. She went back to Ashley, who had not moved. Her breath was coming in short gasps now. "Ashley," Kate asked. "How did you fall?"

Kingston had once again moved closer and broke in. "We were just horsing around! She came up—"

"I'm talking to your wife right now, sir. Please stay back."

"Oh, yeah, sure, sorry," he said, but he edged still closer. "Ashley, honey, I'm here. You're going to be okay, just hang in there, baby." Again he said, "Don't try to talk."

Kate knew she had a limited window of time to question Ashley Kingston, and he was using it up. She stood up and stuck her finger in his chest. "Last time! Stand back, sir, or I will have you charged with interfering in a police investigation."

He put up his hands and backed away, his attention locked on his wife.

She turned back to Ashley, who lay completely still, eyes staring. This time when Kate checked for a pulse, she found none. She was gone. She considered CPR, but it made no sense with so much bleeding. Though she would never show it, she felt helpless, unsure what to do to cause the least harm. Kate heard sirens below them, as the ambulance entered the parking lot at street level. They would handle it.

She looked quickly at Sam Kingston. He was using his tissue to meticulously remove the last traces of his wife's blood from his fingernails. He didn't ask about her condition.

Kate felt a familiar sensation, the slowing of her heartbeat, the sharpness of focus that she got when things didn't add up.

She wrote down in her notebook what she had witnessed so far, and looked for her husband. Paul stood a few feet away, staring at her like he had never seen her before. Well, she realized, he hadn't, not like this. She had no gloves with her, and when she looked at her hands and saw blood and dirt on them, she simply wiped them on her shorts. Before this day was out, her husband would probably insist even more strongly that she quit.

She couldn't worry about that now. She needed help. Normally she worked homicides, where she would have another detective and several patrol cops to control the crowds. She hadn't worked an accident scene like this in years.

Was this an accident?

She wasn't going to find out down here, she decided. And she needed to hurry. Against her orders, people at the back of the crowd were heading up the hill to continue their workouts. If there were any clues up there, they would soon be lost.

Kate gestured for Paul to come over. "I could use a hand." He nodded, and she reached into her fanny pack and pulled out some business cards naming her a homicide detective with Phoenix PD. She handed him the cards and told him to keep people there as long as possible. "Give my card to anyone who might have information, and to the EMTs and the police when they arrive."

"Where are you going?" Paul asked her.

She pointed up the trail, and spoke directly to the husband of the fall victim. "Mr. Kingston, the EMTs will be arriving now. Can you show me what happened up there?"

He gave his wife one last, impassive look. "Sure."

The crowd made way for them and they started their climb. She heard Paul taking charge.

"Okay, folks, let's help the police out on this. Anyone have a pen and paper I could use? I'm going to be asking each of you for your contact information."

This was not procedure, but Kate trusted him, and she simply couldn't do everything by herself. It was important to see the accident scene.

Kate and Kingston climbed rapidly, and the valley spread out before them in a peaceful panorama of rolling landscape ringed with mountains. It was a beautiful day. The air had warmed; the sky was clear and bright blue. Normally Kate would marvel at the scenery, find downtown Phoenix in the distance, breathe it all in, but not today.

Below them, the EMTs reached Ashley Kingston. More people had joined the crowd already there, and some were breaking away and coming up the path.

"What do you and your wife do for a living, Mr. Kingston?" This sounded like a casual question, meant to distract him from his pain, but for Kate it was the beginning of an interrogation.

"She was a teacher. We're both teachers," he corrected. "Shadow Cliff High School." Kate felt some bitterness in his answer, and thought he must not like teaching very much. She also noted that he had used past tense in referring to his wife.

"Been married long?"

"Three years next month." They approached the point at which Ashley had gone over, but Kate kept going. She wanted to start at the beginning. Two women in exercise attire, pushing racing strollers, passed them heading downhill. Kate automatically smiled at the babies, but Kingston looked away.

"Children?" Kate asked.

He didn't answer, so she looked at his face to make sure he'd heard her. He'd been watching her, but lowered his eyes. "No. She understood when we married that I didn't want any. Teaching's great birth control." There was that bitterness again.

They got to the spot where Sam Kingston had gone over. Looking down, they watched as the stretcher bearing Ashley

Kingston was wheeled down the hill toward the ambulance. Her face was covered with a sheet. Ashley's husband watched them take his wife away but said nothing.

Kate said a silent prayer for the strength to do right by the woman. That simple goal, to speak for those who could not, was what kept her doing this job. She asked Kingston to sit on a rock on the other side of the path, while she stayed to look around.

The ground fell away steeply here, and had he not been able to put his foot on that boulder and drag himself back up, or had he not been tall enough to reach up to the edge, he would have been the one to hit bottom, not his wife. *Mr. Kingston, in spite of overwhelming evidence to the contrary, this was your lucky day.* She wondered what the hell had these two been playing at in such a dangerous place.

Getting down on her knees to look over the edge, she spotted a lacy hair tie dangling from a bush below the sight line. Kate reached for it with her pen and dropped it into a clean tissue from her fanny pack. She'd transfer the whole thing to an evidence bag when she could.

"That's Ashley's," Kingston said, suddenly right next to her. Too close. Kate stood quickly and backed a step away. Did she imagine the chilling little smile on his face?

She shook it off, but stayed far from the precipice. "Can you show me what happened?"

He took a big breath and let it out. "We were on our way up the mountain, and we stopped here to rest and enjoy the view. Ashley was in a funny mood, real high energy, kind of dancing around me, making jokes.

"Did you fight? Anything physical happen between you?"

"No, nothing like that. And then I guess she pushed me."

"You guess?"

"She hit me from behind. I wasn't expecting it, and I moved forward. I lost my footing."

"What did your wife do when you fell?"

Kingston smiled, as though at a fond memory. "She screamed. But when she saw I was okay she laughed, and ran away. Like I said, she was in a strange mood."

Kate looked at the steep fall, probably three hundred feet down, and tried to imagine Paul dangling off a cliff like this, and her laughing about it. Strange, indeed.

"Do you think your wife was trying to kill you, Mr.

Kingston?"

He considered the question. Finally he said, "I've been wondering that myself."

"Was she seeing someone else? Had she talked about divorce?"

Again Kingston shook his head. "No."

"Is there an inheritance? Any life insurance?"

Kingston looked down and seemed to contemplate his brush with death before he answered. "When we married, I wanted to make sure she was protected if anything happened to me, and she insisted I should be protected too, so we each got a million dollar life insurance policy. I never thought I'd be the one collecting on it."

Kate made no comment.

A police officer, stocky and breathing hard, made his way toward them. Kate showed her badge and asked for an evidence bag for the hair tie.

"The officer will take you to the station to complete a formal statement, Mr. Kingston, and then you can make the identification for your wife." She dropped the hair tie into the evidence bag and handed it to the officer. "Would you send my husband up, please?"

When Paul arrived, his wife stood at the spot where Ashley Kingston had gone over, arms crossed in a hug, head down, but her eyes were open and staring at where the body had lain. A ground squirrel sniffed a safe distance away, its tail curled and vibrating. When the creature saw Paul, it stretched its tail over its back and chattered angrily before disappearing over the edge.

Paul went to Kate and put his arm around her waist. She turned into him and held on tight. "Let's finish the hike," she said. "I need to work off some stress."

They made it to the top of the peak in silence and sat on a bench that overlooked the city. Kate pulled a baggie of bread out of her fanny pack, and ground squirrels, a full-sized squirrel, and even a large gray mouse came out of nowhere to be fed.

"You okay? Paul finally asked.

"Yeah. How about you? First dead body, and all."

He shrugged. "Not pleasant, that's for sure. Watching her die. Poor guy, what a horrible accident."

Kate shook her head. "That was no accident. He killed her."

"What do you mean? We all saw her. She slipped and fell."

"A death that occurs as the result of a felony is murder, and Sam Kingston attempted to murder his wife." Not for the first time in her career, Kate felt overwhelmed. There were so many victims, and no matter how hard you worked, so few of them got justice.

Paul still didn't seem convinced. "Well, it did seem odd that she wouldn't stay with him. I just figured she knew he was okay, and they played rough. I mean, the guy was pretty broken up."

Kate had seen a lot of distraught people in her time on the force. Sam Kingston was not one of them. "If it were me, would you have left me lying there alone before the paramedics even arrived?"

"Of course not!" Paul said. And then he seemed to get her point. "But Sam Kingston didn't hesitate, did he?"

"He told me they were headed up the hill. If Ashley were continuing a game, she would have kept running uphill. She was trying to get away from him. She might have made it, too, except for that guy tying his shoe." She emptied the last of the bread from the baggie, and one brave ground squirrel came close enough to claim it, tail high and twitching.

Kate continued, "The four most deadly times for a woman are when she's pregnant, when she tells her man she's leaving him, when he has someone waiting in the wings, and when she's worth more dead than alive. Our girl probably hit at least three out of four. She never had a chance." She told him about the insurance policies that Kingston had confirmed.

"You think he has someone on the side?"

"Wouldn't surprise me. And I think she was pregnant. Her husband definitely didn't want kids." Kate thought about Ashley's thin body and bitten nails, and about Sam Kingston not allowing Kate to speak to his wife. "My gut says he was a control freak. He may have suspected she'd had enough. Or she may have told him."

"What makes you think she was pregnant?"

Kate could still see the woman, bleeding, her broken body barely able to move, covering her belly with her hands in one last futile gesture of protection. "Just a hunch," she said.

"You let him go."

"Would you vote to convict right now if you were on the jury?"

"Sounds circumstantial," Paul allowed.

"There's one piece of evidence I don't think he can explain away," Kate said with resolute satisfaction. "Her hair tie." She explained where she had found it. "There were a lot of hairs on it, with roots attached, that will prove it was hers. Maybe that it was yanked pretty hard off her head, too. If she came up behind him and pushed, as he claims, how did the hair tie get three feet out, stuck to a bush? There's been no wind, and those things might get loose and fall, but they don't fly. He lied. He came up behind *her*, and when she was somehow able to keep from going over, and turned to run, he grabbed her by the ponytail. The elastic came off in his hand instead. I'm certain he was clutching it when he slipped over the edge.

"I didn't arrest him because I want him to say over and over again—for the record—that he was facing *away* from her when he went over, with no way to grab that hair tie."

They were quiet for a while, each with their own thoughts.

"Well, my darling," he said, "you make a hell of a detective."

Kate sighed, long and hard, releasing the weight of the world. She turned to Paul and put her head on his shoulder; he put his arm around her. "You know," she said, "I am seriously considering retiring. I really realized today how lucky I am to have you in my life."

Paul gave her a mock wounded look. "Took you long enough."

She kissed his cheek penitently. "Poor Ashley, and so many others like her, had no one she could trust. Whatever time we have left—"

"Whoa, we're not that old!"

"It's not about old. Ashley was young. We just never know how long our particular roller coaster of life will last, and I want to ride it to the end with you."

"Well, you know that would make *me* happy. Are you sure you can play golf with me all day and not miss the excitement? What would you do?"

"I have a lot of stories from this job. Maybe I'll write mystery novels. How hard can *that* be?"

✝   ✝   ✝

ELIZABETH R. MARSHALL is a native New Yorker, happily transplanted to Phoenix almost twenty-five years ago, and a lifelong, avid murder mystery reader. Now that her children are grown she is finishing her first novel, a mystery about a reluctant psychic who travels with a carnival. "Falling Into Place" is the first short story she has ever written, and it was inspired by climbing North Mountain in the Phoenix Mountain Preserve, and being afraid to look down.

MURDER IN THE NINTH
Merle McCann

Scottsdale Homicide Detective Molly Raines backed out of her garage with the air conditioning going full blast. Not yet nine in the morning and the temperature was over one hundred degrees. What did she expect? It was August in the Phoenix Valley.

Through her windshield, she spotted hot air balloons floating above the Tatum corridor. Someday, before she was too old to climb into the basket, she'd have to sail over the valley. Usually the balloons made her smile, but she had a strange feeling today wasn't going to be a good day. Before she reached the end of her street, her cell phone rang. Molly eyed the ID window. It was her Homicide Supervisor, Lawrence Hudson.

"This is Raines."

"Hey, Molly. Got a call from the Violent Crime Supervisor. We've a homicide at a Pima and Happy Valley location. You in the area?"

"Not far. What's the address?" Molly jotted down the numbers. "On my way."

"Wilson and Schmidt are already rolling to the scene. I'll meet you there."

"Any preliminary info?"

"Patrol's there. Crime scene's secured. The vic, Nancy O'Shea, is inside the home—older woman, apparently lived alone. EMTs confirmed death. Vic's neighbor called it in. He checked on the woman because she didn't walk her dog this morning."

"Did he go inside?"

"Yep. Said he spotted O'Shea and made a u-turn for home to call nine-one-one. Backdoor was unlocked. Body's in the front hall."

"I'll be there in twenty minutes."

"I've got the search warrant. See you there."

Five years ago, when Molly joined the homicide division, Lieutenant Lar Hudson treated her as a team member from the first day. Over time, they'd come to understand and trust each other. If there was one thing Molly knew, Lar's judgment was solid and his sixth sense usually spot on. A tough guy who loved animals.

When Molly reached the gate at the subdivision, she spoke with the guard and he waved her through. The vic's house was situated on a quiet cul-de-sac. Molly parked behind three patrol cars. Lar's car sat across the street. She stepped from her vehicle expecting Wilson and Schmidt to arrive any minute. The house and yard had been circled in yellow crime scene tape, and three uniformed officers stood at the curb. Curious neighbors gathered in their driveways, watching.

Molly approached the patrol officers just as Lar finished providing the police aide with the necessary information for his crime scene log. He turned and introduced Molly to the uniformed officers.

"What can you tell us, Lieutenant?" she asked.

He squared his stance. "Scene's secured. EMTs confirmed death. Forensic team's en route. CSS has been dispatched. We talked to the neighbor, Stan Blaire. Said he and his wife were in O'Shea's home many times, but today he cut out pretty fast. He told us O'Shea has no family in Arizona other than a grandson who recently signed with the Diamondbacks. That's it."

"Thanks, Lieutenant," Molly said. "When Detectives Wilson and Schmidt arrive, let them know we're inside."

Molly and Lar slipped under the tape and approached the decorative iron gate to the courtyard at the front of the house. A locked dead bolt prevented them from entering. They circled to the walled backyard and found the gate there unlocked. Molly scanned the silent house and perfectly groomed yard. The sparkling pool water was still, the equipment silent, undoubtedly on a timer. They lingered on the patio long enough to take in the back yard and neighboring land.

Wilson and Schmidt appeared as Molly stared at the cracked glass, sliding patio door standing partially open. Lar gestured to her. "Raines is taking the lead on this one. Let's take a look inside and then we'll figure our assignments."

They put on latex gloves and eased into what she perceived was the family room, average-sized, decorated in gold tones. Molly admired the Kachinas on the bookcases and the needlepoint throw pillows. The room felt homey.

Other than the damaged slider, she saw no sign of violence. Framed photos graced the fireplace mantle. She pointed to the door. "Someone kicked it pretty hard."

Lar nodded. "Yeah, from the inside. Must've been pissed."

They glanced into every nook and closet as they passed through the kitchen into a crossing hallway. Molly said to Wilson and Schmidt, "Once you guys have checked out the scene, I'd like you to interview the neighbors. Wilson, you take Mr. Blaire next door." She turned to Schmidt. "You canvas the rest of the street. People were outside watching when we drove up."

After assigning the detectives, Molly and Lar checked out the various rooms in the house then inspected the victim's body, avoiding the coagulating blood that pooled around it. The deceased lay on her stomach in front of a double doorway leading to a small home office. The collar of her Nike warm-ups was soaked in blood. Molly clenched her teeth and squatted to view up close the crushed skull. *Lar's right. Her killer must have been in a rage.*

The woman's walking shoes appeared new, and her nails were polished. She wore modest makeup. Molly eyed the blood on the white walls and nearby carpet. "Spatter indicates she was hit more than once." Molly rose and slowly pivoted, memorizing everything. The elegant home was meticulously maintained. "She lived well." Molly glanced down once more at the body and closed her eyes. *Poor thing.*

Lar clamped his jaw. "What a cowardly act. Bastard hit her from behind."

"Yep. She never saw it coming." Molly sighed and walked into the master bedroom, opposite the office. The king-sized bed was unmade. She paused to study three pictures hanging above it. Brides and grooms at an altar. *Probably her wedding and each of her childrens'.* Molly recalled her own wedding and her fabulous dress. But then memories of an ugly divorce shattered the moment.

More photos covered the opposite wall. *Grandkids?* Some were of girls, one in a soccer uniform, one in a basketball jersey, and another wearing a karate gi with a black belt. The rest were of a young boy. The first was a freckle-faced kid in a soiled jersey, holding a bat and well-worn glove, too big for his hand. *Our new D-back?* Another showed the same face, this time in a little league football uniform, helmet tucked under his arm. "Check out these pics, Lar. The whole family's into sports."

"Yeah, the vic, too. There're skis, a bike and golf clubs in the garage. I'll look at the photos in a minute."

As Molly moved from frame to frame, the boy grew older and bigger, his uniforms more sophisticated. She stopped before an eight by ten photo. The boy crouched behind the plate in catcher's gear, glove elevated, ready for the pitch. "He's a catcher. Weren't you a catcher, Lar? You gotta see these."

The next enlargement showed the boy hitting, stretched out in a completed swing, the ball exploding from the bat. Having played ball all through school, Molly studied his form then moved on. "Lar, this shot shows the boy pitching as a righty, but he bats lefty. I can imagine how many pro offers he received."

She stepped closer. The last photo showed him accepting his D-backs' jersey. At the far right, almost out of the frame, a gray-haired woman stood, hands clasped beneath her chin, beaming with pride. *The vic.* Left of the photo, the evening's printed program was displayed, dated less than six weeks ago. Using her cell phone, Molly snapped a photo of the picture for identification purposes.

Lar said. "I'm going to check out the closet."

"Be right there." Molly rescanned the room. On a table next to the sofa in the sitting area, a scrapbook rested at an angle. She picked it up and flipped some pages. An *Arizona Republic* article reported the drafting by the D-backs of Jason O'Shea. She noted it for her supplemental report.

"Damn it, Mol." He didn't sound good.

She wheeled around and headed into the closet, stopping short. "Aw geez." A tawny cocker spaniel lay on its side, its head bludgeoned the same way the vic's had been. "I wondered about the dog."

"Me, too. God, I hope Mrs. O'Shea never knew." He sighed. "I figure she's been dead for only a matter of hours." He checked his watch. "When the ME gets here, will you deal with him? I hate his puns." He shook his head. "Glad you're the lead on this one, Mol. I'm up to my ass in cases right now."

"No problem." She opened a drawer of the wall unit above a hamper. "She had a lot of jewelry. Her wedding rings are here." Molly spotted a set of keys then glanced at the hanging clothes. "These furs are real. It doesn't feel to me like a burglary gone bad."

Thirty minutes later, Medical Examiner, Dr. Barlow, showed up with his assistant. He nodded to Molly and Lar. "I understand this is the grandmother of that new Diamondbacks' player."

"Any trouble finding the place?" Lar asked.

"Nope. Finding my way was easy as rounding the bases."

Lar groaned. "You're effin' killin' me, Doc."

Barlow chuckled.

That evening, Molly and Lar, sat at a conference room table for a briefing with Detectives Wilson and Schmidt, their notes spread out in front of them. Two department supervisors sat in. Molly addressed Wilson. "What did you learn from the neighbor?"

"Sounds like O'Shea had a close family. Her children stayed in contact. She and her husband were perfectionists, hard workers, do-it-yourselfers. Never hired outside help. They weren't wealthy but lived comfortably. The husband died of a coronary two years ago." He cleared his throat. "Their two children live out-of-state. O'Shea and her husband followed their grandkids' sporting events from the get-go. The granddaughters eventually gave it up, but not the grandson. Mrs. O'Shea was thrilled with his baseball success and often bragged about his talent. He attended Gonzaga University in Spokane." Wilson sighed. "Sounds like a hell of a kid."

"What about the other neighbors?" Molly asked, turning to Schmidt.

"They didn't see anything. Their houses all orient to the backyards."

Molly clicked her pen several times. "The perp probably came in through the slider and left the same way. The front door and gate were still locked. I found her keys. Once we get fingerprints, we'll know for sure."

Schmidt took a deep breath. "She would have seen him through the glass slider. Either she knew him or he tricked her into opening the door."

Molly nodded while staring at her notes. "One of the crime scene techs found cigarette ashes in a flower pot on the patio. No butt to test for DNA."

Wilson leaned forward. "Blaire, the neighbor, said Mrs. O'Shea enjoyed a cocktail but never smoked."

"Geez," Lar said. "It suggests our killer relaxed by the pool after finishing his work—maybe just the pool man."

Molly looked at Lar. "Blair said they used no outside help. I doubt she had a pool guy."

Molly asked Schmidt, "Any idea on the weapon?"

"Not yet. The glass slider was struck too low for it to have been a knee. Had to be something harder than a shoe. Possibly a metal object."

She glanced from face to face. "A steel-toed boot?"

"It's possible. Could've used the murder weapon on the door," Lar said with a shrug. "It was smashed from the inside. No evidence of forced entry. Looks like O'Shea knew her killer. So why destroy the door before he leaves? Rage? Of course, he might've been high on something, PCP maybe." Lar shook his head. "My gut keeps screaming revenge."

Molly jotted a note. "Let's go with that theory. Lotta signs point to it. We need to discover who was angry enough at her to kill her." She paused. "If he carried a weapon, she'd have seen it through the glass door. Why let him in?"

"Probably left it hidden outside," Lar said. "At some point, went back for it, approached her from behind and swung like Babe Ruth. A crow bar keeps coming to mind."

Molly looked from Wilson to Schmidt. "Canvas everyone in the vicinity. Talk to the gate guards. Bring in O'Shea's computer. Contact everyone in her directory. Go through her bills and bank accounts. Maybe she wasn't as well off as her neighbor thought? Find out who paid for that kid's education. Private schools are expensive, even with a sports scholarship.

"I'll look into the family. I've already notified her son. He and his wife are flying in tonight from Colorado. I'll Google him and his in-laws and business associations.

"The grandson owns a high-rise condo near Scottsdale Fashion Square," Molly said. "Signing bonus purchase. He was blown away when I told him about his grandmother. He's coming into the precinct tomorrow. Somewhere, we'll get a break." Molly hoped that was true. She couldn't get Mrs. O'Shea off her mind. *Nobody should die that way.*

The next day, Molly approached Schmidt. "Find anything new in the O'Shea case?"

"I went back to talk to the gate guards, picked up a computer printout on everyone entering the week preceding the murder.

Most vehicles belonged to residents or their visitors. An RV, several delivery trucks, pool maintenance men, and landscapers also came through."

"Anything stand out?"

"The guard commented on one of the landscapers, new to the community. Said the equipment he was hauling didn't make sense. He gave me the guy's ID. I'll check it out."

That afternoon, Mrs. O'Shea's son and his family arrived. Molly put Jason, the grandson, in one interview room and his parents in another, telling them she'd be with them shortly.

She strode in to meet Jason, a tall, strapping young man. Molly sat opposite him and asked, "Mr. O'Shea, were you on good terms with your grandmother?"

Jason's brow furrowed. "Of course. Why would you ask?"

Molly scrutinized him. "It's my job. Murders are frequently committed by relatives. We eliminate the family members as suspects first." She cleared her throat. "I'd like you to stand, take off your shirt and show me your hands and arms."

"Why?" he nearly shouted.

"To see if you have defensive wounds. Mrs. O'Shea would have fought her assailant, if given the chance."

Jason's eyes filled with tears. He stood and yanked off his shirt. "I loved my grandmother. I'd never hurt her. I would die for her and gramps. They supported me in everything I did. My sisters, too."

"I don't doubt that." She stood. "Raise your hands toward me." She scanned his arms and torso for bruises and found none. His hands and fingernails appeared uninjured. "Turn around, please." He pivoted and she saw his back was unmarked. "Thank you, Jason. You can put your shirt back on." She sat down. "I understand your grandparents were both athletes in their day."

Jason's voice cracked. "They were. Gramps was crazy about sports. Gram, too. She skied with us last winter. But, she loved baseball best."

"You must have brought them great happiness."

"I hope so." He stifled a sob as he sat down. "They came to every game they could. My sisters' games, too." He wiped his eyes on his sleeve. "You gotta catch her killer."

"We're doing our best." Molly asked him a few more questions, thanked him again, and suggested he wait for his parents in the reception area. "They won't be long."

Next, she joined John O'Shea and his wife, introduced herself and expressed her condolences. John looked haggard. He'd taken hard the news of his mother's death. His wife, Diana, held a tissue to her reddened nose.

"When can I see her?" John asked.

"I'll take you over to County this afternoon." Molly showed him the picture she'd taken of the photograph at the O'Shea's home. "Is this your mother?" He nodded. "Can you think of anyone who would want to kill her?"

He shook his head. "I don't think my mom ever made an enemy."

"Where did she grow up? What was her maiden name?"

"Hensler. Her father was German. She grew up in Montana."

"Tell me about her. The neighbors didn't know much."

"Mom's parents are gone. She was never close to them. My sister and I saw them only once or twice. Mom met Dad at San Diego State. They were both there on athletic scholarships. Dad played baseball, she played softball. They married and had me and my sister."

"Did she have brothers or sisters?" He shook his head.

"Where's your sister?"

"She's in the hospital in Montana. Emergency stomach surgery. I'll give you the number. She'll come as soon as she can."

Molly nodded and stood. "This'll do for now. I'll call if I have more questions." She led the O'Sheas to their son and watched as they walked on either side of him, each with an arm around his waist.

The next day, Molly phoned Lar. "I'm on my way to the ME's to read his preliminary report. Dead end on the landscaper. Wilson's doing more canvassing. Maybe a neighbor or a guard has remembered something." They hung up after Lar encouraged her to keep trying.

When Molly walked into the ME's department, Barlow met her at the lab's door. "You here for my prelim?" He handed a paper to her. "Fresh from the printer."

"Anything obvious?"

"There were no defensive wounds, no struggle. She died from blunt-force trauma to her head. Her facial bones look to have fractured on the stone flooring. Repeated blows to the back of her head are evident. Whoever hit her was swinging for the fence. I found traces of a black dye and carbon in her hair, but it wasn't hair dye. Her gray hair wasn't even tinted."

"Any ideas on the weapon?"

"The nature of her wounds suggests the weapon didn't have sharp edges. It was round—like a pipe, or barrel-shaped. Given everyone's focus on baseball, I suspect a bat." He raised a finger. "Wood bats have the maker's label burned into them. Some are rubbed with color following the burning—red, black, just depends."

"Could I trace the manufacturer?"

He stroked his chin. "Doubt it. The percentage of dye to carbon suggests this bat's fairly old. Plus, there was no resin. I doubt it was ever used in a pro game. So, you'd probably strike out, pardon the pun. If you should discover a bat, we'll test it for blood residue, and if it's the vic's, you'll have your weapon. Now that would be a home run, pardon—"

"The pun. I know. Would that evidence fly in court?"

"Good one." He grinned. "It'd fly like a home run."

Three weeks slipped by, and Molly worried the O'Shea case was sliding toward the cracks. The memory of Jason O'Shea's grief haunted her. Molly wanted to get this killer. More than wanted. Needed. O'Shea's entire family longed for answers.

Hurrying from the precinct, she stopped by Lar's desk. "I'm taking the O'Shea file home over the weekend. I'll re-evaluate everything."

For two days, Molly sifted, sorted and listed the facts of the case in columns on a spreadsheet. Nothing stood out. She outlined each of the family members with everything she'd learned about them. Her telephone interview with Mrs. O'Shea's daughter provided nothing additional. Then she realized she'd researched O'Shea's extended family, but not the Hensler side. She put the name into Arizona's database and came up dry. As a last resort, she Googled the name. A Denver newspaper article indicated a Robert Hensler had been arrested recently on assault charges. Molly grabbed her cell phone and called Denver PD. After properly identifying herself, she asked, "Can I speak with the detective in charge of the Hensler case?" She was put on hold.

A raspy voice responded. "This is Farley."

Molly introduced herself. "I'm inquiring about Robert Hensler. I understand you're holding him on assault charges."

"The newspaper got that wrong. Attempted murder is more accurate. Hensler struck a boy with a baseball bat, the grandson of the woman he was living with. Said the teenager didn't show him proper respect. But, we're no longer holding him. He lawyered up. The SOB was released because of an unlawful search. The search was on the up and up, but you know lawyers."

"Any chance you discovered Hensler's parents' names?"

"Hang on." She heard paper shuffling. "Estella and Charles Hensler." Molly listened while Farley provided more details.

"Any idea where Hensler might be now?"

"Nope. He was driving an RV when we arrested him. Could be anywhere."

"Can I have the license plate?"

"Sure." Farley gave her the information.

Molly thanked him and hung up. Next, she phoned John O'Shea. "Hello, this is Detective Raines. Do you know if your mother recently had contact with her brother, Robert?"

"She didn't have a brother. Mother was an only child."

Molly's brow rose. "Really? Can I have your grandparents' full names?"

"Of course. Estella Marie and Charles John Hensler."

"Thanks. I'll be in touch." Using the information Farley provided, Molly requested an APB on the vehicle in Arizona and surrounding states, with an Order To Detain and Notify Scottsdale PD.

Ten days later, she approached Lar at his desk. "Want to go to Salt Lake with me?"

"What's up?" He arched an eyebrow. "I know it ain't nothin', 'cause you're about to bust."

She grinned. "I should lay one of Barlow's puns on you." Her tone shifted. "I just got a call from Salt Lake PD. They're holding O'Shea's brother. I talked to our boss. He okayed the trip. I booked us on the next flight. Salt Lake's picking us up."

Molly and Lar walked into the Salt Lake City Jail. A Sergeant Graham met them and explained that Hensler was stopped for drunk driving. "The officer put the license number into his computer and saw the APB. He brought Hensler in on the D.O.

We've held him until you could get here."

Sergeant Graham obtained a warrant to search Robert Hensler's RV, and rode along with Molly and Lar to locate the rig. It turned out to be a toy-hauler with a Harley-Davidson motorcycle in the back and living quarters up front. In an outer compartment, behind a spare tire, Lar found a baseball bat. He carried it to the RV's open door and showed it to Molly. "Could be the weapon, but doesn't account for the slider's damage."

She grinned. "Right. But, look here." She held up a pair of steel-toed motorcycle boots. "They could explain the damaged door."

On her way out of the vehicle, she grabbed a high school yearbook she found in a closet. It contained pictures and clippings of Nancy Hensler O'Shea and her family. Sorting through the items, Molly found the article and picture of Jason and his grandmother at the Diamondbacks' draft event. Their faces were circled in ballpoint and notations in the margins read, THE TIME HAS COME. I KNOW WHERE YOU LIVE, LITTLE SIS. Another read, ONE SWING OF MY BAT.

When Hensler refused to return to Arizona, Molly prepared the paperwork for his extradition. Then she telephoned John O'Shea and told him about Robert Hensler. She described the scrapbook's contents.

"I wonder why Mother never told us about her brother?"

"She was probably frightened for you and your sister. Growing up with a sociopath must have been horrendous." Molly changed the subject. "Robert played baseball in high school. Made the varsity, but the colleges weren't interested. He must have been irrationally jealous of your mother's success— and now your son's."

John's voice cracked. "The man's a monster. Is Jason safe?"

"Jason needn't worry. With everything we have on him, Hensler'll be locked up for a very long time."

† † †

Award winning author, **MERLE McCANN**, is best known for her Longjohners' Mystery Series for young adults. She is looking forward to publication later this year of her award winning, adult novel, *Vagabonds and Kings.* Born in the Yukon, raised in Seattle, she has traveled the United States and Europe with her husband pursuing their Arabian horse business. Before settling down to write serious fiction, McCann worked as a scenic photographer. She lives with her husband in Scottsdale, Arizona.

SOMEONE WON'T LEAVE ALIVE
Margaret Morse

Tuesday evening, the final tour group for the Haunted Hacienda followed me in silence. When I described the square dances and sock hops given in the ballroom, they yawned. On the tower balcony, I gushed about the lights of Phoenix. They frowned. Viewing the Coke memorabilia, they muttered about its worth.

Outside the master bedroom, the air chilled me. "Ready for the haunted bedroom?" I stood sideways in the doorway to let them see into the dimly lit interior. White curtains swayed around the bed.

I scanned the ten visitors, who were dressed in shorts and T-shirts. "How many of you have heard about the ghosts in this bedroom?" My voice echoed off the tile floor and plaster walls. Four people raised their hands.

My godmother, Sophie Fortner, moved through the group to me, her soft-soled shoes making no sound. She liked to tag along for the last part of the tour. Light from a copper sconce created shadows across her wrinkles.

I put my arm around her shoulders. "This is Sophie Fortner, the home's owner. Have you seen the ghosts?"

Sophie scanned the group. "The presence of those I have loved. I have felt that, yes."

Crossing the threshold, I inhaled a lavender scent. "Okay, let's go into the bedroom. Please don't touch anything."

As they followed me, a lady jumped and looked over her shoulder. "I felt something brush against me."

Sophie drifted over to us. Wearing a black pantsuit, she blended with the room's half-light. "The spirits of the departed linger in their homes." Two women shivered and rubbed their bare arms. "Don't be frightened. It's good that our loved ones are with us." She smiled at a picture on the nightstand. "My husband, Joe. I feel his presence."

The group swirled through the room, chattering. Sophie's talk about the dead had enlivened them. Three women asked about the sepia-toned pictures of Sophie's parents and grandparents. After I pointed out the long-jawed face she inherited from her mother's side of the family, I turned and found Derek Merwin scowling at me from the doorway.

Sophie's nephew had her hawk nose and blue eyes. "Don't let me interrupt. Go right ahead with the tour, Patricia Ann."

I focused back on the pictures. "This is Rosalie Fortner. She spent one night in this room and was never seen again." I sensed Derek's eyes drilling into me. Sophie squeezed my shoulder. Ever since my mother abandoned me and my dad ten years ago, Sophie had ramped up her godmother role, taking me out to lunch or on special shopping trips. This summer she kept me busy as her tour guide so I'd have no time to worry about law school in the fall.

Herding the group out of the darkness, I ushered them downstairs to the great room. Derek stalked after us. Three generations of Fortners had gutted the original structure to create this space, big enough to hold three leather couches, four recliners, and a pool table. On one wall, Sophie had displayed Joe's collection of Colt .45s.

I gestured for the group to gather round a coffee table that held a velvet jewelry box with five drawers. "This is something new on the tour. The box contains the jewelry that Sophie's husband gave her over their forty years of marriage."

Derek's face went from healthy tan to hot red as I opened the drawers one by one. Rings, bracelets, and necklaces sparkled with rubies and diamonds. When I opened the last drawer, Sophie reached for the concho belt gleaming there and fastened it around her waist.

"Is that the concho belt that killed a man?" A pudgy bald guy stared at the silver ovals studded with turquoise.

My feet aching in the cowboy boots Sophie liked me to wear, I launched into my final anecdote. "A year after they married, Joe wanted to buy his first used car lot. He wouldn't let Sophie mortgage her family home. Sophie pawned this belt instead. That night, the pawnshop owner was found dead, the concho belt clutched in his hands. A failed robbery."

"How could you stand to wear it?" a red-faced lady asked.

Sophie squared her shoulders. "It belonged to my grandmother. Wearing it makes her live on in me." Her eyes went to Derek's clenched jaw. "This completes the tour. Thanks for coming. Your admittance fees help support a trust to keep the museum running."

Having let the group out, I returned to the great room, where Sophie and Derek faced each other across the coffee table. Tired after four hours of tours, I headed for the vintage candy dispenser, a glass case mounted on a pole. Grabbing a wooden token from an ashtray, I inserted it in the metal slot, then scooped up the chocolate-covered candies that flowed out. Sugar and cocoa soothed me. A sign on the front of the glass case warned, NO PEANUTS. All of the Fortner men had severe peanut allergies, so the family needed to be vigilant.

Sophie loved chocolate-covered peanuts. Looking in her dresser for a scarf a month ago, I had found her secret stash.

I hastily swallowed a second dose of chocolate. "I'll leave you two alone."

"Wait, Sparky." Sophie used my nickname when she wanted to grab my attention. She held a paper at me, her hand shaking. "Could you review this as my legal representative? Tell me what you think it means."

Derek reached for the paper. "She hasn't even started law school."

Sophie's chin went up. "Her father is my lawyer."

I got to the paper before Derek. "I've been around the law all my life." Reading the document made me burn with anger. "This is a guardian petition, Sophie. It's asking the court to say you're not competent to handle your affairs." I glared at Derek. "You can't be serious."

He snatched the paper from me and turned to Sophie. "I've considered this for months, ever since you started this tour nonsense, making a horror show of our family history. Now you're being irresponsible with the jewelry. You should never have removed it from the bank."

Sophie fingered the concho belt. "I have a burglar alarm."

"I've kept quiet about things like you neglecting to pay your utility bills."

"She was on a cruise." I raised my voice to match Derek's loudness.

"Hearing her babble about seeing ghosts tonight convinced me I'm doing the right thing."

I got in his face. He towered over me. "My dad is her lawyer. We'll fight this."

Sophie made a soft moaning sound, then pressed her hand to her mouth. I moved to her side.

Derek pulled another sheet of paper from his pants pocket. "Sophie, there's a way out. I won't file the guardianship petition if you sign this power of attorney." He offered her the document.

Sophie slipped an arm around my waist, holding the paper so we could read it together. Biting my lip, I frowned at the flow of legal words. "Sophie, this would give Derek the authority to handle your business affairs. Supposedly, you could take it back anytime."

Derek offered Sophie a pen. "Make it easy on yourself, Sophie. Sign the power of attorney."

She sank onto the cold leather of the couch. "Joe always made these business decisions for me. Give me time. I need to connect with Joe."

"We'll talk to my dad tomorrow," I said.

"No, this ends tonight. Let me figure out what Joe would do. You two leave me until I call."

Derek took out a fat cigar and headed for the second level. I passed him as he flicked on the light to the room with the Coke collection. Replaying the scene between Derek and Sophie, I felt I'd let her down. I should have argued with her or used some counter threat against Derek.

Sophie had a liquor cabinet in the tower room, where each night this summer we'd enjoyed a nightcap on the balcony. Helping myself to a tequila shot, I stepped outside to sit on a wooden bench. The tequila's heat uncoiled my stomach muscles.

"Mind if I join you?"

I jumped at Derek's growl. He raised the tequila bottle and a shot glass. I shrugged and held out my glass. Behind me, the house creaked. Below, the wind rustled creosote bushes.

Derek tossed back the tequila. "I'm doing the power of attorney to help Sophie. With my own mother, I let things slide. We had to go to court to get control of her affairs. It was ugly. Tell your dad I'll give Sophie a monthly accounting."

I didn't care about his past problems, because he had hurt Sophie today.

In silence, we shared two more shots. The breeze messed my hair but didn't cool me.

The city lights below were a puzzle I couldn't put together. Derek leaned on the balcony's stone ledge and smoked his cigar.

Rather than yield the tower to him, I moved upwind and studied the nighttime desert. I recalled when I was a kid, how I feared terrible shapes would form out of the darkness and swallow me.

Sophie called up to us after Derek and I had spent half an hour in uncompanionable silence. We found her in the great room sitting up very straight on the couch next to the jewelry box.

She dropped the power of attorney on the coffee table. "Joe has told me what he thinks is right. I've given you power of attorney, Derek. I suppose it's legal, even though you claim I'm not competent."

That was a good point. I wished I'd thought of it. From what I'd seen of the document, it also needed a notary's stamp. I kept quiet about that flaw.

Derek's lips twitched almost in a smile. "Competency is a matter of opinion. I find you quite rational at this moment."

"Since you're so worried about the jewelry, you can take it back to the bank tomorrow." She arose unsteadily, accepting my arm. "Before you take the jewelry, write out a receipt listing each item."

"Why can't Patricia Ann do it?"

Sophie tightened her grip. "Sparky will help me to my room. Give her the receipt before you leave."

As we walked out, I looked back and saw Derek heading for the candy dispenser. I'd tipped off Sophie to Derek's habit of raiding the chocolate when he thought he was alone. My frequent trips for a fix showed me the candy level was noticeably down after his visits.

By the time we reached the bedroom level, Sophie's grip on me loosened and she walked on her own. "Give Derek some time. Don't forget the perimeter check."

That was our joke. After the last tour, I went round the house to see if any visitors were loitering. Tonight, I met only a nervous cottontail who darted across the path circling the house. Lights illuminated the white walls of the Haunted Hacienda, making it a beacon to those on the streets below. With each interior addition, the Fortners had maintained the stucco exterior. The white walls projected a unified front, hiding the jumble of rooms inside.

I paused at a window to look into the kitchen. Sophie, her back to me, pushed something to the rear of a cupboard. I whirled at a fluttering sound behind me, but saw nothing. By the time I turned back, Sophie had disappeared.

Black Mountain loomed over the house. Stepping onto the patio outside the great room, I gasped at the sight of Derek. He stood over the jewelry box, his hands clutching his collar, his eyes popping out. His mouth gaped open, lips drawn back from his teeth. His face flushed purplish red. Bumps swelled on his cheeks and forehead. Running to the patio door, I yanked at it. It held firm. Even in his agony, Derek must have heard me, because he staggered toward the door. Half way to me, he crumbled onto the tile.

I stabbed 911 into my phone. Static garbled the voice that answered. "Help, a man is having a seizure," I screamed. "We need an ambulance." I told her the address and louder static replied. I ran to the front of the house, knowing I'd have better reception away from Black Mountain. When I reached the front door, I yanked at it. Locked, although I knew I'd left it open. Hearing the operator more clearly, I begged her to send an ambulance.

While she jabbered at me about Derek's symptoms, I entered the security code for the door. My fumbling fingers hit the wrong numbers. Biting my lip, I tapped in the numbers more carefully. Still locked.

"Wait a minute, I'm putting the phone down while I try to get inside," I told the operator. With fierce concentration, I stared at each number as I touched the security panel. I had to get the password right the third time or the system would refuse me entry. The electronic lock clicked, yet the door didn't budge. Someone had used the keyed deadbolt.

I pounded on the door with my fists. "Sophie, Sophie." I snatched up the phone and ran. "I can't get in the front door. I'm going to try to break the patio window."

The operator's response dissolved into static as I turned the corner. On the patio, I grabbed a chair and hefted it, but I stopped at the sight of Sophie kneeling beside Derek. His face was a purplish black, and his tongue stuck out from his gaping mouth. He lay still. I knocked on the glass. Sophie jerked and turned a pale face to me. She heaved herself up and moved stiff-legged toward me. When she tugged on the handle, the door didn't move.

"The stick!" I pointed down.

She bent and fumbled with gnarled fingers at the broom handle wedged in the slot for the door. She couldn't dislodge the stick. I pictured the ambulance crew breaking the patio door, spraying glass over Sophie and Derek.

"Sophie, open the front door. I'll go around. Get the key for the deadbolt." Sophie seemed to understand, because she tottered away. Running to the entry, I heard the faraway cry of a siren. The howl of dogs—or coyotes—joined in the rising high-pitched call.

I waited at the front door. Sweat poured down my face, mingling with tears. The house had shut itself against me. I wanted to rush inside and pound on Derek's chest and make him breathe. I didn't like him, but I couldn't just watch him die. "The owner of the house is opening the door," I told the 911 operator. I locked my eyes on the brass handle, willing it to turn. A click. The door swung in, slamming against the wall.

Sophie stepped back as I charged into the great room. I kneeled beside Derek and blurted into the phone, "I'm in the house. Do I do chest compressions?" Crackling obscured her answer. "What?" Listening intently, I still couldn't understand her. I bent lower and caught the smell of peanuts coming from Derek. Over the sound of the operator's broken-up voice, footsteps pounded into the house.

I backed away from the paramedics as they clustered around Derek. Sophie collapsed onto the couch. The paramedics spoke in clipped, commanding tones. A wheeled stretcher rattled over the tile floor. A woman paramedic came over.

"Is it some kind of seizure?" I asked.

The paramedic opened her hand. On her palm rested three round chocolate-covered candies. A fourth candy, bitten in half, was a peanut coated in chocolate.

"These were next to him. Does he have a peanut allergy?"

Sophie's face scrunched up. "Yes, it almost killed him once."

I stared at the candy dispenser. "Sophie is very careful about his allergy. The manufacturer must have messed up and let some peanuts get in."

In one swift movement, the paramedics lifted Derek onto the stretcher. "We're taking him to St. Vincent's."

Fifteen minutes later, the hospital attending physician called and told us Derek died before he reached the emergency room.

I hugged Sophie lightly, afraid I'd hurt her by pressing close. "Should I call my dad or one of your sisters?"

"Let them sleep. We're better off alone." Sophie, who hadn't wept since Joe passed, drooped, sagging earthward.

My muscles knotted up, as if trying to hold me together. Not able to find words of comfort, I heated milk for Sophie. When I added the hot chocolate mix, the cocoa smell brought back the candy and Derek's tortured face, leaving a bitter taste in my mouth.

Sophie drank placidly and reminisced about family funerals. "This will be a closed coffin." She planned to take a sleeping pill. I planned to get drunk.

Sophie wanted to smash the candy dispenser. Thinking like a lawyer, I said we should keep it as possible evidence for a lawsuit against the candy manufacturer for mingling peanuts with plain candies. After I escorted Sophie to her room, I wanted to call my dad, but respected her wish that we be alone.

Not anxious to pass out too quickly, I sipped white wine rather than tequila. The air conditioning grunted on. Sophie liked the house cold, because she didn't give "a gosh darn" about saving energy. My head pounded. I kept on drinking.

Prowling around the kitchen, I heard muffled voices and figured Sophie must be watching TV while she waited for the pill to put her to sleep. The sweetness of the wine made me hungry. I poked around in the cupboards for a salty snack. When I checked the one I'd seen Sophie open, I nearly dropped my wine on the counter. A half-filled bag of chocolate-covered peanuts stood behind cans of pinto beans. Heart pounding, I knew I needed to check the candy dispenser.

In the great room, I strained to listen, fearful that echoes of Derek's strangled breaths lingered. Kneeling in front of the dispenser, I searched unsuccessfully for the irregular shape of the peanut candies. I gripped the metal pole supporting the glass container and shook it. Red, green, and yellow round candies swirled. After inserting two tokens, I was rewarded with one chocolate-covered peanut and five plain candies. While Derek and I were in the tower, had Sophie deposited some of her private peanut stash in the dispenser? If so, she had murdered Derek. In a hurry, she hadn't returned her stash to its normal hiding place. I clamped my hand over my mouth and rocked back and forth as I gaped at the glass bowl filled with sweets.

The voices from Sophie's room cut off. On the patio, the wind clanged and tinkled copper chimes. I wanted to tell somebody about Sophie, her wish for us to be alone no longer seeming so important. I'd call my dad, who'd once been a prosecutor. He could tell me if I was right about Sophie. I reached for my cell phone, which I'd left on the coffee table. It was gone.

I raced to the den for the landline phone. No dial tone. Sophie had probably forgotten to pay the bill. I grabbed my purse, planning to drive to the nearest phone, a convenience store ten minutes away. At the front door, the keyed deadbolt again held the door shut. Sophie kept the key in her room. I wasn't ready to see her, knowing my face would reveal I suspected she'd killed Derek.

Bending to remove the stick in the grove of the patio door, I pictured Sophie waking up while I was gone in spite of the sleeping pill, wandering through the house looking for me. Alone and frightened, she might grab one of Joe's guns and shoot at the first strange noise. So far, the spirits of the house had been those who loved her. What if Derek's angry ghost came to her? I wanted to stay in case the house turned against Sophie.

I headed for the room Sophie had set up for me when my mother took off. White furniture, lace, ribbons, and flowers, this was a sweet girl's space. Sophie's collection of antique dolls sat upright on a pink chaise, their glass eyes open at me. Whenever I stayed here, I couldn't rest until I turned the dolls face down. Settling into a rocking chair, I decided to outstare them.

What if Derek's ghost appeared to me? I'd never experienced a ghost. If Derek's angry spirit formed out of the shadows, I didn't want him sneaking up on me asleep. I just had to make it to the dawn, when the outside world would connect with us. As my arms and legs grew heavy, I flexed my fingers and toes. I bit my lip, trying to activate my brain. To keep my lids up, I blinked furiously at the dolls. I locked eyes with a blonde one, an antique baby. She blinked back. I shot out of the rocker, hand clamped to my chest. The baby's gaze fixed on me until I turned her face down.

When I tried to sit still in the rocker, my legs twitched. Itchy spots crept along my arms. The dry desert air made me cough so badly my nose ran and my eyes teared up. My tongue tingled and swelled. I gasped, trying to force air into lungs that felt stuffed. I was allergic to the room, after all these years. Convinced I'd die horribly like Derek, I forced myself up and stumbled into the hall. By the time I reached the bathroom, the itching had stopped. I swallowed two allergy pills, even though my breathing was back to normal. I sat on the tub and patted my flushed face with a cold wet towel.

"Sparky?" Sophie held onto the bathroom doorjamb, wearing a red kimono over a white nightgown. "Are you okay?"

"I couldn't sleep. The house scares me."

"I scare myself sometimes."

My eyes locked on the Colt in Sophie's hand. Knees shaking, I forced my gaze to her face. "I know what happened. You have to make it right."

She nodded and headed down the hall, her slippers swishing on the tile. I started when the cold air of her room hit me. Sophie dropped her kimono on the bedspread, a red splash on white. I went limp with relief when she placed the Colt in her nightstand drawer.

The bed creaked as she sat stiff-backed. "I told Joe that Derek wouldn't have stopped with the power of attorney. He would have taken everything from me. Joe said, 'Don't get riled. Let your lawyer help you.' I ignored him and handled Derek myself."

"Where's Joe's picture?" The nightstand looked empty without it.

"I didn't want him to see me like this." A spasm rippled through her wrinkles.

Joe grinned at me from the top drawer of the nightstand, the first place I looked. "You know Joe would say to finish what you started." I put the photo on the bed next to her.

Sophie spread her fingers over his face. "Call your dad, Sparky. He can tell us what to do about notifying the police." She withdrew my cell phone and the front door deadbolt key from her kimono pocket. "Please wait outside, dear. I need time alone with Joe."

I walked into the night with the touch of her soft cheek on my lips. Wiping my eyes and nose on my sleeve, I turned on the phone. A gunshot banged inside the house. The loud crack hung in the air as I pressed my hands to my chest, sensing the bullet rip through Sophie's heart. I spun around. Every window in the Haunted Hacienda blazed with light.

† † †

MARGARET MORSE lives with her husband Duane and nine rescued dogs in South Phoenix. After working as an attorney for twenty-five years at the Maricopa County Public Defender's, she retired and began a second career as a writer. She is working on the sequel to her first murder mystery, WELL DEFENDED. She's had four short stories published—two in *Arizona Attorney* and two in Desert Sleuths anthologies.

THE POWER OF BOOKS
Kris Neri

In the five months that Plum Tardy had owned High Desert Books, the only bookstore in the small Arizona town where she was hiding out, she'd learned to recognize every type of book customer. The ones who strutted around with their hands clasped behind their backs to prevent them from buying anything. The people killing time while waiting for their dinner reservations at area restaurants, who drifted about aimlessly. And the voracious readers, who looked like they wanted to grab every title shelved in Plum's store, so they could read uninterrupted for a long time.

She'd learned to recognize all those book browsing types and many more.

But never had she seen anything like this.

For the last three weeks, a man had come into the store before closing on Tuesdays. While Plum and Tuesday-Man had never been introduced, she knew he was Mick Dougherty, a flinty-looking guy who worked for Jake Fremont. Jake ran a successful vitamin company around the corner in Old Town Applewood.

Initially, from the street, Dougherty always stared pointedly at the bookcase that stood in the window. She shelved her favorite mysteries there so passersby could see them from the sidewalk even when the store was closed.

Once inside, he zipped around, hastily scanning titles. Without even reading the dust jacket descriptions, he yanked some books from the shelves, stacking them in his arms.

He never commented, as others did, at Plum's eccentric organization. She'd never before been a bookseller in her thirty-odd years, but she had her own ideas how bookstores should be set up. Customers often found it odd that romances with dogs were shelved in the pet section, and books about bringing peace to multi-cat households were was just as likely to be found among the personal growth books.

After Dougherty collected eight titles exactly, he carried

them to the storefront bookcase. There, he stripped her selections from the first two shelves, replacing them with his own choices—which usually weren't even mysteries. Without acknowledging her, he walked out.

Every Tuesday just before closing…always the same…never an explanation.

She wrestled with whether she should tell Jake what Mick did. Jake was not only her best customer, he was her closest friend there, even if he was old enough to be her grandfather. Not that she ever shared that much about herself with him—there were things about her past that she couldn't tell anyone, such as her reason for lying low. But she and Jake had formed a warmer bond than she'd felt with anyone for a while.

Besides, what could she say? That Dougherty rearranged her inventory? Sure, it was nervy, but was it dangerous? She knew Jake, an eternal optimist, would dismiss it as nothing. People did reorganize bookstores occasionally. She'd also learned that in these months. But that was just a matter of readers turning their favorite authors' books face-out, so the covers would attract buyers, not spine-out as Plum had placed them.

Nobody ever had the audacity to rearrange her store as aggressively as Mick Dougherty did. Besides, he frightened her. He looked unassuming enough, with his perpetually beige clothes and mousy hair, but there was something about the way his murky eyes looked, not *at* her, but *through* her, that gave her a chill.

Last week she'd finally found the nerve to talk to him. While he arranged his newest collection in the storefront bookcase, she shouted from the safety of the cash wrap, "The green always rises."

"Huh?"

"The green. The best always rises," Plum explained. "You must think you're choosing better books for that display."

Plum was a great one for spouting adages, which she'd learned from her mother. That other people never quoted them the same way didn't bother her. Neither did learning that her mother had been hard of hearing for most of her life.

"Don't you mean the cream always rises?" Mick said with a derisive sneer.

Cream? Cream rises? Like the moon? That was ridiculous.

Without another word, he marched out, dropping Plum's

mysteries in a sloppy pile on the floor.

She knew Jake regarded Dougherty as a decent manager, even if he did need a personality transplant, but she suspected that was because Mick had taken over most of Jake's job functions, allowing Jake more leisure time.

Now it was Monday. If Dougherty pulled that stunt again tomorrow, she wasn't sure what she would do.

The door opened, forcing Plum out of her funk over Dougherty. Gina Lowell, another good customer, came in. Gina, a plump, silver-haired woman, was a member of the bookstore's mystery book club.

"Howdy, Plum," Gina called. She grabbed their next book club choice from a display and carried it to the register.

"This is a surprise, Gina. You always pop in on Tuesdays after volunteering at the youth center."

Gina grimaced sheepishly. "The last two Tuesdays that I've stopped, that awful Mick Dougherty was here. I'm embarrassed to admit I avoid him, but the guy gives me the creeps. I would never have taken that weirdo for a reader."

Would she take him as a book arranger? "Why do you think Jake keeps him on, as his manager no less?"

With a dismissive sweep of her hand, Gina said, "Jake's a complex man. He's all about the west, yet he's a peacenik at heart. What do you expect? He sells supplements, after all."

Jake was a big-hearted guy with a generous spirit, who saw the best in everyone. Plum didn't know how he'd remained that open. She'd learned the hard way that some people's best wasn't that good.

† † †

By the time Plum trotted upstairs to her tiny apartment above the bookstore, she wondered whether she was being too suspicious. She no longer trusted her judgments. Five months ago, her whole life had exploded. She'd lost her job to a bad economy, her boyfriend, Noah, cheated on her. If that wasn't bad enough, he also kept the money she paid him for her half of the mortgage and let the house they bought together fall into foreclosure. Trust didn't come easily to her anymore.

She'd picked Applewood, Arizona as a place to lick her wounds. But her hands weren't totally clean, either. When she ran out of the California house that she and Noah owned, she did something unscrupulous, though justified considering his betrayal.

Her apartment above the bookstore wasn't as lavish as their house had been. Plum slept on a mattress manufactured during the Carter administration, read on a couch that sagged in the middle, and cooked on a stove with only one working burner. Applewood was just as comfortably homey as her funky apartment. It was a tiny, historical town, nestled between Cottonwood and Jerome in Arizona's high desert. Plum had come to love its broad expanses and the prickly pear, desert willow and mesquite that grew everywhere. Mostly, she loved the peace she'd found there. But if anyone looked too closely at her past, she could find herself in trouble.

Jake stopped by the next morning. The wiry old man looked like Plum's idea of an Arizona cowboy, with his Western hat and bolo tie and perpetually scuffed boots. As always, he carried a take-out container of breakfast for two, forever reminding her that she didn't eat enough.

Jake was the most successful business owner in town. In addition to the storefront vitamin store he ran around the corner, he owned the large warehouse that stretched behind all the stores on Main Street, where Plum's bookstore was located. From there, his staff manufactured and shipped huge amounts of supplements across the country. But Jake had confessed to her that he'd grown tired of running the operation. All he wanted was to sit back, sipping a scotch, while he whittled his way through his towering to-be-read stack of books.

"Jake, I sure appreciate your business, but I worry about all the time you spend reading. Are you certain Mick's up to managing your business?"

"You worry too much, Plum. Mick might not be the warmest person, but he is efficient. Besides, I haven't shirked *all* my responsibilities. I change the password in the central computer every week, which controls all phases of my operation, as well as the door alarm code. The old man still has something on the ball." He tapped his temple. "Now, what new books do you have today?"

Even after Jake left, Plum let his optimism carry her—right up until the time that Dougherty yanked open her door and went into his peculiar ritual. After a menacing glance that caused her to cower, once again, Dougherty gathered an armload of books and proceeded to arrange his own display.

Plum took a deep breath. *In for some penne, in for some pounds*, as her mother always said. "No!" Plum shouted. "Don't you dare move those books."

She dashed out from behind the cash wrap and ran to his side, yanking the last one from his hand.

Mick directed those enigmatic eyes at her. With no warning, he shoved her against a bookcase, until the shelves cut so deeply into her back, they took her breath away. "It sure would be a shame if there was nobody here to open your bookstore one day. And you'd never know *which* day it would be."

Had he just threatened to make her *disappear?* When he released her, she collapsed to the floor. Dougherty placed the final book where he wanted it on the shelf.

He looked down at Plum. "Leave them," he warned. With that he walked out.

The instant he was gone, Plum rushed to the door and locked it behind him. She flipped the closed sign around and turned out the lights. But rather than going upstairs to her apartment, she sat on the floor in the darkened store and stared at the books Mick had moved to her shelves.

Finally, Plum felt a glimmer of an idea. She grabbed the phone at the cash wrap and called Jake at home. "Jake, do you trust me?"

"What's this about, honey?" When she didn't answer, he said, "You know I trust you."

She took a deep breath. "Then give me your computer password. Tell me what you changed it to today." She wouldn't share what she suspected until she was certain.

Jake hesitated. "I told you I changed my password every *week*. I didn't say I changed it *today*. How did you know...?" After a pause, he sighed. "Okay, it's CSSWRNTG."

"How about your door alarm code?"

"Same thing. Lazy, huh?" He chuckled.

She looked over the titles Dougherty had arranged, where her half-formed theory panned out. "Jake, I have something to tell you. You should come to the bookstore. Now."

† † †

Jake and Plum stood before the storefront bookshelf. "You see, Jake, if there was never any logic to the books Mick Dougherty shelved there, then he had another reason for that arrangement. If you look at the first letter of each title, you'll see they spell out your computer password and alarm code. Anyone passing by could know it just by scanning those titles."

She decided not tell Jake about Dougherty's attack on her unless she had to. She didn't want him feeling protective. If she was right about Dougherty, a woman and an elderly man were no match for such an aggressive thug—they had to come at him another way.

Jake frowned. "That forms my password, all right, but it's got to be a coincidence. Why would Mick want to spell out my password?"

Plum shrugged. "It's a doggie-dog world."

Jake chuckled. Why did he always laugh at her adages?

He stared at the titles Mick had arranged. Jake was a reader. She knew that assortment of books had to seem as pointless to him as it did to her. One was a do-it-yourself plumbing manual, another a biography of a long-dead local librarian that no one remembered. The others were equally poor choices if scintillating reading was the objective.

"Okay, maybe this is a bit too fishy," Jake conceded.

With no idea how to proceed, they decided to wait at the darkened window of the unused second bedroom in Plum's apartment, which overlooked the shadowy parking lot behind her store and the back of Jake's warehouse. Maybe something would happen to show them how to proceed. If something was up, Plum suspected they'd see it there.

Jake took a pillow from the guest bed and made himself comfortable on the floor. "You ever noticed anything odd out here?"

"I never look out this window. This room contains Flo's old junk, which she left when I bought the bookstore." Flo was the bookstore's former owner.

Jake sighed. "I don't believe anything is going to happen. This is sure to be the most boring night of both of our lives," he muttered. "And I've had a lot more boring nights than you have."

"A woked pot never boils."

Jake laughed. "Surely, that's a 'watched' pot, Plum."

That didn't sound right to her.

While they waited, Jake talked about the changes he'd seen in Applewood. "It's become more modern, but it's still the same friendly town it's always been. I wish you'd let me bring you to a merchants' mixer. It's past time you knew more of your neighbors."

Beyond her customers, Plum hadn't met many people in Applewood. After Noah's betrayal, she wasn't ready to let new people into her life.

Jake also told her about Arizona history. "With so much space between towns, we Arizonans couldn't always rely on the law. Sometimes we had to make our own desert justice."

They stayed there at that window for a good part of the night, fighting sleep. But just after one A.M., their wait ended. In the dim lighting of the parking lot, the rear door of Jake's warehouse, beside the Dumpster, opened.

"What...?" Jake sputtered.

A man peered out the door. Then he and two other men emerged, their arms filled with large boxes. The last guy shifted his boxes to one of the others, and punched in a code on the alarm keypad beside the door.

Jake's natural cheer vanished. "You think Mick was one of those guys?"

"Not a chance," Plum said. "Mick is probably at some bar establishing a good alibi. Otherwise, there's no point to this game. Look, Jake, Mick has created a way to share your password with others, without needing any contact with them. The only way to keep his hands completely clean is to have a way to prove he was somewhere else during these hours."

With a weary sigh, Jake said, "Plum, why don't we check my inventory to see how much they've made off with?"

She knew those men had robbed more from her friend than just money.

At the rear of his warehouse, Jake entered the same code, and he and Plum went in. It took another couple of hours, but they discovered that dummy orders had been set up in the computer to match a corresponding decline in inventory. The scam would have worked well, only Dougherty's cohorts didn't know Jake's bookkeeper loaded a duplicate set of the books in his laptop, which wasn't wired into the company network. The siphoning had only been going on for three weeks, but the men

Jake and Plum had seen creeping from the warehouse had already siphoned off over eighteen thousand dollars in merchandise. There were fake entries in the computer for every night of the week over the last three weeks.

†   †   †

Plum and Jake finished the night back in her apartment, where she made her friend an omelet on her one-burner stove.

Jake sounded sad when he said, "I guess we've confirmed the theft from every angle. Now it's time to turn it over to the cops."

Plum bit her lip. Should she say something? Could she expect him to make another choice because of her? "Jake, I'm not exactly on the grid here."

He raised one graying eyebrow questioningly. Plum finally shared how she left her life in California. With Noah cheating her in every possible way. "Not only was he boinking his coworker, he took my half of the mortgage payment, and kept it, while he stopped making payments to the bank. And it was a huge sum. I never wanted a house that big, but he had to have it."

"It's not that I'm not sympathetic, Plum. But what does any of it have to do with being on or off the grid."

"When I caught them—Noah and that woman—I wanted to run out of the house and to start driving somewhere. Anywhere. I stopped long enough to grab a roadmap from Noah's man cave. And there, beside his giant TV, I found a satchel of currency. I don't know whether that was the money he'd saved from not making house payments, or if he was involved in something that required illegal cash." She bit her lip. "Don't know, don't care. I hope it wasn't his and he got in trouble for losing it."

"Just grabbed it, huh?"

Plum nodded. "Yup, grabbed it and ran. Applewood was just a name on the map to me, but when I passed through, I liked it. I noticed there was a bookstore for sale. What better place could there be for a reader to hole up?" She shrugged. "Anyway, there was exactly forty grand in the satchel. I paid Flo thirty in cash, for the business and the building. That left enough to get me started. But you see, I begged Flo not to register the new deed on the building yet. You know, in case Noah came looking for me. Although I paid for it, my ownership of this place isn't quite legal."

Jake pushed his plate away. "And if we tell the cops how you happened onto Mick's scheme, they might look too closely at you? You could find yourself in some hot water."

"Yeah," Plum said dismally. "Noah was in commercial real estate. That wasn't the first time I noticed he had large amounts of cash. I feared it was his boss's money—you know, to pay bribes to city officials. I never asked, though."

"Never wanted to know, huh? We're a lot alike, my girl."

They sank into silence.

After a while, Jake said, "Okay, I won't rat you out, Plum. I'll fire Mick, but otherwise, we'll let 'em get away with it."

She could see that pained him. "He'd know I warned you. Besides, we can't let them get away with it."

Jake seemed hesitant.

"Come on, Jake. You talked about desert justice. Surely this crime cries out for it."

"Kiddo, that's history. This is the modern world. We can't do things like the old days."

Plum stood firm.

Finally, he asked, "You have a better idea?"

She snapped her head emphatically. "I do. And you were right before. It is time I met my neighbors here."

Jake looked confused about what meeting her neighbors could possibly have to do with bringing Mick and his pals to justice, but he promised to let Plum's certainty carry him along.

Jake agreed to maintain his cordial relationship with Dougherty. He also sent an email to the members of the neighborhood merchants' association, inviting them to a party to be held in the parking lot behind Plum's store and Jake's warehouse on Friday night. It was Wednesday now. So far, Dougherty's crew had entered the warehouse every night. Plum hoped their pattern would hold.

She didn't open her bookstore on Friday, spending much of the day cooking food for their guests. She prepared it at Jake's house, a few blocks away from their stores, where all of his burners worked.

She and Jake met again in the back lot Friday afternoon to decorate for the party.

"I don't know about this, Plum," Jake said. "Don't you think people will resent being invited to a gathering where you can smell the Dumpster? Can't we move it somewhere?"

If her plan was to work, they had to slow down the men who kept invading Jake's warehouse, rather than letting them slip away. Her idea was to wheel the heavy Dumpster in front of the warehouse's back door, but only after she felt sure the men were inside. Now Plum pursed her lips thoughtfully. "Maybe we should put the food table on the other side of the alley, away from the garbage scent." After she spread out the food, she asked, "You remembered to invite Mick, right? To insist he join you here."

"You bet! He's going to be right at my side when this goes down."

† † †

Plum's plan was simple. The businesses on their block closed at five P.M. According to Jake's company computer records, the pilferers' entries always began right around seven. Dougherty's boys obviously waited until all the business people had cleared out before gaining entry to Jake's warehouse. Plum was the only person who actually lived in the neighborhood. On the assumption that they would do the same tonight, she gave her party a late start.

None of the guests seemed to mind that they couldn't arrive until after nine P.M., nor care about the location. Jake was right—their neighbors were great. She wished she hadn't waited so long to meet them.

Plum kept busy throughout the night, replenishing food and drink, and meeting folks and chatting. If anyone wondered why their hostess kept a tote bag on her shoulder, one clearly weighed down by something heavy, they were too polite to ask about it.

Jake kept Mick within arms' reach. He did it by continually bringing Mick more drinks and plates of food. Keeping him so comfortable he wouldn't want to leave.

At a point well into the evening, Plum and Jake made eye contact. With the slightest of nods, they agreed to put their plan in motion.

Jake called the Applewood Police Chief. "Ben, it's Jake Fremont. I'm at a party behind my warehouse, but I'd swear I hear noise coming from inside." After a break, he added, "Right.

Nobody should be there now." After another silence, he said with a self-deprecating chuckle, "Forgetful old man—I might have left the front door unlocked, and I know I left the alarm off. I'd appreciate it you could send someone to check it out. Your guys can go through the front door."

After Jake snapped off his phone, he nodded to Plum. The desert justice mission was underway.

She had counted on the weight of the Dumpster outside the warehouse door slowing the pilferers down until the cops could reach them. Instead, no more than ten minutes after Jake's call, the Dumpster suddenly flew aside and the door jerked open. From somewhere deep in the warehouse, Plum heard someone shouting, "Police! Freeze!"

The gathering disintegrated into chaos. Partygoers started screaming. Three men lurched out the warehouse door. Instead of that heavy metal garbage dump stopping them, the party guests did. The three terrified men began frantically looking about for a way to escape, but too many people blocked their path.

When one man's gaze fell on Dougherty, his face registered relief. "Mick, man, you gotta help us out here. This was all your idea, you know."

By then two officers had emerged, and they took in the situation in a flash. Within moments, they'd corralled the bad guys, including Dougherty, and handcuffed them.

Before they herded the four men away, Plum pulled a hardcover book from her tote bag, one of the books that Mick had used to send the code. She straightened her arm, holding the book like a gun.

"Dude," she shouted at Mick. "Use a book—go to jail."

Plum turned to Jake, as the police officers took the four bad guys away, and asked, "Now that adage has to be right."

Throwing his head back in laughter, Jake said, "It is now, Plum. It is now."

† † †

KRIS NERI writes the Samantha Brennan and Annabelle Haggerty Magical Mysteries, *High Crimes on the Magical Plane* and *Magical Alienation,* and the Tracy Eaton Mysteries, the latest of which is *Revenge for Old Times' Sake*. Her novels have garnered Agatha, Anthony, Macavity and Lefty Award nominations—she's a three-time Lefty nominee. Kris has published more than sixty short stories and is a two-time Derringer Award winner and a two-time Pushcart Prize nominee for short fiction. She teaches writing for the prestigious Writers' Program of the UCLA Extension School and co-owns The Well Red Coyote bookstore in Sedona.

A KILLER MONSOON
NANCY HART NEWCOMER

Dark storm clouds built up into towering thunderheads over the Superstition Mountains east of Fountain Hills, Arizona. The blonde weather forecaster on the office TV said a monsoon storm was coming early this year, just after the Fourth of July, and it was coming hard. "Temperatures are falling ahead of the storm—it's down to one hundred and five degrees now," she announced in a perky voice, "and winds are gusting up to forty miles an hour."

"Be back by five," Jill Stewart told the receptionist as she grabbed her rain jacket and hurried out the door of Sonoran Winds Real Estate. She hopped into her oven-hot white SUV to drive to the empty short-sale house on Trevino Drive. Her clients, the Jenkins couple, were to meet her there in twenty minutes, her last appointment this Friday afternoon. Hard splats of rain pelted the windshield as she took a right onto Saguaro Boulevard. She turned the wipers on high and cranked up the air conditioner.

After parking in front of the 1980s split-level ranch house, Jill pulled up the hood of her jacket and ran through the rain to the front door. Her thumbs worked the tumblers on the combination lock-box on the doorknob and finally popped it open with ten minutes left to get the lights on before the clients arrived. The rain grew heavier as she turned on the outdoor illumination and stepped onto the covered patio to look at the backyard. She screamed when she realized what was in the water feature.

A young man in a gold Arizona State T-shirt lay face up. Blood ran from slashes all over his body as the rain soaked his clothing. He was draped over a boulder, his upper torso lying in the pink-water pool. The waterfall tumbled onto his face.

Jill heard a faraway doorbell. She covered her mouth with her hand, ran back into the house and threw up in the kitchen sink before answering the front door. When they saw her face,

Ryan and Fran Jenkins gasped.

Sheriff's Deputy detectives Matt Blake and Frank Bowman arrived shortly after Jill's 911 call. Both in their early thirties, they had been with the department for eight and six years, respectively. With other investigators on their way, Blake interviewed Jill and the Jenkins couple immediately and after getting their contact information, said they could go.

The storm stopped as suddenly as it had begun but the humidity made everything feel even hotter than before. The Coroner and crime scene specialists arrived and began their work. In the victim's pocket they found an ASU Sun Card identifying him as Sahir Kumar.

While the crime scene techs were examining the backyard, Blake, Bowman and two other deputies interviewed neighbors up and down the street. They found only one person who might be "of interest."

Stan Winter lived two doors down from the house where the victim's body was found. He answered the doorbell using a cane and invited Blake and Bowman into his frigid living room where he sat heavily in a worn brown tweed recliner. Bowman pulled out his cell phone, tapped the screen and showed Stan the ASU ID photo of Sahir. "Ever seen him?" he asked.

"Yeah, I have," Stan said, running fingers through his thinning white hair. "My grandson Greg is a student at ASU and was living here last year. My son and his mother died in a car accident six years ago so Greg came to live with us. With me, my wife died recently…"

"But you met Sahir?" Bowman asked.

"Yes, last semester Greg moved into an apartment off campus with Sahir. They came out to the house a couple of times—used my tools to work on Greg's old pickup truck and chowed down on home-cooked meals. Over winter break, they went their separate ways."

"What happened?" Blake asked. "Why did they move apart?"

"I can't keep up with all that," Stan said, shaking his head and raising his palms in a sign of resignation. "Might have been girlfriend trouble. Think I remember something like that. I really don't know. Greg's got a new roommate now named Johnny." He reached for a pad of paper beside his chair and wrote down the address and Greg's phone number.

"Thanks, Mr. Winter," Blake said giving him his card. "If you think of anything else, please let us know."

Around eight PM the crime scene techs were about to pack up when a deputy shouted, "Got something here. Looks like it could be the weapon." He was in an overgrown rocky wash behind the backyard fence.

Blake and Bowman joined him as a tech shined his flashlight into the vegetation. Lying in a puddle under an overgrown prickly pear cactus was a bloody knife.

"Shoot it and bag it," Blake said. He ran his flashlight over a wider area and discovered a twisted bicycle lying nearby. "Shoot the bike and grab it, too."

Seated around a conference room table the next morning at the Maricopa Sheriff's substation, Blake and Bowman waited to bring their sergeant, Manny Ortega, up to speed on the case. Manny entered and settled his short, sturdy frame in a mesh chair.

"What do we have for cause of death?" Ortega asked.

"Multiple stab wounds to the torso. But also a bad contusion on the skull and the right leg has a fractured tibia. Medical Examiner's running more tests now," Blake said.

"The stabbing looks like crime of passion," Bowman said.

"Yeah, but the head and leg almost look like an accident or fall."

"Also, there was blood between the driveway and the back yard. Body could have been dragged back there," Blake said.

"What do we know about Sahir Kumar?" Ortega asked.

Blake passed a summary sheet across the table. "We talked to the ASU student records office as well as campus and Tempe police. The vic was twenty years old, a sophomore in computer science."

"What else?"

"Well, he was a good student, has a three point five grade average," Blake said. "He's from a small town outside Mumbai, India. His parents are still there. He lived west of the campus in a house with a roommate, Yoshito Sato. No wants or warrants on Sahir."

"But a neighbor to the crime scene, Stan Winter, thinks there might have been some trouble between his grandson Greg and the victim," Bowman said.

Ortega handed back the document. "Okay. Why don't you head over to Sahir's place and see what the roommate says. Track down this Greg Winter too."

The detectives got into their black SUV with the Sheriff's insignia and bold gold logo on the side. Bowman punched Greg Winter's Tempe address into the GPS. When they arrived, they parked on a side street and walked to the apartment complex.

They found Greg's door on the first floor of a seedy 1970s building with a parking lot out back. Blake rang the doorbell. The door opened and an overweight young man looked up at them. He wore a stained T-shirt and boxer shorts, had a shaved head and sported several visible piercings. Blake showed his identification. "We'd like to ask you a few questions. About Sahir Kumar. You heard what happened?"

"Yeah, I heard," he mumbled in a deep voice.

"Mind if we come in?"

"I guess not," he said, stepping back into the apartment. The deputies followed him to a dinette table with the only chairs in sight not covered with rumpled clothing and pizza boxes. Empty beer cans and liquor bottles overflowed the kitchen garbage can and were strewn around the living and dining room. The place reeked of stale beer and cigarette smoke.

"What's your name?" Bowman asked.

"Johnny. Powell." Blake found it difficult not to look at the silver ring in Johnny's left eyebrow and tried to look him in the eyes instead.

"And your roommate is Greg Winter?"

"Yeah."

"Any other roommates?"

"Nope."

"Where is Greg now?"

"At class," Johnny said. "He usually gets home about one o'clock, unless he has a study group."

"What were you and he doing Thursday afternoon and evening?" Bowman asked, trying not to look at the silver ring attached to Johnny's lower lip.

"We were both in a computer statistics lab class from four

till eight."

"What about after that?" Bowman flipped open a notepad and wrote down the time of the class.

"We went to a party, man, over in the high rise at Apache and Rural. Some rich kids up on the tenth floor. It was a crazy scene."

"Crazy how?" Blake asked.

"Well, typical Thursday night bash, tons of people crammed together wall-to-wall inside and out on the terrace, loud sound system pumpin' music."

"Anything happen there? Any fights or anything?"

"Well, Greg's ex was there, Brittany." He wrinkled his nose in disgust. "That wasn't too cool. She was lookin' hot and hangin' all over Sahir which was *really* not cool—he was Greg's old roommate from last semester."

"So what exactly happened?"

"I don't know, man. Greg called him some names. Then there was some pushing and shoving but nobody got hurt. The cops weren't called."

"Then what?"

"Sahir and Brittany left, man. That's all that happened."

Bowman picked up a programming textbook on the table and thumbed through it.

"What's Brittany's last name," Blake asked.

"Nyes, I think. Yeah, that's it. With a 'Y.'"

"Okay, thanks," Blake said, handing him his card. "We still need to talk to Greg. Please have him call us as soon as you see him."

"I'll tell him, man, but Greg kind of does what he wants, you know?"

"If he doesn't call, we'll find him," Blake said. "Tell him that."

Just as they were standing, they heard a key turn in the front door lock. A tall skinny kid with long limp brown hair walked in.

"Greg Winter?" Blake asked.

"Yeah. So what."

"We'd like to ask you a few questions. I'm Deputy Blake, this is Deputy Bowman."

"Okay," Greg said, moving a pizza box to sit on a stained armchair. He threw one leg over the arm in an attempt to look nonchalant. The move didn't work for Blake.

"We're investigating the death of Sahir Kumar Thursday night. When was the last time you saw him?"

Greg twirled a few strands of his hair and stared out the front window. "I guess he was at a party we went to Thursday night."

"You guess?" Blake said.

"Yeah. He was there."

"Did you talk to him?"

"No, man. He's a nerd." Greg glanced at his roommate. "I was hanging with Johnny, here, and some other dudes. Then, we left and came home."

"I heard you called Sahir some names. Had a shoving match."

"Yeah, but it was no big deal."

"So you didn't hurt Sahir?"

"Naw, man."

"And you're sure you didn't follow Sahir and Brittany?"

"Hell, no. I couldn't care less about them."

Bowman asked Greg and Johnny to write down names and phone numbers of anyone they knew at the party. Then the deputies stood and Blake handed Greg his card. "If you remember anything else, please give me a call."

"Right," Greg said as he tossed the card on the table among the empties.

Upon leaving Greg's apartment, the deputies drove to Sahir's home on the other side of campus. It was a typical run-down student rental house with a missing shutter and overgrown bushes. Blake rang the doorbell, which set off a dog's yipping. Soon, a young Asian man with large glasses peeked out the window in the door and opened it.

"Hello. I'm Detective Blake and this is Detective Bowman," Blake said, showing his badge and credentials. "We're sorry to hear about your roommate. Can we come in and ask you a few questions?"

"Sure, I guess," Yoshi said, opening the door and stepping back. His eyes were rimmed with red and looked swollen from crying. The small living room was neat with two futon couches, a coffee table, a couple of lamps and a flat screen TV. A pair of video game controllers lay on the table. "Would you like some tea?"

"No thanks," Blake said, sitting on one of the couches. "We

just want to talk a few minutes." A shaggy white Shih Tzu pranced into the room and sniffed his boots with great interest. He scratched its ears and received some tiny licks in return.

"How can I help?" Yoshi asked.

"How did you know Sahir?"

"We were in freshman classes together. We formed a study group and became friends."

"We're trying to piece together the last forty-eight hours or so before Sahir died," Bowman said. "What can you tell us about that?"

"Well, nothing really happened on Wednesday. Just classes and studying…Oh, wait. There was an incident at the Memorial Union. We were chowing down on some rice bowls and Johnny Powell came up with a couple of his skinhead friends. He looked at Sahir and said something like, 'Didn't know they let the Taliban eat in here.'" Yoshi said the last phrase in a low, scratchy voice.

"Nice guy," Blake said.

"Yeah, he's a jerk. So are his friends. We just ignored them and they finally went away."

Blake jotted Johnny's name and "skinhead friends?" in his notebook and nodded for Yoshi to continue.

"We went to classes together on Thursday as usual. Then we split up to study and have lunch. I got home about five o'clock and Sahir got here around six. We ordered a pizza and then decided to go to a party at the high-rise apartments at Rural and Apache on the other side of campus."

"Those apartments are kind of notorious for parties where law enforcement is called."

"Yeah, but we went early, around ten o'clock so we didn't think we'd get hassled."

"Did either of you take a date?"

"No, sir, it wasn't that kind of party."

"But Sahir ran into Brittany Nyes."

"Yeah. It was like pre-ordained or something. I think they'd been attracted to each other for a long time."

"And Greg Winter was there?"

"Oh yeah. That was the bad part. Greg did not take it well. He'd had a lot to drink. And who knows what else. Started calling Brittany names and pushing Sahir around."

"And…?"

"They got into it—"

"What do you mean 'got into it?'"

"Just shoving, pushing. That's all. And then Sahir and Brittany left."

"And Greg?"

"He left right after them."

Blake turned to Bowman. "We need to talk to Brittany."

"Yep, we do."

They found Brittany tanning in a very skimpy red bikini on a lounge chair by the pool at the new Sierra Vista apartment complex south of the campus. Blake and Bowman approached her, faces shaded by their broad-brimmed brown deputy hats. She looked up cooly as if expecting them and smiled. They introduced themselves.

"Hello, deputies," Brittany said in a soft southern accent. "What can I do for you?"

"Are you Brittany Nyes?"

"Yes, officers, are you here to cuff me or pat me down?"

"We'd like to talk to you in the lobby. Please put some clothes on first," said Blake.

"Oh, all right," she said getting up and pulling on an oversized, maroon ASU T-shirt and slipping into rhinestone encrusted flip flops. "How tall are you," she asked Blake. "Six two? Or three?"

Blake ignored her.

Inside the building in a study lounge off the lobby, the deputies sat on overstuffed chairs across from a couch where Brittany perched, legs tucked under her, fluffing her long blonde hair.

"Miss Nyes, we're here regarding the death of Sahir Kumar Thursday night. When did you last see him?"

"I was at a party over on Apache and ran into him there. It was crowded and loud."

"What happened then?" Blake asked.

"A former acquaintance of mine, Greg Winter, was there and was quite rude to us. Along with his foul-mouthed roommate, Johnny. Both obviously drunk. Greg called Kumar disgusting names. They almost got in a fight. But Kumar, always the gentleman, led me away and we left the party. He walked me back here and left on his bike. I assumed he went home. I was devastated, of course, to learn of his death."

"Were Greg and Johnny still at the party when you left?"

"Yes they were. Staring daggers at us."

"Can you remember anything else?

"No, I wish I could help, but that's all I know."

When Blake and Bowman got back to the station, Blake had a message to call the crime lab.

"Hey Cheryl, what have you got?" he asked. "Okay, that's great, thanks for getting this done so fast."

He turned to Bowman. "We must have done something to make the cop gods happy."

"Got a hit on the knife print?"

"Yep. On the bike, too. Our good friend Greg. Got himself arrested last year for DUI so they had his prints in the system."

"Let's go get him."

The detectives drove back to Greg's apartment building and parked out front. Within a minute the Sheriff's SWAT team arrived and coordinated their next steps with the deputies. They approached his door and rang the bell. No answer.

"Maricopa County Sheriff's Office Search Warrant," Blake announced.

As two SWAT officers kicked open the door and entered the apartment with guns raised and ready, they heard brakes squealing and gravel flying in the back parking lot. They ran to see Greg's battered red pickup truck speeding away and turning left. The deputies ran to their vehicle and took off after him. Bowman cranked the steering wheel and turned to follow the truck as Blake hit the lights and siren.

"I'll call Tempe Police and DPS," Blake said.

Bowman turned onto Rural Road, heading north. They could barely see the dusty red truck ahead of them. It took a right onto the 202 Loop Highway heading eastward. The rush hour traffic was heavy, slowing them down. They lost sight of Greg briefly but saw him again after they passed the 101 Highway north and south exits. The truck abruptly swerved off the highway onto an exit ramp leading to the Beeline Highway. Then it turned left. The road ran ten miles north to Fountain Hills and up to northern Arizona. The deputies followed across the Salt River Pima

Reservation where the virgin desert stretched for miles to the Superstition Mountains under dark stormy skies.

"Holey moley, look at that," said Blake.

To the east a wall of dust a mile high was moving at thirty to forty miles an hour across the open desert. At that speed it would reach them before they got to Fountain Hills.

"Yep, it's a Haboob all right," Bowman said.

Cars were already pulling off to the side of the highway and turning out their lights to wait out the dust storm.

"The monsoon rain will be right behind it, and we don't want to lose him," Bowman said as he stepped on the accelerator.

They were almost to Shea Boulevard when the dust began to hit the car. They saw the suspect in the red truck blow through the red stoplight and continue north on the Beeline. Bowman hit the gas but the dust was getting thicker and the wind more fierce. They were forced to slow as the storm engulfed them, bringing visibility to zero. They had no choice but to pull off the road and turn off the lights.

"Think he's pulled off the road, too?" Bowman asked.

"Be crazy not to."

"Probably is though…crazy."

They waited out the dust storm which pounded on the car like a million nails creating a deafening roar. Finally, it began to diminish. The visibility opened up a little. Bowman crept the car forward and back onto the highway.

As the dust dissipated and the sky grew lighter, the monsoon rains came. They picked up speed. Cars were stopped all along the side of the road, drivers gauging when it would be safe to venture back onto the highway.

They could see a half mile ahead now through hard-driving rain. Bowman gripped the wheel with white knuckles as gusts of wind rocked the car and thunder cracked above them. There was no sign of the beat-up red pickup.

Ahead on the left they could see the soft glow of the two-story electronic sign for the Fort McDowell Casino. As they neared the stop lights at the intersection, Blake wondered if Greg would go left over the back roads to Fountain Hills. Or would he continue north toward Payson and the high Rim Country beyond?

"Straight or turn?" Bowman asked

"Turn."

Taking a left, they passed the big casino, glowing pink and green in the stormy light. At Mohave, they turned onto the winding road to Fountain Hills. The rain continued steady and strong with gusts slamming the car every few minutes.

Just around the first curve they saw it. A bent and twisted dirty-red truck, looking more like a metal sculpture, resting upside down against a twenty-foot tall saguaro cactus. The cab and front end were smashed in.

"Looks like it flipped and rolled," Blake said.

"Let's check it out."

They found Greg, what was left of him, entwined with the twisted wreckage, his face barely recognizable. The rain poured down and a lightning bolt shot through the sky above. As thunder followed, Blake said, "Call it in."

While Bowman made the call, Blake walked around to the passenger's side and squatted down to look inside the mangled cab. The glove compartment had sprung open. Scattered among shards of glass and dotted with blood were dozens of photographs of Brittany—walking down the street, sitting by the pool, talking to a friend—apparently taken without her knowledge. Blake shook his head as the rain dripped in on the soggy mess. He thought, *it's going to be a long monsoon season this year.*

† † †

NANCY HART NEWCOMER was an award-winning advertising copywriter for twenty-two years on brands ranging from Apple Computer to SPAM. After retiring she turned to fiction writing and had her first short story "Coyote's Bones" published in last year's Desert Sleuths anthology, *SoWest So Wild*. She grew up in Iowa and went on to live in Boston, Brussels, New York, London, Chicago and Minneapolis. She currently resides in Fountain Hills, Arizona, with her husband John and gray tabbies Thelma and Louise.

SEEDS
TONI NIESEN

Florence – Arizona Territory, 1892

Thomas Azule inhaled the pungent scent of the freshly cut creosote branches he gathered with his children, Gloria and Charlie. He liked teaching them the ways of their O'odham heritage. So many white people now lived in the area, he didn't want his children to lose the wisdom of their ancestors or their closeness to the land.

Today he would show them how to cook the creosote to create the sticky substance needed to seal his seed pots. His fields had suffered along with his neighbors' from the drought that had caused the area so much misery for the last two years. Despite his best efforts to plant his crops in the most water-saving way, recent harvests had been meager with barely enough *kaiij,* the seeds from his corn and wheat to feed his people and to sell to the whites who passed through the area.

In good years the food had been in such abundance that his people learned to rely on the luxuries they could buy with the profits they made selling the excess. Now they had barely enough to feed themselves. His first priority, however, was to save the *kaicka* or seeds he'd need to plant future crops. These seeds were never eaten, and it was for the *kaicka* that he and his children now worked.

After carrying their load of branches home and boiling them down at their mother's kitchen fire, the children filled clay pots with grains of wheat and ears of the best corn from the harvest. They cooled the sticky creosote glue and used it to fasten lids on the pots to make them airtight. As they finished, Thomas rode up leading two ponies. He dismounted and pulled small homemade wood and leather saddles from the shed beside their adobe home. The children cinched the saddles on their mounts. Their father loaded the pots in saddlebags made of knotted maguey fiber and secured them behind the saddles.

"Where are we going, Father?" Gloria asked as she filled her canteen for the trip.

"To a special place in the mountains to the east. To a place of coolness. We must travel two days to reach it. Someday, it will be your responsibility to care for the *kaicka,* so remember the way."

"I will, Father. I'll remember that prickly pear cactus patch over there. And the javelina tracks around it," Gloria said and giggled.

"Don't be silly," said Charlie. "Those tracks will be gone with the next wind. You must look for things that will stay the same."

"I know that, Charlie," she said. "You're so serious. I was just trying to make you smile."

Carmen Sanchez gave Thomas Azule change for the nails he'd just purchased at the trading post her father owned in the Arizona desert. A few minutes later Thomas returned and paid for a length of calico. A third trip to the register resulted in his buying two sticks of hard candy. He handed one stick to the small girl beside him. Carmen smiled and counted out his change, then turned to help George Feeney, a local rancher.

Feeney muttered and scowled at Azule as he went out the door. "Doesn't the man know how inconsiderate he is to buy only one thing at a time?"

"Tom Azule is a good customer, and his children are students of mine at the school," Carmen replied. "He just does business in his own way."

"I thought the Indian brats got sent to boarding school. And where's he getting his money anyway? Haven't heard about anyone around here hiring him."

"Since he's already done a good job teaching his children English, he wants them to go to the same school as the other kids around here. They're good students," she said as she measured out a pound of beans. "And, I don't think Thomas needs anyone to give him a job. His family grows and sells corn and wheat to the miners and the military. We buy from him too sometimes." She tied up the package of beans. "Can I get you anything else?"

Feeney pulled a soiled handkerchief from his pocket and loudly blew his nose. "Are you telling me he's the Indian responsible for stealing my water by building those damn mounds of his? I'm sure he's using those mounds to hide the wells he drills to steal the water before it gets to my property. It's been going on since the drought started and our irrigation ditches dried up."

"I don't know anything about that," Carmen said, handing him his purchase. "I think everyone's suffering from the drought."

"If that's so, why doesn't everyone have enough water to grow their crops and feed their families? He's a damn thief." Feeney threw his money on the counter and stomped out of the store.

Carmen shrugged and went back to the books she was trying to balance for her father. She yawned, tired from working all her week-ends at the trading post leaving her little time to prepare for the coming weeks' classes.

"Teacher?" a meek voice said.

"Gloria, I didn't know you were still here. Do you want me to send someone to get your father?"

"No, he's coming back for me after his errand. Who was that nasty man who told you those lies about my father?"

"Oh, he's an angry person who doesn't have enough water for his fields. He's just looking for someone to blame for his troubles. Don't pay any attention to him."

"But my father's not drilling more wells or stealing his water. He builds mounds to help save as much water as he can. It is the way of the desert people when the rains don't come."

"Do you think your father would come to our school sometime and tell the students how he's learned to farm the land?"

Gloria looked down at her bare feet before giving Carmen a mischievous smile. "I don't know teacher. He doesn't like to talk to people much but I'll ask him. If he won't come, I'll tell you his stories myself."

"That would be wonderful, Gloria. Thank you."

The following week, Gloria stood at the front of the one-room school house. This morning she seemed a little shy, especially after her brother scolded her in loud whispers before she began.

"Our people are great farmers," she said. "The *Hohokam*, the ones who came before us, built canals to bring water to our fields. Usually, the canals would bring all the water they needed. When there was no rain, they planted their fields in spiral mounds with rocks to hold the moisture around the plants, and they planted special seeds that grow in only two moons so they could be harvested sooner. Most important of all was the *kaicka*, the seeds they saved to plant future crops. They put these away first, even before they used their crops for food.

"My favorite trick was the one they used to keep rabbits from eating their crops. They planted lettuce and greens the rabbits liked around the edge of the fields to keep them too busy eating those things to eat their other crops. That trick kept both the rabbits and the people happy, but sometimes the rabbits were caught and eaten for dinner."

The children laughed at the rabbit story and clapped as Gloria returned to her seat in the classroom.

"Thank you Gloria. It was wonderful of you to share the ways of your people with us. Maybe our class can try planting using your methods in the field behind the school."

The following Monday, neither Gloria nor Charlie were in class. At lunchtime, Carmen noticed the sky to the west where they lived was dark with smoke. Worried, she struggled to keep her focus on her class. Toward the end of the school day, Gloria and Charlie rode up, tied their horses in front of the school and took their seats in the classroom.

"Sorry we're late, teacher," Gloria said, her eyes red-rimmed.

"Is everything all right?" Carmen asked.

Charlie looked up at her with a frown. "Our fields are burning. Mother said we would be safe here, but I wanted to stay with Father."

"Is there something we can do to help?" Carmen asked. "We could round up the men in town."

"No," Charlie said in a loud voice. "They would not be welcome."

"There is no water to fight the fire with anyway," Gloria added. "Only a miracle of rain could stop the fire."

As the afternoon wore on, Carmen spotted dark clouds in the sky and the wind picked up. For a while, she thought maybe it would storm, but no, the air remained dry.

When school finally ended, Carmen pulled Gloria and Charlie aside. "It may not be safe for you to go home yet. Why don't you stay with me? We'll make some hot chocolate."

"Mother said to stay until they come get us," Gloria said. "We won't be trouble."

Carmen took the children next door to her small house. She sat them down in two spindle-backed chairs at her kitchen table and grabbed some cookies from her cupboard. After stirring up a fire in the wood stove, she poured milk into a saucepan to warm and turned to the children. She kneeled beside their chairs and drew them close. "I'm so sorry this is happening to you," she said. "Can you tell me how the fire started?"

"It was that Feeney fellow," Charlie said. "He broke in looking for our seed corn. Said he heard we had some." Charlie frowned at his sister. "It's all her fault for talking to everybody about our ways like that."

Gloria's eyes brimmed with tears. "No one from school would be that mean. He just saw father out planting."

"So did he take any seed?"

"A little," Gloria said. "Then he set the fields and even our house on fire. He said we deserved it for stealing his water."

Carmen poured each of the children a cup of the steaming chocolate. "Be careful, it's very hot. While you drink it, I'll go see if anyone can ride out and check on your family."

With a sense of foreboding, Carmen burst through the door of the sheriff's office. "Sheriff Rhoads, I need you to ride out to Thomas Azule's place as fast as you can. The children tell me Feeney has ransacked their home and set everything on fire."

"I'm on my way. I saw the smoke and was getting ready to ride out that way. I'll round up some fellas."

"Please hurry. It's been burning all afternoon. I'll keep the children with me until you get back."

"Mama," Gloria cried running to her mother as she rode up to the school beside one of the sheriff's deputies. Covered with soot, the woman was barely recognizable. Wide vertical lines reached from her eyes to her chin where tears had coursed down her face. She slowly dismounted and went to her children.

"My babies," she said. Hugging them to her chest, she started to sob.

"Where's Father?" Charlie asked.

The deputy who had accompanied their mother turned and looked at her before speaking. She sobbed harder, but nodded slightly to him. "I'm sorry," the deputy said. "I'm afraid your father was shot and killed in his field while trying to put out the fire."

"Oh no!" cried Gloria. "Not Father. He can't be dead." She buried her face in her mother's skirt.

"Did the sheriff arrest Feeney and the men who helped him?" Carmen asked.

"Not exactly. The sheriff will be along soon and will tell you what happened when he gets here."

Several hours later, after Carmen had settled the children for the night on pallets in her home, and their mother had washed up and dressed in clean clothes from Carmen's closet, the sheriff knocked on the door.

"Sorry to break in on you this time of night," Rhoads said. "I thought you'd want to know what happened."

"Did you arrest Mr. Feeney?"

"Hold on now, Carmen," the sheriff said. "Let me tell this. We tried to ride from Azule's place over to Feeney's, but the wind shifted, and the fire started up in that direction blocking us. We tried riding around it, but it was no use. We had to wait it out."

"I wondered what was taking so long. Did you manage to get through? Did he get away?"

"Yeah, we got through all right," Rhoads said, tapping his hat against his thigh. "We thought we'd lost him, but Feeney didn't go anywhere. We found him dead outside his house. Wasn't much left, but enough that we could tell who he was. Guess he sealed his own fate when he started that fire."

Two weeks later, Carmen and Sheriff Rhoads found Charlie, Gloria and their mother raking the charred ground outside what was left of their house. The smell of impending rain overpowered even the stench of the scorched crops surrounding them.

"You've made a lot of progress cleaning up," Carmen said. "Looks like you're getting ready to plant another crop soon."

"Oh, we are," Gloria said. "It's September already. We want to be ready to harvest by the beginning of November."

"That's only sixty days away," the sheriff said. "What can you grow that fast? And where will you get more seed? Didn't you say Feeney took yours?"

Gloria and Charlie looked at each other. Gloria smiled and said, "Yes, he stole our seed, but Father taught us where to go for more. He made sure we would always have our *kaicka*."

TONI NIESEN was born in Arizona. She lived in Alaska for over two decades before returning to live in Scottsdale with her husband and grandson. She has written a weekly newspaper column, several short stories and is working on an aviation-themed mystery.

A THORN IN HIS SIDE
Virginia Nosky

Central Arizona juices stirred with vernal life. Spring-like temperatures had come early—everybody commented on it—exclaimed over the untimely blossoming of Phoenix gardens, the desert plants. The yellow foaming mists of the palo verde trees and sweet acacias, ubiquitous golden brittle bush, lacey mauve flowers of the ironwoods burst on the landscape over a month early. The first of May customarily saw the stately saguaros crowned with their snowy wax blooms, but this year saw the glowing flowers the first of April. Migratory birds had headed north, desert birds were busy romancing and nesting. Ground squirrels unburrowed themselves and scampered everywhere. Coyote puppies whelped, rattlesnakes chasing winter torpor curled languidly on sun-warmed rocks. Already the daytime temperatures were climbing, not unpleasant in the arid landscape that hadn't seen rain since January. The air was soft, silken.

It was weather to be outside, doing. Hikers climbed in the rugged preserves, mountain bikes competed, zigzagging over dizzying courses. Motorcycles crisscrossed the warming earth, roaring up and down arroyos, through rocks and vegetation, cutting unlovely ruts that would survive in the malleable, acquiescent soil for centuries.

The rolling foothills of the Superstition Mountains stretched for miles with saguaro cacti, from fingerlings to two-hundred year old behemoths. Towering, blooming, multi-armed giants reached to the cerulean sky, pockmarked with the round holes of cactus wren and woodpecker nests and bullets from the local target practicers.

Tyree Crum was enjoying the pleasures of the spring-like afternoon. He and his girlfriend, Chastity Dee Breed, had wrapped up their kissing in the bed of his Dodge Ram—he was tamping down his urges, staying respectful of Chastity Dee—how could he not with a name like that?—and had brought out his firearms to practice sharpshooting. His pistol was an

American Eagle Colt .45 Classic, his rifle a lever action .30-ought-six Winchester Springfield. The former was a recent purchase at the Maricopa County Fairgrounds Gun Show, the latter a gift from his old man on the occasion of Tyree's ninth birthday, over the objections of his mother, Bethesda Crum. *"You're crazy,"* she had yelled *"Givin' a young child the means to kill hisself and maybe somebody else."* Tyree's father, Malachai Crum, had shouted, *"Shut up."* And that had been the end of that.

The upshot: Tyree had grown to be an expert with the rifle, but had decided he wanted to branch out to small arms. He needed to develop his technique. Out under the open blue skies was the perfect place to hone his skills like the other devotés of the Second Amendment—the one about the militial right of American citizens to bear arms—a Bill of Rights right strongly espoused by the aforementioned armed enthusiasts targeting desert vegetation in the spirit of patriotism.

Now Tyree Crum had big plans, excited perhaps by the precocious fecund sap running through the flora and fauna of the Arizona spring.

The sun had begun to settle over the Superstitions, streaking the sky with rosy pinks and golds. Six or seven contrails also striped through the blushing sunset, remnants of flights in the navigational patterns of flyovers from the West Coast.

Chastity Dee sat on the tailgate of the truck, swinging scrumptious legs, admiring her boyfriend drawing beads on various rocks and cacti. "Golly, Tyree, you're sure amazing."

Tyree stood taller at her praise, aimed the pistol at an impressive boulder and pulled the trigger. A chip flew off the ancient latite. He blew on the muzzle. "Now watch this. See that there big saguaro yonder?" A majestic six-armed saguaro stood about twenty yards away. "See them flowers on the top?" He took aim. There sounded a sharp crack and the waxen crown of flowers exploded in a shower of pearly petals.

Tyree turned with pride, only to see Chastity Dee's alarm. "Oh gee, Tyree. I don't think you ought to do that. I'm, like, for sure there's some kind of law that says you can't."

Tyree moseyed over to nuzzle his girl. "Nah. Lookit. There's saguaros all over the place. What's one little old cactus. How about another smootchie kiss?"

She turned coyly and his kiss landed on her shell pink ear.

"Well, I don't know. It's just that…that the flowers are so pretty and special-like."

Tyree grinned at Chastity Dee, hitched up his sagging Lee jeans a fraction, popped a Bud Lite, took a satisfying swig, twirled the Colt with his finger, then whirled, aimed, pulled the trigger, did a 360° and fired another from the hip. One of the arms of the saguaro trembled, then tumbled to the ground. He tipped his chin up and polished off the Bud, crumpled the can and tossed it over his shoulder. "C'mon, babe, how does a Big Mac sound?"

Chastity stared at the fallen arm, then shrugged. "Why, just fine. I was feeling a little peaky."

"Cool. There's something I want you to do for me. Us."

"Us? Oh, Tyree. Whut?"

"It has to do with our future."

"Our future? Oh, my." Chastity Dee, all smiles, jumped off the tailgate and slid onto the truck's bucket seat.

The Ram roared off, leaving behind a cloud of greasy exhaust; twelve crushed cans of Bud Lite; two Econo-size Fritos bags; an oily box that held the sugary remains of a half dozen Krispy Kremes; twenty-six spent shells; fifteen cigarette butts; one snotty, faded red bandana; a lipsticky Kleenex; a slick of black seepage from the crankcase of the Ram; seventeen chipped rock fragments; a wounded, five-armed saguaro; plus, at its base, one shot-off arm—a sad green scrap in the dust. And, deeply etched for posterity, the tracks of four heavy gauge tires.

As evening came on, the random cracks of gunfire grew sporadic over the mountains and died down. The whine of motorcycles quieted as a pearly dusk settled over the rugged Superstitions.

† † †

Tyree and Chastity Dee held hands over the red, white and yellow detritus of their super-sized burgers and fries. Chastity's expression was skeptical. "Gee, Tyree, I don't know. It, like, maybe doesn't sound as easy as you say."

He frowned. "You want an engagement ring, or not, Chast?"

"Oh, Tyree. I'm just so way overcome. But couldn't you just, like, buy it?"

"Chast, I want you to have the best. Don't you want the best? You do want us to get married, right?"

"Oh, I do. Really. I do." She looked around and dropped her voice. "But robbing a jewelry store? What if we get caught?"

"No worry there. Piece of cake. I've scoped out the prospect in that Fashion Square Mall. On a Saturday. Big shopping day. Crowds. Easy to disappear. When's the last time you heard about a jewelry store getting knocked over? It just ain't done much anymore. It would be unexpected-like." He stroked her hand, then singled out the third finger and squeezed it. "Wouldn't it be the most romantic thing, gettin' engaged with a beautiful diamond ring? What do you say, Chastity Dee? We'd always remember a big day like that over the years. So special-like." He squeezed again. "We'd tell our kids. Tell our grandchildren."

Chastity giggled. "Wellll..."

Tyree hunched up closer. "Here's my plan. We dress up real nice and go into the store holding hands, looking real happy...you know. Lovebirds. Wear that blue dress that shows your tits. I've checked. The salesman is a guy, so you lean over a lot. We ask to see the diamond engagement rings. It won't look funny that we're a mite nervous. We'll just keep asking to see more rings, you know, unsure of what we can afford. That sort of thing."

"Oh, Tyree. I'd be scared to death."

"See what I mean? But that will look normal."

Chastity swallowed hard. "Then whut?"

Tyree brushed the air with his hand. "Oh, that. Why I just suggest that he opens other cases, scoop out the jewels and put them in a bag I'll give him. Then we run out of the store and get lost in the crowd." Tyree sat back and waved his hand again. "Like I said. Piece of cake."

"Why would he do that? The jewelry store man."

Tyree's face was serenity itself. "I'll show him my Colt. He won't make no trouble."

Chastity gulped. Squirmed. "Then whut?"

"Remember where we were today? Out on the desert?" He sat back and slapped both hands on the table. "I'll go there, dig a hole for us to bury the swag. We'll sit on it for a few months...all except, of course, for the humongous diamond engagement ring you like that will be on this little finger right here." He picked up her ring finger. "The one that tells the world Chastity Dee Breed is going to be the bride of Tyree Crum."

"Oh, Tyree." Chastity Dee's face took on a dreamy look.

"When? When will we get married?"

"After a few months, when we can safe-like sell the stuff. Then we'll go to, say Las Vegas. To one of them wedding chapels, then have a way cool honeymoon. Would you like that? We can go anywhere your li'l heart desires 'cause we'll be rich."

Chastity Dee's gaze drifted out the window as her brow furrowed in thought. "I think I'd like to go to Hawaii."

"Hey, me too. Go down there and stretch out on that there white sand and drink us some Mai Tais. That's a terrific idea, Chast."

"Whut are 'my ties?'"

"They're some kind of Hawaii fruit juice, and I think rum and sugar, real sweet. And they go down so smooth-like." He playfully tapped her nose. "Gotta be careful. They sneak up on you. Make you feel," he pinched her cheek, "real lovey."

She giggled, then was lost in thought for a few seconds. "I want to do one of those hyphen things in my new name. I'd really like that, so fancy-like."

Tyree's face fell into concentration for a full minute. Then his face brightened. "Yeah, that would be real good. Chastity Dee and Tyree Breed-Crum. Yeah. I like it. Classy."

"Well, then…I guess I'll do the jewelry store thing."

Tyree leaned over and kissed her cheek. "Atta girl. Aloha, baby."

† † †

Chastity Dee's nondescript beige Chevy Nova nosed around the parking lot of Fashion Square Shopping Center in downtown Scottsdale. When a spot opened, Tyree zipped the car into the tight space. "Now remember, Chastity Dee. We get the jewels and get out fast. When we get away from the store, we slow down, mingle with the crowd, then dip into Dillard's. We sorta separate and look like we're just shopping, but make our way normal-like out through the men's department. It's real simple. Then we drive away, casual, before anybody catches on."

"What if somebody does catch on and chases us?"

"Darlin', we'll be in and out before you know it. Or anybody else. The trick is to be quick and not get rattled and screw up. Smooth." He chucked her under the chin. "We gotta be smooth. Look. See how crowded it is? And it ain't like we're tryin' to hide somethin' big. My little old purple bag will be full of the jewels. Not big atall. I'll put it in this Dillard's shopping bag here, and nobody will think anything of it. We'll just walk right out of there as nice as you please."

"Okay, okay, okay. I get it." Chastity swallowed hard and wiped her hands on her blue dress.

Tyree grinned at her. "Always did admire you in that outfit, baby. You remember now what I told you. About leaning over a lot. Ain't a man with a heartbeat'd look anywhere else." He turned the motor off. "Okay, here we go."

"Oh, Tyree! I'm scared."

He patted her arm. "Just think of Hawaii, them flower leis around your neck and them Mai Tais." Surreptitiously he patted the Colt .45 jammed in the belt under his fancy fringed jacket. No sense in worrying Chastity Dee any more'n she already was.

Tyree and Chastity Dee joined the throngs of shoppers—tourists enchanted with the dizzying array of merchandise, locals looking for specifics, platoons of prowling teenagers. They made their way to the jewelry store Tyree had cased for their caper. Its windows glittered enticingly, the big glass door stood invitingly open. A lone salesman carefully buffed glass counters, glancing up, eyes full of hope at any passerby who had slowed to gaze at some sparkling temptation.

Tyree felt Chastity slow down and he pushed firmly on her elbow to propel her into the hushed store. Tyree sniffed appreciatively. The store was fragrant with taste, opulence, and money. Rich-like.

The delighted salesman's smile spread across his face. His eyes travelled over Tyree's Resistol cowboy hat to his ostrich boots, with their pointed filigreed stainless steel toes. He took in Chastity Dee next—blonde curls, big blue eyes and matching blue dress out of which sprang a toothsome, creamy bosom. He moved forward. "Howdy," he said. "I'm Charlie Newsome. And what can I show you today, sir? Ma'am?"

Tyree assumed a bashful grin. He squeezed Chastity Dee's elbow in encouragement—or warning, since the girl looked a tad nervy. His emotions were a bit mixed up in his mind. He answered Charlie Newsome, making his voice strong and manly. "I'd...we'd like to see what you got there in the way of engagement rings. For the lady here." He bashfulled again, shuffling his boots. "We're getting married."

The salesman bowed. "Do you have something in mind, sir? A price range, perhaps?" He swept behind the case in invitation.

"We want the best. Don't we, darlin'?"

Chastity Dee's eyes were big. Tyree gave her elbow a worried pinch and jerked his chin at the case. The girl frowned and rubbed her arm, but leaned over the counter to point to a sumptuous pillow cut diamond. As Tyree had hoped, the salesman gazed appreciatively down at Chastity's *décolletage*. He brought out a key, fumbling to unlock the case, whipped out a black velvet pad and brought out the ring. Tyree reached for the bauble and slipped it on Chastity's finger.

The girl gasped, waggling her fingers as rainbow sparks shot out of the stone. "Oh, Tyree. This is the one I want."

Tyree's annoyance at her forgetting they wanted to try on *lots* of rings made his voice testy. "That's probably too much. Uh...maybe something else?"

"Of course, sir, though the lady has wonderful taste. That's one of our finest stones." He held out his hand for the ring. Chastity Dee reluctantly wiggled it off her finger. Her eyes followed the dazzling diamond as Newsome placed it back in the case and locked it. Tyree frowned.

The salesman gestured. "We'll try the case over here.

Tyree like to have exploded with impatience. He thought the man would be leaving the jewels on the counters. They didn't have all afternoon to diddle around with this one at a time thing. He'd been so confident and calm, but he felt it slipping away.

Chastity Dee made her way over to the other case, glanced nervously at Tyree, then leaned over for the salesman's admiration as she pointed to another glistening gem. "Can I have that one, Tyree?"

The salesman suavely unlocked the case and plucked out the new ring, again placing it on a black velvet square, again turning the key.

Tyree had not counted on all this locking and unlocking. His hand went to his pocket for the Colt as his temper burst into the open. "Get out of the way, Chast...we ain't got all day." He pointed the .45 at the salesman. "You, there. Just open up all them cases and put the stuff in this here bag." He fumbled with a purple velvet bag with a gold drawstring, the elegant former casing for a special-issue bottle of Crown Royal whiskey.

"Begging your pardon, sir. Are you robbing the store? We can't have that. I'm afraid I'll have to ask you to leave."

"Oh, Tyree! Let's go!" Chastity backed toward the door.

Newsome raised his voice. "Sir, you must leave!" He reached under the counter.

Tyree pulled the trigger of the Colt. The shot, muffled by the thick carpeting, soft music, and the din of the shopping crowds, struck the jewelry salesman in the chest. He was thrown back against the wall, then slumped to the floor, groaning. Tyree scrambled over the counter for the keys to the cases.

Chastity stood by the door, sobbing, wringing her hands, wailing, "Oh, Tyree. Oh, oh, oh."

Tyree was a blur, unlocking, scooping jewels into the Crown Royal bag. The *whoop, whoop* of a security alarm sounded over the bustle of the mall.

Tyree gave a last swipe of blazing diamonds, emeralds, rubies and pearls into the bag and scrambled over the cases to the door. He shoved Chastity out of his way and ran.

"Oh, Tyreeee!" she cried in desperation as she saw her fiancé melt into the crowd.

Momentarily in shock at her happy future vanishing in a wisp. Chastity remembered the prostrate salesman behind the counter. Her sweet nature came to the fore. She ran and knelt beside the wounded man, who was unfortunately now unable to appreciate the vision that Chastity Dee presented to him again spilling lushly out of the bodice of her blue dress.

Mall security came moments later. The moaning Charlie Newsome was wheeled off on a gurney. Considering Chastity Dee's near hysteria at the perfidy of her "fiancé", the police spoke among themselves that the girl couldn't really be considered a true accomplice, that the thief had obviously just been using her as a decoy to get to the diamonds and other jewels. Could she tell them where they might find the criminal? Tyree Crum was it?

She could.

†   †   †

A convoy of blue and white police cruisers with Chastity Dee in the front seat of the lead car turned onto the rutted dirt road that led into the Superstition Mountains.

"It's a coupla miles in," she said. "I think I can find it if we get close. I been out here before with that rotten Tyree Crum a coupla times. I'm telling you the promises that boy made to me!"

"If you can help us find him, ma'am, that'll look good to the judge," the officer at the wheel said. "You'll get off real light, I can promise you."

"I'm not holding much to men's promises any more, but I thank you for that." Her voice was firm as she pointed. "It's right up ahead over that little hill."

It was decided that since Tyree was armed and likely dangerous, the approach to the spot the girl indicated would be slow and careful. The police cars parked in a half circle. Three officers and Chastity Dee climbed up the rocky hill until they could look over the top of the rise. Down below, Tyree, shirt off, was energetically digging a hole at the base of a tall, five-armed saguaro. The Crown Royal bag lay on the ground beside the hole. Chastity Dee's Chevy Nova sat nearby.

Chastity whispered to the officer, "That's him, there. Where he said he was gonna bury the jewels. Looks like that's what he's doing. This is where he'd come to shoot off his gun. He'd practice on the cactuses and the rocks. Look. See there. That there's one of the saguaro's arms he shot off, so proud-like. And there's my car. The dirty rotten, thievin'…oh, don't know whut all!"

Suddenly Chastity Dee broke away from the officers to stand at the top of the hill. "Tyree Crum," she yelled. "I've brought the police, you skunk, you rattlesnake. I've told them all about you and robbing the jewelry store and shooting Mr. Newsome, that poor man. You're gonna go to prison big-time and I'll just laugh and laugh."

Tyree stopped digging.

Chastity Dee warmed to her subject. "And I'm gonna buy me a ticket to Hawaii and I'll lay me down on the beach there and drink me some 'my ties' and think about you in prison. Ha! Ha! Ha!"

The officer stepped up, gun raised, and called out. "Lay down your arms, Mr. Crum. We've got you surrounded."

Tyree looked right and left, his face a study in panic. He snatched up both the Colt and the Winchester. Behind him the tall saguaro began to tilt, its base undermined by the hole he had dug.

The five-armed cactus swayed, its delicate balance

compromised by the loss of its sixth arm to Tyree's casual target practice two days before. It tilted.

Chastity screamed. "Oh. My. Lord. Tyree. Watch out!"

Tyree froze at her alarm, looked up, mouth agape as the two-ton saguaro lurched, then toppled onto him. His scream echoed off the hills as the huge plant's cruel thorn clusters slammed into his body, crushing him to the desert soil.

All to be seen were Tyree's twitching hands and ostrich cowboy boots with the filigreed stainless steel toes pointing at the sky.

"Jeez," the cop said. "Not a good way to go."

Chastity Dee, her arms folded, looked on. "Told Tyree he oughtn't be shooting at that cactus. Serves him right." She turned to the policeman. "You think we better see if he's alive?"

"Ma'am, there isn't likely to be much left to tell. I think you'd best look away while I go down and take a look."

"Oh. Oh my. Tyree. Imagine. Squished, just like that!"

The officers swarmed down to the unfortunate Tyree.

Chastity Dee watched for a moment, then shrugged, turned and walked back down the hill toward the police cars. She whispered to herself, "That first ring was sure pretty, though." She put her hand in her pocket and fingered the ring hidden inside. "But this one's almost as nice."

VIRGINIA NOSKY is an author, poet and screenwriter. Her seven novels have won the Independent Publishers National Gold Medal, five Arizona Book Publishers Association firsts, and two Arizona Authors Association firsts. Her poems and short stories have appeared in several anthologies. Arizona's cities, mountains and mesas appear prominently in her work, though it is the desert she finds most interesting—its topography and climate. "The desert is a violent place; it bites and scratches." Virginia lives in Paradise Valley with her husband, golden retriever, Barkis, and Labrador retriever, Peaches. Visit her at www.VirginiaNosky.com, and YouTube.

DUST TO DUST
R K OLSON

July 6, 2011

Her alarm blasted its usual rude awakening to the latest local news. Ruthie rolled over and felt for the snooze button, hoping to stop the announcer's booming voice. "Last night's massive dust storm has…" She pulled the covers over her head and then the words sunk in.

Jumping to her feet, she peeked through the blinds onto her patio and saw no evidence of more than a typical dust storm, a predictable part of the monsoon season. Arizona was sometimes like that in July, always like that in August. The heat dropped to an almost pleasant low 100's while the humidity rose. Thunderheads developed during the day and by evening reached full force, ready to drop swirling rain and dust on anything in their path.

She pulled on her yoga pants and an old T-shirt. She hit the remote and glanced at the one word headlining the national news. HABOOB.

Grabbing her Diamondbacks' baseball cap, she stepped outside to check for any real damage. The air was already heavy with moisture; last night's storm had been anything but a relief.

Outside her front door, she saw that the coating of dust was unusually thick. The oversized windows wore a film of silt; she noticed a quarter-inch layer of build-up on the metal frames. Beyond her low-walled patio, the condo complex looked like a ghost town. She walked through the cactus garden separating the private spaces from the street in front. Filmy napkins and plastic bags waved from cactus spines. In the distance the lone jacaranda tree lay uprooted.

Having neglected to bring her keys, Ruthie hopped up and down to check over the block wall that enclosed the swimming pool. The usually clear water was brown. Chairs were upended. Several umbrellas lay on the deck, sheared off, looking like abandoned tropical drink adornments. A thick layer of powdery dust covered everything.

"Hey, Ruthie," Carl, the pool man, hollered out the window as he pulled his van to the curb. "You survived the dust storm? Hah-boob is what they're callin' it on the TV." He emphasized the first syllable, as if it was something to laugh about.

"I can't believe I slept right through it. I worked late all weekend and then again Monday night. Went riding yesterday morning. I think I got heatstroke."

"It was somethin'. You could see that wall of dust coming from clear over by Queen Creek." He moved toward the pool enclosure, propping the gate open with a large rock. "No escaping it, just waiting for it to get here, like a slow moving train…with no brakes."

Following him as he unlocked the gate, Ruthie could see that the pool was a lake of sludge. She lifted her baseball cap, wiped the sweat from her forehead and tugged the hat down. "What a mess."

"Don't I know it. Every complex I service in town has been calling me. I'm scheduling jobs on how quick they pay me. This place always sends my check right on time, so here I am. Like the Bible says, 'Them that's got shall get.'"

Ruthie bit her lip and willed herself not to engage further. She knew from past experience, once Carl began spouting his own version of Scripture it became impossible to break away politely. She turned back toward the gate. "You've got your work cut out for you, Carl. See you later."

Walking the perimeter of the buildings she saw that most of the damage was minor. There was trash scattered everywhere. An omnipresent, thick layer of dirt caked every surface.

The landscaper's truck rolled up, accompanied by the screech of worn brakes, and five men jumped out armed with rakes and blowers.

"Hey, Miguel." She waved at the driver. A stint on the HOA board had familiarized her with every worker and every owner on the property. "Don't tell me the Scottsdale Siesta is your first priority too."

Miguel appeared confused.

Ruthie gestured toward Carl. "The pool man is already here."

"But today Wednesday morning," he said in a heavy Spanish accent. "We here always Wednesday morning. Pool guy gonna be angry. We blow the dust." He hooked a thumb backward. "He supposed to be here Monday and Thursday."

"I guess he's doing us a favor. Just do the best you can, Miguel." She walked on.

The property consisted of separate, two-story rows of identical condos composed of cinderblock, painted the color of the earth. Crushed colored stone was spread over the dirt to keep the dust down. The monotony was broken by trails of river rock, footpaths in contrasting smaller granite stones, and a plethora of desert plants which had overnight become snares for bits of blowing detritus.

The interior walls of the condos were constructed of the same block as the exterior, making the units nearly soundproof. Each unit boasted a wall of windows at the front which not only let sound escape, but allowed a stunning view of Camelback Mountain. This time of year almost all of the windows stayed shielded day and night against the onslaught of heat. For as tightly connected as its units were, the Siesta's residents maintained a great deal of privacy.

Ruthie slowly wound her way around the perimeter of the complex to her enclosed front patio, #4 on the bottom. She looked down the row right and left. Extensions of the interior block walls made it impossible to see her neighbors' units from her front door. Standing out on her patio, she could see the front door of #6, her closest neighbor to the east. Esther Solomon was still in town. It was her custom to visit her son's home in San Francisco for the months of July and August, but this year her granddaughter had some sort of function in Italy and her parents had accompanied her. Mrs. Solomon's declining health kept her from joining them.

No sign of Mrs. Solomon this morning, but that was not unusual. During the other seasons, she would venture out early to water her flower pots and enjoy a cup of coffee. This time of year, there was nothing to water. Only the hardiest desert plants were still alive, and they survived on whatever was left by the monsoon rains.

Stepping back into her condo, Ruthie closed the door against the morning's heat and humidity. Lifting a slat in the blinds, she again surveyed the untidiness outside, realizing it was pointless to tackle the mess until the landscapers had come through with their noisy blowers, rearranging the debris.

The television was still on, a local reporter repeating the same story she had seen as she walked outside earlier. She made a cup of coffee, turned up the volume and sunk into her favorite chair. As she watched the footage of "the wall of dust" for the third time, the sound of sirens nearby broke her attention. She caught sight of two cruisers pulling up outside behind an ambulance.

The sirens stopped. Stepping outside, she followed as she saw the officers heading for the pool area.

Carl stood at the far end of the pool, holding the extended vacuum handle, flanked by all the landscapers, kneeling over the edge looking into the pool. A crowd of uniformed officers, paramedics and three people wearing shirts that read CRIME SCENE SPECIALIST were huddled at the deep end.

The two officers walked quickly toward the EMTs. "What have we got?" one officer asked as the other took out a notepad.

"Nothing for us here. This is strictly a recovery operation." He pointed toward Carl. "Pool guy has been here for over half an hour, the body's been mired in the muck the whole time. It's all yours." The pair began packing their equipment to leave.

Ruthie stood listening as the officer turned to question Miguel and Carl.

"It appears someone has met their Maker," Carl mused. "I hope they had—"

"How long since you found this?" the officer asked.

"I been working about a half hour, I could feel something down there but I thought it was some furniture maybe blew in, or a tree limb. Couldn't see nothin' but mud when I got here. It wasn't till I got some of the muck out that I seen it looked like a body. Then I called you boys."

Ruthie walked toward the edge and peered in. She clapped her hand over her mouth.

Carl continued. "Miguel here and I was just talkin'. If I use the skimmer and you fellas use the rescue pole, maybe we can work it up to the shallow end."

Miguel had already walked to the end wall where a variety of pool equipment hung on brackets. He held a skimmer and a long pole, carrying them like a tight rope walker, trying not to hit the others or the few pieces of furniture still standing as he made his way back to the deep end.

"Hey." One of the crime scene technicians pointed to

Miguel. "Leave that. Everyone take a seat over there by the barbeque. And don't touch anything. Just leave everything where it is."

After they slowly worked the body up to the shallow end, what Ruthie had already guessed was confirmed. Mrs. Solomon, who didn't swim, didn't even keep a pool key, had somehow ended up at the bottom of the Scottsdale Siesta swimming pool.

Detective Bo Bowen squirmed as he sat in Ruthie's favorite chair three days later. Whether he found the chair or the situation uncomfortable she couldn't tell, but it was obvious he didn't want to be in her house, listening to her. His cowboy hat teetered on his knee.

Ruthie paced. "You realize Mrs. Solomon had no pool key. And the gate is always locked."

"I understand that…"

"She lost it last year and said if she ever had a reason to go in there again she'd borrow mine. So she couldn't have got in on her own. You don't think that's suspicious, detective?"

"Look, there's no evidence of foul play."

"There was a wound on her head!"

"Consistent with hitting the Cool Deck on her way in. Or maybe flying debris. The coroner says she had been dead between twelve and fifteen hours. That's consistent with her being out in the middle of the…the dust storm." His fingers worked the rolled edge of his hat. "Her front door was unlocked, and nothing was disturbed as far as we could determine. You confirmed that yourself."

She had entered #6 with the detective shortly after the coroner had left on that terrible day. Everything seemed to be in order in the tidy condo. A glass of wine had been poured, the corked bottle placed back in the fridge. It was no secret Mrs. Solomon allowed herself one glass per night for her health. Also on the counter sat a bowl of oranges. A note, handwritten in fine black ink, was tucked under the container of fruit. Ruthie didn't have to read it. She had written it on Monday morning.

> *I'm here if you need anything. Breast cancer is*
> *scary, but I know you will soon be a survivor*
> *like me.*
> *Ruthie*

Ruthie had stared at the note. "I'd appreciate it if you'd keep that to yourself. I've never told anyone but her."

"Anything look out of place? Anything missing?" Detective Bowen had directed her to Mrs. Solomon's bedroom, then the small bathroom.

Ruthie looked around. "No, but I'm telling you she would not have been in the pool area."

"Let's see what the coroner has to say," he had said. Now he stood and handed her the note that she'd delivered two days before Mrs. Solomon's death. "And don't worry. Your secret's safe with me."

"I thought you had to leave everything in place?"

"Not a crime scene. The coroner ruled it an accident. They aren't going to reopen the case, ma'am. I'm sorry." He set his hat on his head as he walked out.

Ruthie sat on her patio enjoying an almost cool September morning when Miguel and his crew pulled up in a shiny blue pickup.

"New wheels?" she called.

He waved. "Yes. New for me. Is five years old." He directed the men, then walked over to her patio. "I haven't seen you since..." He examined his work boots. "It's sad about the old lady, yes?"

"Yes," she said. "I miss her. I looked forward to seeing her each day." She glanced at the neighboring patio. Empty inside, no furniture or plants outside. Mrs. Solomon's son had come, taken a few personal items, and given the rest to charity. Cleaned out in two days. Her mail was being forwarded to his address in San Francisco.

"What the police say?" Miguel asked.

"Accident." She brushed her hands together. "Case closed." As he walked toward his truck, she eyed him with just a bit of suspicion.

Ruthie went inside and made a list of everyone who had a key to the pool gate. Miguel's name was number two on a short list of suspects with no motive. She hated the list; made up of individuals for whom she had developed a fondness.

Two days before, she had seen Carl whistling as he adjusted the pool's chemicals. She tried to view him as a killer, but she just couldn't make the connection. "You been saved?" he had asked her.

"From what?" She knew what he meant and regretted her response immediately.

"Washed in the blood of the Lamb." He was on his knees, hands held to the sky holding colored water samples up to the light, looking like a penitent begging forgiveness. He squinted at her. "Once you been saved all your sins are forgiven, by the Grace of God."

"I'm good," she said, turning away.

She had stopped Steven, the I.T. guy, shortly after Mrs. Solomon's death. "You heard about the drowning, I guess?"

"Yes," he said, shoving his glasses up with his index finger. "I didn't really know her."

"You didn't happen to see her heading to the pool on the night of the haboob did you?"

"I worked late that night. Which was cool because the office, well my cubicle is nowhere near the window, but from my boss's office? You could see that thing coming from miles away. A big brown wall just getting closer and..." His glasses slipped down again. "I got home about three A.M. It was all quiet here."

She hadn't even put him on her list.

The list included the neighbors, the management company rep, along with Miguel, Carl, and the handyman who only came when called. Ruthie phoned him.

"Hey, this is Handy Andy. Got a problem? I can fix it. Leave your name and number at the beep."

He returned her call twenty minutes later. He hadn't been to Scottsdale Siesta since April. Ruthie's dilemma was one problem Handy Andy could not fix.

She contemplated the possibility that the pool gate had been left open. Had it been a calm night, it was unlikely but possible that the gate had not latched. But the heavy, solid metal pool gate opened from inside and out with a key and was self-latching unless it was propped open, which was strictly against the HOA rules. The gate was meant to stay closed. And if it had been left open, it would have been blown shut and locked tight by the first gust of wind.

The question continued to nag at her: What happened? She had seen Mrs. Solomon on that Monday morning. Dropped off the note and bowl of fruit. The elderly woman was in good spirits. They complained about the heat. Tuesday morning Ruthie had set out on her bike, up the green belt path to her favorite breakfast spot and had become lost in a book. It was afternoon when she headed back, her body drained by the time she made it home. She took a cool shower and a dose of electrolytes, then sat in front of the fan before heading to bed. Too exhausted to turn on television or radio, she had seen no sign of the storm, missed every warning.

The fourth Wednesday night in September, Ruthie hosted book club. She shared the summer's drama.

Sherry, the sleuth of the group, squinted over her reading glasses. "Did Mrs. Solomon have many visitors?"

"She had friends but they rarely came over. She'd meet them for lunch or dinner, shopping, that sort of thing. She always offered the workers a cold iced tea. Sometimes they went inside for a few minutes."

"Aha." Sherry raised an eyebrow. "And this Miguel just got a new truck? Any chance he got into Mrs. Solomon's private stash, then threw her in the pool? Waited a couple of months before he spent the money? It's possible."

"Ruthie, you said it was a fairly new truck. Do you think the old lady had fifteen to twenty K hidden in her condo?" Lena, the accountant looked at Ruthie. "Was she well-off?"

"I think she had some money, but her son kept her on a pretty tight budget. I got the impression he was concerned she might outlive her assets. She had tons of jewelry—some costume, some real. Fabulous pieces."

"That's it!" Sherry jumped up. "A jewelry heist."

Ruthie shook her head. "She told me she kept it all in a safe deposit box. And she still had her wedding ring when she drowned."

Sherry sat down. "Did you follow up on the I.T. guy's alibi?"

"I don't even know where he works." Ruthie was beginning to regret sharing her misgivings.

"Does he have a parking pass on his windshield? He works in a big building downtown, right?"

"I'll check," Dodie said, jumping up from the sofa. "What parking space number is he?"

She was back in two minutes "Ta-dah! "Ta-dah! His parking sticker is for the Chase Tower in downtown

Phoenix."

"Well that narrows it." Ruthie's voice dripped sarcasm. "I'm sure I can find his office on one of those forty- plus floors."

Sherry was undaunted. "So the pool guy? Maybe Mrs. Solomon noticed he was having an affair with…" She leaned forward, "I don't know…you?"

"How disgusting!" Ruthie shot Sherry a dirty look. "Be serious. I would be the one who would know if Carl was fooling around with someone here." Ruthie rolled her eyes. "Have you seen him? Not a chance."

Grabbing the bottle of wine, Dodie topped off their glasses. "Well, maybe it really was an accident."

Ruthie lifted her wineglass and stared into the dark liquid. "It wasn't."

The phone rang as Ruthie added dollops of caviar to an *hors d'oeuvres* tray at her annual holiday open house. Everyone who knew her well enough to phone was in attendance. "Hello?"

"Ruthie? This is Robert Solomon. Esther Solomon's son. I hope I'm not catching you at a bad time."

"No," she said tucking the phone under her chin as she lifted the tray of *canapés*. "Is everything all right?"

"I'm a little stumped here and I hope you can help me. I received a card in the mail today from a jeweler in Scottsdale. It was addressed to my mother, wishing her a happy holiday and thanking her for her business. To your knowledge, had my mother been buying any jewelry lately?"

"More jewelry?" Ruthie set the tray down, then made her way to her bedroom, closing the door. "I can't imagine…"

"I tried to call the store but they're closed. I just wondered if you could shed some light."

"I wish I could. She had so many beautiful pieces, collector's items. Why would she buy more?"

Robert sighed. "Well, she was a spender, you know. Shopaholic. That's why I handled her money. My father left her with a pretty comfortable retirement fund, but she would have been broke years ago if I hadn't taken over. Anyway, I'm sure I'll have the answer after I reach the store tomorrow."

"I'm so sorry I couldn't help." She set the receiver on the bed, and stared at the wall that she and Esther Solomon had shared.

Detective Bowen arrived on Monday afternoon, sat in the same chair, fidgeted with his hat. "I may have to eat some crow."

"How so?" Ruthie asked.

"It seems your neighbor had sold some jewelry on the third of July, two days before she died. She was paid five thousand dollars in cash. There's no record of a bank deposit."

"And there wasn't any money in the condo when you *investigated* on Wednesday morning."

"Nope. And her son didn't find any cash when he went through her things," he said, fingering the brim of his hat.

"So someone took the money and then killed her to cover it up?"

"You might be the prime suspect, except I don't figure you would have kept pestering me to investigate if you had actually killed her."

"Well, that's a relief." Ruthie rolled her eyes, and opened the top drawer of her desk. She pulled out a sheet of paper. "I made a list of suspects."

"You what?" He stopped squirming.

"She didn't have a pool key. It had to be someone who was in town and had a key, so I made a list."

† † †

One week later she called Detective Bowen. She paced her patio as she spoke. "I've been thinking about Mrs. Solomon's murder. She must have known who took the money."

"But unfortunately we don't. I've talked to everyone on your list. In person. I'm guessing at least one of them's a very good liar. Unfortunately, it's not difficult to hide cash. And it's way too late to process any fingerprints. Whoever did this got a good head start." He sounded contrite. "To be honest, and please don't quote me, but I don't think we have a prayer of solving this case."

"So that's it?" Ruthie asked.

"I'm afraid it's a dead-end. We know what, why, when, and where, but we don't know who. I'll keep workin' it, but right now? I don't have a clue."

She hung up and considered the empty space next door that had been so full of life. She reached in her door, grabbed keys off the hook and made her way to the pool area.

Unlocking the gate, she tried to recall that unpleasant July morning. She wondered again who killed Esther Solomon and prayed to remember any small detail that might provide an answer.

Everything was now the same as it had been before the storm—furniture lined up around the deck, broken umbrellas replaced. She sat on a chaise longue, staring into the water. If only Detective Bowen had taken her seriously he could have found the killer by now. He should have listened to me, she thought. "Damn him." Hot tears spilled onto her cheeks. "Damn him!"

"Who you damnin'?" Carl walked in, swinging his tool box. "Good Book says you better get yourself right with the Lord before you damn somebody else, girl."

"Not in the mood, Carl." Ruthie stood to leave.

"The hand of God is not short."

"Uh-huh." She headed for the gate.

"You'll see." Carl said under his breath. "Mind what I say or you just might get that cancer back."

Ruthie stopped in her tracks. She believed Detective Bowen when he said her secret was safe. Only one other person knew, Esther Solomon.

She fought the urge to turn back, to tell Carl that the Good Book also spoke about greed. And liars. And murderers. She fought the urge to hit him on the head, push him in and hold him under the water, watching him struggle until he "met his Maker." She hurried toward her condo to let the detective know who killed Esther Solomon.

She offered up silent thanks as she ran. Her prayer had been answered.

† † †

Having spent most of the last four decades raising her four children, author **R K (RONI) OLSON** has recently altered her lifestyle to focus on her lifelong desire to write. Transplanted from the Pacific Northwest, Roni enjoys life in downtown Scottsdale, AZ with her dog, Jemima. She is former President of the Sisters in Crime Desert Sleuths Chapter.

CAT PISTOL HOODLUM
CATHY ANN ROGERS

Drool oozing from the side of his mouth, Kelvin Meekim pressed his lips to his long shirtsleeve to damn up the dribbling fluid before it made its way onto the carpet or onto his gloves. On his knees, leaning forward to listen through the shuttered closet doors, it annoyed him that he had not learned to control his nerves and the drooling that followed. In these days of DNA and forensics, this gross condition was unsightly, but also a self-divulging telltale sign that placed him on the scene. Disastrous in his line of work.

Concentrating on keeping his mouth closed, Kelvin peered out from the bedroom closet. The damn house was supposed to be empty, but he had heard the front door open downstairs a few minutes before. Here he sat, feeling caged in as he imagined the indignity of being unmasked as a common thief and led to the back of a police car. With his luck, Downley and Carmichael would be the cops to get that satisfaction.

With his usual "get-in-quick-get-out-faster" philosophy, reaching the second floor master bedroom in record time where a wall safe held the mother lode of jewelry and cash, he had arrived to find no safe and nothing of much value. So far, the only part of the plan he had achieved was the "get in quick" part. Now that he was in, he was spending precious minutes calculating a way out, with nothing to show for his trouble. Even as he hid like a wild animal waiting for an escape route to open, he added to his mental to-do list to speak with Ginny about her screwy tip this time. Instead of getting a cut of the takings, she was going to owe him.

Reaching into his right pants pocket, he wrapped his hand around the wooden grip of the Ruger Bearcat pistol he had found at a pawnshop several years ago. Looking like one of the guns he saw in the thirties gangster movies and the cowboy movies he watched as a kid, he treasured it like a good luck charm. He took it with him on every job, but never loaded it with bullets. Just because he carried the twenty-two did not mean he was willing to fire it. That idea had not come to him before now, but he had not been in this situation before. As a vision appeared before him of shooting his way to freedom, he realized the fallacy of waving his unloaded Bearcat at someone who might have their own weapon loaded with real bullets.

Without warning, a piercing scream reverberated throughout the house, echoing on slate floors, granite counters, and marble tabletops, arriving in the density of the carpeted bedroom, as if the last sound wave had lost its struggle to survive, just as the issuer of the sound must have done in response to the loud pop he recognized as a gunshot.

Uncertain if he would crap his pants or throw up first, Kelvin's knees quivered while chills ran up his neck and prickled the short spiked hairs from his nape to the top of his head. Motionless, Kelvin felt a skewed awareness of reality. Maybe it was a minute or an hour since he heard the woman scream. He tried to think, but decided that fact was not as important as avoiding getting himself shot. In the middle of the worst fright of his life, he thought how all the clichés made sense: frozen in his step; feet glued to the floor; paralyzed by fear. He caught himself from laughing aloud at how life kept putting him in his place, mocking his arrogance. Getting a grip on his emotions, he raised his sweaty body upright and found the courage to ease himself into the room by following the momentum of the moving closet door.

At first, the absence of sound gave an unoccupied feel to the house, but as he moved toward the open doorway, he made out muffled movements under the long staircase in the hall. Dealing with this new panic made him breathless now, every nerve in his body on fire. Not until the sounds stopped and he considered how he might jump from the balcony, did he feel his tension give way. Turning away from the double door entry, he crossed to the arcadia door, slid it open, and moved outside onto the narrow balcony.

With a quick estimate of the distance he had to jump, he considered it a risk worth the taking when a voice from behind said, "I wouldn't do it. You'll never survive the impact."

"Holy crap," Kelvin said, hearing a girl's voice coming from his throat.

In his sickened fright, Kelvin turned around to see the

polished crime boss he knew as Nick Harley. On the streets, Nick, known as Slick Nick, was someone you did not mess with if you knew what was good for you. Knowing how he dealt with others who crossed him, Kelvin figured Slick to be the last person to see him alive.

"Slick, I didn't know you lived in this house," Kelvin managed to say.

With the demeanor of a man who is accountable to no one, Nick said, "Before you piss your pants, why don't you come downstairs? We can have a drink and talk about why I shouldn't put a bullet through your head."

Feeling the heat of Nick's stare, Kelvin felt the inevitability of his situation as they approached the top of the stairs. Life was like that, he thought. Of all the times you get by out of sheer luck, the job that nails you is the one that goes wrong right away. Giving in to his destiny calmed him while Nick followed behind as they walked downstairs.

Once at the bottom of the stairs in the opulent paneled foyer, Kelvin came to a stop remembering the shot and the woman's scream. Trying to conceal his searching glances from Nick, he did not see evidence of a dead body. With a sense of relief, he hoped what he heard was just a loud, physical argument and the woman was not hurt.

"What were you doing up there, Kelvin? If you wanted to visit me, all you had to do was ask," Nick said, breaking into Kelvin's thoughts.

"Oh, man. I'm sorry for this, Slick. I got Ginny to scout for jobs for me in the neighborhoods where she cleans houses. She told me this house would be empty for a month while the owners were on vacation. She even gave me the combination to the bedroom safe where the couple who lives here keeps their stash. She never said you was the man that lived here. I swear to God, Slick. I know better than to mess with you."

"You know, I believe you, Kelvin. And because I believe you, I'm going to let you off the hook for this. You don't do damage when you break in. I admire your technique."

Believing that he might get out of this after all, Kelvin said, "I sure appreciate you taking this so well, Slick. Anything I can ever do for you…"

"There is something you can do. Today."

"Sure, what is it?"

"Your timing is perfect for the favor I need. You see, I've had a little accident that needs cleaning up."

Recalling the gunshot and the scream, it did not take Kelvin's limited imagination to figure out what was coming next. "I'm listening."

"I need you to do a real job for me. Make this place look like a sloppy burglary all over the house. When you get to the kitchen, you'll make it look like the burglar was surprised by a woman who wasn't supposed to be here and she got shot in the process."

"Is she dead?"

"Yeah, but it was an accident. She was mistaken at how long she could get away with being with another man and misjudged her ability to get away with it. Complete clumsiness on her part. So, you see my predicament. What cop is going to believe it was an accident with my reputation? You're my best chance to beat this thing. What do you say?"

Knowing he did not have the option to say no, Kelvin nodded.

Moving toward the dining room, Nick jerked his head, directing Kelvin to follow him through the swinging door connecting the formal dining room to the kitchen. The first thing that caught Kelvin's eye was a tangled mass of bright yellow hair that covered part of a soft white face, but had separated to expose a feminine nose and pouty red lips. On approach, he saw the rest of her body behind the island. Long, toned and tan, Kelvin thought she looked like a mannequin from a dress shop window.

A sickening fear rumbled in Kelvin's stomach making him light-headed. For as long as he had burglarized homes, he had never once put a face to the victim. She was not *his* victim, but he felt guilty just the same. Without a doubt, his instinct told him she had not deserved an end like this. Setting his feelings aside, he had a job to do if he wanted to get out of here alive. Later, he would barter with his conscience.

"Get started in the rest of the house," Nick said. "This will be the last room, but you see what we have to deal with here. Make it look good, not staged. The cops will see through that."

After a quick nod, Kelvin went back upstairs and began going through each bedroom to create his version of an amateurish burglary. Opening drawers, tossing their contents, and tilting pictures, Kelvin was glad he still wore the gloves, waiting until Nick was out of view before he pulled the handkerchief over his mouth. As embarrassing as the drooling was, he kept the face cover a secret from everyone. For the first time since he began that habit did he feel its importance. Like, what kind of fools did Nick take the cops to be, Kelvin thought. He was sure a forensic team could sniff him out by his choice of laundry detergent. The last thing he wanted was to make it easy for the cops to identify him by sweaty paw prints and drops of slobber everywhere.

Considering his odds, Kelvin figured that if there was a positive to this situation it was that he did not have a reputation for sloppy jobs like this. The fact that they had not caught him yet did not mean they did not recognize his work. This was not his style, he thought, shaking his head as he continued to fuss around in drawers. Knowing before the job where you were going and what you intended to take, made the job easy. The fact that no one had ever been present, much less harmed on any of his jobs was another reason he figured he was on the list of low priority criminals.

If someone told the cops this was one of his jobs, he wondered if they would believe it without an eyewitness. It was the random acts of junkies and crackheads to wander around in hopes of finding something valuable. If he decided to operate blind, he was not sure he would choose this way to do it. This left too much to chance. Feeling like a man stuck on a down escalator, he moved through the downstairs rooms working his way back to the dining room. Within ten minutes, he was back in the kitchen with Nick who had used something to put pry marks on the kitchen door that now stood open to the airy back yard.

Leaning against the island counter, a drink in one hand and his other arm crossed over his waist, Nick said, "I've been thinking. It would be even better to have a witness when the cops come. You can be someone I've hired to help me out with something or other around here. We were out, came back, and found the house tossed, with Traci dead. They won't be so suspicious if I have a witness. Can you handle talking with the cops?"

Caught off guard by Nick's revised scenario, Kelvin hesitated. Fear was back, accompanied by a sense of dread. The deeper he sank into this nightmare, the closer he came to believing he would not get out of this house alive.

"Listen," Nick went on. "You owe me. I could be calling the cops on you for attempted burglary. Instead, I'm giving you an opportunity to help me out of a sticky situation."

Feeling the pressure from Nick reminded Kelvin of the times his mother tried the same tactics to get her way. Not appreciating the pressure from Nick any better, but not sure what other option he had, Kelvin said, "What do you want me to do?"

"That's what I want to hear, a cooperative tone. When the cops get here, you'll be standing with me while I tell the story of what happened. I'll look over to you once in a while. All you have to do is agree with what I've said. That's easy enough, right?"

"Sure," Kelvin said, trying to look convinced though he did not think it sounded that easy or believable. Just because they called him "Slick" Nick did not mean he was smart. It meant he was slippery and dishonest to the core, but how smart Nick thought himself to be did not come close to how smart he was, Kelvin thought.

"Okay. I'm calling them now," Nick said, holding up his right index finger as he relayed to the person on the other end of the line that someone broke in and killed his girlfriend. Then he said, "Hell no, I won't wait on the line. Get someone over here. Now!" Nick flipped his phone shut and turned to Kelvin, "Oh, wait a minute. Didn't I hear they call you the Cat because of that Ruger pistol you carry around with you?"

"I guess some people call me that."

"You better set that out on the island counter. Cops get nervous when they find out someone has a concealed gun," Nick said.

In a blinding flash of clarity, Kelvin believed he understood what Nick was angling for to get himself out of his trouble over the girl. Knowing he had to be fast or he would not make it, Kelvin started the motion of going into his pocket for his gun, but instead he pushed passed Nick, now off balance and falling backward, and escaped through the back door.

"Hey, you little son-of-a-bitch," Nick yelled. "Get back here."

Feeling the heat on his back from the desert's afternoon rays, Kelvin ran out of the yard between towering twenty-foot oleanders and down a dusty alley. This part of Carefree was a ghost town during the summer when homeowners returned to their native states until the first signs of winter. Making this the ideal location to get away without the worry of witnesses, Kelvin had parked under a carport open to the alley in a stretch of homes Ginny said were vacant. Using his electronic door opener and engine starter, he jumped into the waiting car and was down the alley and out onto the highway before he looked back.

"I guess it's time to visit Mom in Wickenburg for a few days," Kelvin said to his alter ego he liked to think gave a crap. "These are the kind of days that make you think you should find a new line of work."

Disappointed at the lack of response, he settled back into the seat to concentrate on the road and settle his nerves. As he reached for one of the water bottles he kept in the center storage bin, his hand touched the scrap of paper with the address Ginny had given him. Glancing at the house number, he lost his grip on the steering wheel for a moment when he realized he had reversed the last two numbers of the address. Nick's house was not the target house at all. That mistake had almost cost him his life and still might if Nick came looking for him. Blowing out a puff of air exaggerating his frustration at the irony of life, he turned west on the Carefree Highway toward Wickenburg.

† † †

When the dispatcher sent out the call about a burglary at the residence of Nick Harley, police officers Downley and Carmichael looked at the other with matching sardonic expressions.

"So Slick Nick was robbed, huh?" Downley said. "Sounds a little, what's the word, unbelievable. Dangerous guy like that, who'd have the guts?"

"After all the victimizing he's done, I might have to pinch myself to keep from smiling if he starts complaining about police action and justice for the victim," Carmichael said.

Driving the short distance between their current location to the Harley home, they pulled up to find Slick Nick running from the side of the house toward the alley waving a gun in his right hand. Downley screeched his cruiser to a halt and both men, guns drawn, called out for him to stop and put down the gun.

"He's getting away," Nick said, flushed and angry. "The jerk is getting away. Don't just stand there looking stupid. Go after him."

"Drop the gun. Now," both officers said in unison.

As if the reality of the scene occurred to him that instant, Nick stopped, released the gun from his grip, and raised his arms over his head.

After kicking the gun to the side, handcuffing Nick and patting him down for other weapons, Downley said, "Calm down and tell me what happened."

"This sorry-ass hoodlum by the name of Kelvin came in here to rob me. He killed my girlfriend when she wouldn't tell him where my money is. She's on the kitchen floor," Nick said, wrenching his head to the north side of the house.

Exchanging furtive looks, Carmichael headed toward the side door Nick indicated, while Downley continued to take notes on the sequence of events he was hearing from Nick.

"It all happened so fast, I couldn't react in time. Then he was gone. I picked up my gun and started to go after him. That's when you got here."

"You say he went after your girlfriend for the hiding place of your money, and when she wouldn't or couldn't tell him, he shot her. Did the lady live here? Is that why he thought threatening her instead of you was more effective? If your gun was so handy, why didn't you pull it on him to defend her?"

Having seen that hesitation before when asking a suspect an unexpected question, Downley knew there was more weeding necessary to come up with the truth. From inside the house, he heard his partner yell out, "She's alive. Paramedics are on the way."

The blood had drained from Nick's face. The cocksure attitude had left with his color, telling Downley that a well-constructed plot had fallen to ruin.

"Wait a minute. I'm the victim here. This isn't fair. I was the one who was violated."

After seating a petulant Nick in the back seat of the patrol car, Downley took out an evidence bag and scooped up the Glock 21 he had kicked away moments ago. Smelling it, the odor of gunpowder told him someone had fired the gun and not long ago. Whether Nick or Kelvin used this pistol to shoot the girl, the lab would have to figure out, but someone used this gun for something.

Within minutes, the property was crowded with an

ambulance, the forensics team, and detectives who would take over the case.

Inside the police car, Carmichael said, "I don't know if our boy Kelvin was here or if that was part of the lie Nick created for an alibi, but if he was here and got away…well, this has got to be the luckiest day of his life."

† † †

Born and raised an only child in Cincinnati, Ohio, **CATHY ANN ROGERS** spent her early years listening to vivid stories by parents, relatives and other elders. With firsthand insight into historical events, she developed a keen interest in the art of storytelling. In her fiction, as in life, characters suffer from a skewed sense of justice and bittersweet victories. After establishing her accounting and tax business, she resurrected her writing career with various short stories and her first novel. In the arid climate of the Arizona desert, she shares her home with two Bichon Frisés, Whitney and Sophie.

THE RATTLE OF DARKNESS
MARTIN ROSELIUS

The unbearable heat of mid-July pressed down on Pancho as he crept among the rocks of the dry desert hills south of Sonoyta, Mexico, his home the past seven years. Whenever an urge called to test his manhood, reaffirm his superior position in the hierarchy of God's creatures, he went in search of cold-blooded reptiles. Those with prized rattles on one end, venomous fangs on the other.

He overturned rocks, pushed his long stick into holes and beat on the creosote bushes, driving a startled serpent from the safety of its shelter. A rush of adrenalin raced through him as he pinned the hissing head to the ground with a forked staff and advanced on it with his machete. A quick whack filled him with an excitement almost as satisfying as those frequent visits to the whores.

Pancho experienced few times in life when he alone was in total command. With the snakes, or with the whores, *he* was the man.

After a two-hour killing spree, Pancho succumbed to exhaustion. He'd collected two fat trophies in a burlap sack but hadn't been satisfied until he'd butchered an even dozen. Carcasses lay scattered about and would soon be picked over by predators, their remains left in the sun to bake and rot.

Later that evening, after a plate of beans, a grilled steak of diamondback and a six-pack of cold *cervesas*, Pancho left his house and stumbled down the dusty road toward the towering steel-reinforced fence that meandered along the border between Sonoyta, Mexico and Lukeville, Arizona. To those from the north, it was a protected barrier that separated two worlds of divergent cultures, lifestyles and politics. To those from the south, it was a barrier that separated the willing workforce provided by Mexico from the opportunities provided by America. And to Pancho, it was a barrier he took advantage of to separate those workers from the *pesos* in their pockets.

Where the street came to a dead end at the dirt path that ran parallel to the border, Pancho turned left and approached an unpainted concrete block building. He glanced up and down the deserted road. The moonless night remained quiet, interrupted only by his crude burp, a rumble from his bare stomach that ballooned beneath a stained T-shirt. After retrieving a set of keys from his pocket, he fumbled with the locks on the wrought iron gate and the wooden entrance behind it that wore a shy coat of flaking green paint.

Pancho stepped in, shut the door and felt for the chain on the bulb hanging from the ceiling. He pulled it with a heavy hand. The room lit up as a harsh light bounced off the bare windowless walls. He plopped down on the only piece of furniture, a rickety wood chair in the corner. Checked his watch. 11:07. He tipped his hat to shade the light from his eyes, closed them. Rocked back.

A tap on the door startled him, even though he had been expecting it. He shuffled toward the entrance, cracked the door, and looked out into darkness.

A face met him. Dark complexion. Scrubby beard. Soiled baseball cap. Other faces appeared behind the first one. Pancho stretched his neck. Studied them a moment. Counted heads, then nodded.

He opened the door wider and the six men, two women and three children stepped up and onto the concrete floor. Pancho closed the door behind them and locked it.

After collecting a substantial number of *pesos*, Pancho gave them their instructions. He grunted, bent over and pulled up a corner of the Mexican rug, exposing a wooden panel, three-feet square. He lifted a handle built flush into the trapdoor. It swiveled upward on two rusty hinges, exposing a pit of darkness beneath it.

He stepped over to the wall and flicked a switch. Light appeared from the hole in the floor. In silence, Pancho descended a crude handmade ladder. The workers and their families, each with a small sack or tote, followed closely behind and soon disappeared into the shaft leading to a subterranean tunnel that stretched for 150 feet. It came to a dead end where another vertical shaft and a ladder led them up to a trapdoor that opened beneath the star-studded sky of Arizona in an area thick with creosote bushes and scattered rocks.

After the last person disappeared into the night, Pancho pulled the door with the camouflaged cover back down, secured it and returned to the one-room building. He replaced the rug, turned off the lights, then shuffled off to his house, breathing heavy from a long night of hard labor.

When Pancho arrived home, he reached out to unlock his door but two shadows appeared from behind to startle him. "Ah, who—"

"Shut up, pig." The two men hustled him through the doorway. Pancho fell to the floor. Tumbled onto his back. His assailants remained silhouetted against the glow of the corner streetlight.

"*¿Qué pasa?* What…what do you want?"

"Luido sent us to collect his money. He is becoming impatient. He said you needed a reminder."

"No! *Por favor!* Don't hurt me. I will pay. Look." Pancho dug into his pocket and pulled out a wad of *pesos*. "Here. I have *mucho dinero*. Take this. I will get more."

The man reached down, grabbed the money and flipped through the bills taking a rough count. "When will you pay the rest?"

Pancho scooted back. "*Pronto.* Very soon. I have more crossers tomorrow. I will have it then."

The first man stepped forward, leaned down and pushed his scruffy face next to Pancho's. His breath smelled of cheap tequila, his body of cheaper women. He held up a long blade that glistened as it caught the faint light coming through the window. "Luido will not be happy. But I will try to persuade him that you are a man of your word. I will be back *mañana*. If you do not have the rest of the money by then," he pressed the knifepoint into Pancho's paunch, "I will make you squeal like the stupid stuffed swine you are."

The man rose up and replaced the weapon in a sheath on his belt. He paused a moment, stared down, then with a swift kick jammed his boot tip into Pancho's side. Pancho lost his breath. He gasped for air as he grabbed his ribs. Pain radiated throughout his body.

"*¡Botas, pronto!*" the man yelled.

Pancho squirmed. "I…I…"

The man reached down, gripped Pancho's left boot with both

hands and wrenched it off with a quick twist. He tossed the boot to the second man, then yanked off the other one from the right foot. "A pig doesn't deserve boots."

The man turned and the two intruders disappeared through the doorway, leaving nothing but dust rising up in the glow of the streetlight.

The following morning Pancho lay on his stained mattress, nursing the ache from the man's kick. He glanced at his socks with the holes in both toes. Last night Luido's men had taken his money and his boots.

He owed Luido money. He knew that.

So what if Pancho smoked a little of Luido's expensive stuff? Who didn't? What if he did visit Luido's whores? Who didn't? But the money Luido's men took from him last night did not belong to Pancho. The money they took was Manuel's. Pancho worked the tunnel for Manuel Baptista and his boys. It was they who supplied the runners. Pancho only received compensation of a few *pesos* for operating the underground border crossing. Manuel would want the money due him for last night, and now Pancho didn't have it.

If he did not pay these *pendejos*, Pancho would be a dead man. He had one day to think about his desperate situation. Twenty-four hours to come up with the *dinero*.

He stared at the ceiling. His stomach growled as he lay on his back, thinking, following the money trail. Then, in a rare whiff of ingeniousness, it came to him. *Yes! The money trail.* He'd show these thugs he was as smart as they were.

He had a plan.

That night, after putting on a worn pair of leather sandals he snuck from his neighbor's doorstep and went to see the one person who had the means to help him out. The man passed him a heavy bag. Pancho passed him the last of his savings—a stash of *pesos* he had hidden under his mattress.

After leaving the man's house, he walked toward the one-room block building by the border fence. Arrangements had been made for four men to do a crossing that night, and Pancho recognized this as an opportunity. A business opportunity. If his plan worked, he would have enough to pay off all his debts with both Manuel Baptista and Luido and have a little something left over for himself.

He waited on the chair once again, until alerted by a soft knock. He rose and went to the door. A face appeared. Then more. He looked them over. Counted four heads. Nodded and opened the door for them to enter.

"I am Rafael," the first man said. He pointed to a younger man. "This is my nephew, Fernando, and my two friends, Javier and Emilio."

Pancho exhaled a heavy burst of stale breath. "*¿Tienen el dinero?*"

"Yes. We have our money." Rafael went to his bag as did the other three. Pancho collected from them, stuffed it in his pocket and recited instructions as he had done many times. When he finished, he paused, then asked, "You have the money for the contact in Ajo and the transportation?"

The four replied, "Yes. Yes. We have the money."

Pancho nodded. He turned to conceal a smile as he uncovered the door to the shaft. He flicked on the light, picked up the sack he had brought with him and led the men down the ladder. At the other end of the tunnel, he climbed up, unlatched the door, then stepped out under the stars of Arizona.

The men assembled around him. He pointed. "The Americans patrol over there." He turned. "Tonight you should go this way to the wash. I will lead you until I believe you are safe." He lowered the trapdoor then headed off into the darkness. "Follow me."

They pushed their way through the scrubs guided by the faint glow of a late rising moon. After thirty minutes, they stopped in an area of thick desert brush along a dry gulch. As the men gathered, Pancho stuck his hand into the sack and withdrew the pistol he had purchased earlier that evening.

The men jumped back.

"What is this!" one man said. "What are you doing?"

"What do you want?" another asked.

"*Por favor*," they pleaded. "Don't do this. We have families."

Pancho stared at them. Cowards, he thought. They are *patéticos*. "Empty your pockets. Drop everything." He pointed at the ground. "And toss your bags over here. *¡Rápido!*"

Without hesitation, the men did as he asked. When they finished, they stood, fidgeting. "We need the money to get to Phoenix. How are we going to—"

"*¡Silencio!* Where you are going you will not need money." Pancho glanced down where paper *pesos* and silver coins were scattered next to their booted feet. Boots! Yes. Pancho would get *las botas* tonight, too. He grinned, raised the gun. "Turn around. Do not make this difficult."

After stuffing their money into his bulging pockets, Pancho removed two sets of boots that looked like they might be his size. He kept the pair with the silver tips that looked more expensive even though they didn't fit as well, then collected the men's bags and raced back to the tunnel. Once inside, he secured the hidden entrance, hurried to the block building, locked the two doors and quickly returned to his own house. He knew Luido's men would come, but he was prepared to pay. He had enough money to cover all his debts plus a bit extra for some smoke and some whores. He chuckled to himself. *Those fools. Now, who is the smart one?*

† † †

Gabriela Sanchez and her husband, Juan-Carlos, lived just off the bus line in south Phoenix, a neighborhood of modest homes with a high concentration of Hispanic families. They had immersed themselves in the American dream, were fortunate enough to have entered the United States with green cards and had recently become naturalized citizens.

Knowing her husband would soon arrive home from work, she busied herself preparing a dinner of green chili burritos. The kitchen was a place she normally felt happy, but today she was filled with nervous anxiety. She had been expecting her brother and a nephew from Mexico. They were overdue. Her brother, Rafael, had called on a cell phone three nights ago to let her know that he and Fernando were at the border waiting to cross with a man named Pancho. It would be the last time they could use their cell phone, as it wasn't programmed to function in the States. They expected to be at her house by the following day, or the next at the very latest. Everything had been arranged she had been told, although she didn't want to know any details.

She set out extra tortillas, hoping the two family members would soon show. But her concern deepened with every passing hour. *Where are they? Why is it taking so long? Has something happened?*

Her two children ran through the living room in a game of chase. "Kristina! Paulino! Stop that running." She glanced at the wall clock. "If you're not watching cartoons, bring me the remote."

They ignored her. Racing past, they disappeared into the back bedroom leaving a trail of giggles and laughs.

"When are you going to listen to me?" Gabriela grabbed a dishtowel as she headed into the living room. "Arugghh! Those kids are gonna drive me crazy." She glanced around and noticed the remote on the coffee table. Picking it up, she aimed it at the TV and set the channel for the evening news. She turned up the volume, set down the remote, then headed back to the kitchen. She was half-listening when something caught her attention. She stopped. Peered back through the doorway. Stared at the newscaster as a sense of fear grew into a rush of terror.

"…is continuing to investigate the death of four unidentified Hispanic men just north of Lukeville, Arizona. The Border Patrol has indicated the bodies may have been lying in the desert two to three days. They also report that based on evidence collected at the scene they are treating this as a robbery and murder of undocumented aliens. No witnesses have come forward. Tonight they are asking anyone with information concerning this incident to contact the Border Patrol or your local authorities. Coming up next, Campaign two-thousand twelve and the…"

Gabriela dropped the dishtowel. She leaned against the doorjamb. Her head swirled. She dropped to her knees. A pain shot through her body as a cry of agony escaped her lips. "No! No!" she wailed. "Not my Rafael. Not Fernando. Please, God, don't let it be them."

Juan-Carlos found her slumped on the floor, her body racked by sobs. Their two small children had attempted to comfort her, but failed to understand. He rushed over, took her in his arms. "Gabriela, what is it? Are you hurt? Who did this to you?"

She sat up, wrapped her arms around him and between sobs, explained what she had heard on the evening news. He listened and soon understood her concerns. "Maybe it is not them?"

"Then where are they? I have this terrible feeling it *is* them."

Juan-Carlos held her tight. "We should call the police. We will ask them."

"No! We can't."

He looked at her. "I understand. But we have to know. Let us wait one more day to see if they show. If we do not hear from them, we will have to go to the authorities and see what we can find out."

Gabriela buried her face in Juan-Carlos' shoulder. Her body shook and her shoulders bobbed up and down from an uncontrolled rash of sobs.

Two days later Gabriela and Juan-Carlos contacted the authorities. After discussing the circumstances behind their concern and providing a physical description of her brother and nephew, they were told to visit the morgue in Casa Grande to view the bodies. It was a terrible moment when sheets from two of the men were removed, and Gabriela, in a burst of tears, nodded. She and Juan-Carlos drove home knowing they would have to share this heartbreaking news with relatives who remained in Mexico.

† † †

Pancho had just left the *cantina* when two men approached. They told him they wanted to cross into the United States. Did he know somebody who could help them?

Pancho's eyes lit up. "*Sí, amigos.* You have come to the right man. I alone, in all of Sonoyta, can help you cross safely. But, my friend, it is very expensive. Do you have the money?"

"Yes," one of the men said. "We can pay." He glared. "As long as it is fair and reasonable. And our safety is assured."

Pancho crossed himself. "My friend. I am an honest businessman. And I am taking a great risk. I must be compensated. But I can assure your safety." They turned and continued walking. "Now, let me tell you what you must bring with you tonight."

Pancho filled in the two strangers on the plan to move them across the border. And, of course, the cost of doing so. After agreeing on a price and a time and place to meet, they separated, walking off in different directions. Pancho grinned, and for the first time since the fortunate crossing of the four foolish men, he felt light on his feet. *These two will pay handsomely. And Manuel Baptista and his boys will not know of this little piece of side business. All the money will be mine to be used for smokes and whores.*

That night, as expected, a knock came while Pancho rested on his chair, dreaming of how he would spend the money. He rose, opened the door and peered out. The two men he had spoken to earlier in the day stared back. Pancho opened it wide. *"Hola, mis amigos.* It is good to see you."

The men nodded. Once inside with the door locked, Pancho held out his hand. "The money."

"How do we know you have this tunnel?" one man asked. "I see nothing but a chair."

Pancho withdrew his hand and gestured toward the worn rug. "It is here. Let me show you."

He peeled it back, lifted the trapdoor and flipped the light. "You see. I am an honest businessman. Now, the money."

The man reached behind his back, then with a swift motion drew his hand in front of him, holding a firm grip on a gleaming knife with a six-inch blade.

Pancho jumped back. "What! What is this? A robbery? I have no money. What is the meaning of this?"

The man without the knife stepped forward. "Ten days ago you took four men across the border through your tunnel. One was a younger man. Do you remember?"

Pancho began to panic. Sweat beaded on his forehead. He started to shake. "I…I don't remember."

The man with the knife moved in, pressed it against an overlapping fold of Pancho's neck.

"Ah, ah, yes, now I remember. Four men. They went through the tunnel. I saw them go out the other end. They disappeared into the darkness. I never saw them again."

The man slapped Pancho. He fell back against the wall. "Liar. We know you killed them. We know you stole their money. Confess and we will let you go."

"Who…who are you?"

"You don't know me, but you have met my family. My name is Juan-Carlos."

Family? Pancho had little time to think beyond that single thought before the man continued.

"So, do you confess? If you do, my cousin and I walk out of here. Or do we have to kill you for no reason, like you killed those four men?"

"*¡Por favor!* Please, I beg of you. I have family too. Ten little *niños* who depend on me. Have mercy."

"Like the mercy you showed my wife's brother and her nephew?"

"What do you say? Brother? Nephew?" Pancho's heart raced. He felt light-headed.

Juan-Carlos glared at Pancho as hate tested his patience.

Pancho's eyes shot from the man to the knife. "I...I didn't mean it. Manuel Baptista made me do it." He crossed himself. "As God is my witness, he made me do it."

Juan-Carlos exhaled, lowered the knife, then looked toward his cousin. They nodded in agreement. His cousin stepped over to the trapdoor and disappeared down the ladder. Juan-Carlos backed up, sat down in the chair. He checked his watch, remained silent as Pancho stood motionless against the wall, sweating, and having succumbed to an urge to pee.

Juan-Carlos's cousin hurried down the tunnel, then upon reaching the vertical shaft, climbed upward, unlatched the door above his head and stepped out into the night air. He glanced around. Noticing an area of boulders nearby, he began to roll and push them toward the closed trapdoor. He placed the heaviest rocks on top of the camouflaged panel, making certain they wouldn't roll or slide. He went back, gathered smaller ones, stacked them on top of the larger ones, creating a pyramid of substantial weight.

After he was satisfied no one would be able to lift the trapdoor from inside, he headed off through the desert brush. He set a direction parallel to the border fence until he reached the highway, where he stepped out onto the warm asphalt pavement and began walking toward the border-crossing where he would once again enter Mexico.

As Pancho stood in silence, Juan-Carlos glanced at his watch, then looked up at him. "It is time. You can now make your escape." He tipped his head toward the opening to the tunnel entrance. "Down." Pancho remained pinned against the wall. Juan-Carlos waved the knife. "Now!"

Pancho eased away, took one small step toward the trapdoor. *Is he going to let me go? The other man already crossed to America. Is he letting me go too?* He took another step. Juan-Carlos remained seated. Pancho hesitated a moment, then shuffled over, bent down and half-tumbled down the ladder as quickly as his footing allowed. When he reached the bottom, he looked up. Juan-Carlos appeared at the opening, silhouetted against the harsh bulb hanging from the ceiling. Pancho took a few steps backward, unsure of his next move.

Juan-Carlos leaned over. In his hand he gripped the bag he had brought with him. He untied the cord that held it closed. Tipped it upside down. Shook it. Dark ropes rained down on Pancho. Two. Three. Coiled ropes. He jumped back. The hisses froze him. The chorus of rattles sent fear exploding through his body. He turned. Ran. The trapdoor clicked shut. The lights went out. Darkness enveloped him.

Nobody heard his screams.

MARTIN ROSELIUS, following a career in graphic design/ illustration, has channeled his creative energies into the art of writing, having completed a memoir, SAND IN MY SHOES, ROCKS IN MY HEAD, an espionage thriller, YELLOW BLOOD, RED FEVER, and a suspense novel, LAST SHADOW OF THE CROWN, set in Esfahan, Iran, where he lived in the late '70s. His publishing credits include: *Caribbean Travel + Life* magazine, the *Mystery Readers Journal* and short stories published in anthologies by Sisters in Crime and the Society of Southwest Authors, the latter which took third place in SSA's 2010 writing contest.

THE WRITE LIE
AMY SCHUSTER

Jack Blunt stepped into the humid haze and raised his head toward the hot blackness that filled the Phoenix sky. With roiling shades colliding, white daggers slashing, the monsoon gathered steam. He inhaled the last puff of a cigarette as the deluge dropped, the spanking rain calming the asphalt and christening the air with the scent of creosote. Smashing the butt, he went back into his office, leaving the door propped open to watch the rain.

Three Emmy awards were the brightest things in the otherwise austere room. They stood watch along the edge of the industrial desk, waiting for the clients that would eventually show up in need of a private detective. He twiddled his Mont Blanc pen, a gift from his widower father back in Philly before he headed to Tinseltown to make his mark writing for television. A grand mark he made too, as evidenced by the awards.

Out of nowhere a man appeared in the doorway. He wore creased jeans, a western shirt with mother of pearl snaps, a Bolo tie with matching collar stays, boots and plenty of rain drops. He approached the desk, his hand outstretched in anticipation of a shake. Jack obliged.

"I'm Harley Bradshaw. I need a private detective," he said wiping off his lenses.

"Have a seat, Harley. I think you've found your man."

"Are those Emmy awards?"

"Yes, they are. I used to write for TV. Maybe you've seen the show, *Nun with a Gun*?"

"Packing heat beneath her habit for righteous reasons," Harley replied. "Yes, I loved that show."

"Thanks. I was partial to it myself."

"So, how did you end up here in Phoenix working as a private detective?"

"Well, after the show ended I began to think that perhaps life could imitate art. I was very good at solving crimes on paper.

Why not try it for real? Hollywood is fickle and they were more than happy to move onto the next greatest thing. I had to reinvent myself. I chose Phoenix for the dry heat and those smoldering sunsets my ex turned me on to before the love ran out. Coffee?"

"No thanks. If it's all right with you I'd like to get down to business."

"Okay shoot," Jack said leaning back into his padded chair.

"My wife, Rosiland, died in our home eight years ago. I was on the road selling encyclopedias for *Britannica*. When I returned I found her dead in the bathtub. There was no sign of foul play and the police were quick to rule it an accident. At the time, I couldn't disagree with them."

"And now?"

"I found this." He reached into the satchel he had placed on the desk and pulled out a bundle of cash wrapped in a sheet of paper that had something written on it.

"Where was it?"

"Stuffed inside the case of my wife's accordion in the closet. She knew her way around a polka. It's sort of embarrassing but I've just now started going through her things. I guess I didn't want to let go."

"How much is here?" he asked raising the bundle and removing the handwritten paper.

"Fifty thousand."

"That's a lot of Franklins." Jack smoothed the paper and read the note, "Egomaniac on the stage, phony phenom stealing the scene. Manuscripts materialize, a loquacious charade. Cash and crust arrive in tandem, whilst the proliferate patsy questions her due." His eyes wrestled over the words again as he scratched his temple. "Is this your wife's handwriting?"

"Yes."

"Does it mean anything to you?"

"No. Poetry puzzles me," Harley said.

"What did your wife do for a living?"

"She was a research assistant for the fiction writer, Amanda Merriwether."

"Ah, the mystery writer. Did they get along?"

"There was plenty of creative tension between them. Amanda was a fierce taskmaster who expected perfection but I don't think there was any ill will between them. She was all broken up about Rosiland's death. Blubbered like a baby at the service."

"Was there anyone else your wife worked with?"

"Yes, Amanda's literary agent, Trisha Tovey. Between the two of them she had her hands full, but she never complained."

"This phrase 'manuscripts materialize' maybe that's what all this cash is about? Any idea where I can find Trisha Tovey?" Jack asked.

"She's no longer with the literary agency. I heard she purchased the Shangri-la nudist resort in New River. You'll most likely find her there. So, you'll take the case?"

"Is the Pope Catholic? Two-fifty a day plus expenses. Shangri-la here I come."

Jack parked his '79 Pontiac Lemans in the shade of a mesquite tree and gazed toward the entrance of the Shangri-la Resort before fumbling through the glove box for his notebook and pen. The nonchalance of his gait belied his nerves as he strolled along the tree-lined path and under the ivy that hung low from the arched entrance. He could hear water splashing and laughter from the other side of the dense wall of flowering oleander while bare flesh flashed around the periphery of his vision. He felt like a hesitant voyeur.

He entered the office and approached a woman who wore nothing more than a string of puka shells and cherry pink fingernail polish. She carried her age with beauty and he found himself intrigued by the faint cellulite tutu that graced her hips and hinted toward a certain *savoir-faire* that comes with experience.

"I'm here to see Trisha Tovey," he said, diverting his eyes off to the right of where she stood.

"Not dressed like that you're not. You can remove your clothes and drop them in that bin over there. Trust me, no one here will bother them," she said, flipping her long braid over her shoulder.

"Oh damn," he muttered.

"What's that?" She smiled, her playful tone toying with him.

"Well, I was hoping to avoid undressing but I suppose it doesn't work that way here."

"No. It doesn't. We'd have all sorts of perverts hanging around if we allowed clothed visitors. It's not nearly as traumatic as you think. Go on, get naked," she said with gusto.

Jack stumbled in the corner removing his clothes, mumbling to himself. When all of his clothes were off he stepped back into his cowboy boots before bending down to remove the note Harley had given him and a pack of cigarettes from his shirt pocket. "I feel naked without my boots on," he said, snapping the pack to release a cigarette which he pulled out with his lips. "Now may I please see Trisha Tovey?"

"You're looking at her. What can I do for you?"

"Now that was a dirty trick. My father always said, never trust a naked dame. I'm detective Jack Blunt. Can I ask you some questions about Rosiland Bradshaw?"

Her full lips fell into a flat line as her brow furrowed. "That sad affair. Let's go to the salon. It's private there."

He followed her through a beaded curtain and into the salon which resembled an earthy cocoon. A rust-colored woven rug adorned the far wall while water gurgled over the glassy rocks of a fountain. A large picture window looked out over the pool and beyond to the volleyball court where a nude game was in progress. He paused, mesmerized by the action as an odd sense of solace came over him in a warm flush. He felt young and innocent. A cork exploded behind him, he turned to see Trisha standing there with a chilled bottle in her hands.

"Would you like some champagne?"

"Yeah sure, it isn't often I'm served fancy wine by a naked lady," he said, tucking the unlit cigarette behind his ear. "Rattan? Interesting choice," he said as he pasted himself onto the sofa.

"Here you are." She handed him the glass before sitting down in a chair opposite him. "Now what's this all about?"

"Rosiland's husband found this." He laid the poem on the table between them. "Have you ever seen it before?"

She picked up the sheet of paper and raised it eye-level, her head shaking no before handing it back to him.

"Does it reveal anything to you?" he asked.

"Only that the author is in dire need of a poetry workshop."

"When did you leave William Morris?"

"About a year after Rosiland's death," she said running her finger around the rim of her glass.

"Why?"

"Tired of it, I guess."

"Was the money good?"

"It had been. The three of us, Amanda, Rosiland and myself,

worked really well together. It was a magical time. The writing, the research, the editing. To give birth to a novel is a creative endeavor like no other. The galley proofs, revisions, martini lunches, deadlines, launch parties, all-expenses-paid book tours, and the climb up the bestseller list. All of it, pure magic."

"It sounds intoxicating the way you describe it. What I can't figure out is why you left it all behind."

"Nothing lasts forever. I could see the handwriting on the wall," she said with a sigh.

"Sort of like the handwriting on this piece of paper. I can't help but think it doesn't mean anything to you. It didn't take you long to move on after Rosiland's death." He swirled the wine, staring her down.

"It wasn't the same after that. Amanda made lots of promises she couldn't keep and then came the excuses. It's no secret that great writers are almost always a few sandwiches short of a picnic. Amanda was no exception. Something happened, writer's block, mania, psychosis, maybe murder."

"Murder?" he asked.

"Look, the money speaks volumes."

"I never mentioned any money. Funny you should bring it up."

"Oh." Her face flushed and she turned to cough into her hand. "Just a slip of my literary tendencies. Isn't there always a red herring in a mystery? I don't know anything about any money," she scoffed.

"Listen sister, this isn't my first grammar rodeo," he said swallowing the last of his wine.

"Detective, I don't want to point any fingers, but the person you should talk to is Amanda."

Jack stood and made his way toward the beaded curtain. Before passing through he paused and asked over his right shoulder, "How long has it been since Amanda's published anything?"

"Eight years."

The distressed red door had a satin sheen that cozied up to the inlaid stained glass window like a lover. It opened slowly to reveal the lady of the house, Amanda Merriwether. She was tall and buxom but not fat. Her hair rose up from the widow's peak on her forehead and fell down in large soft loops that framed her well-maintained face. A splash of smoldering shadow drew out the green flecks of her eyes. A mole, settled just above her lip on the right side of her face, screamed sex appeal. She wore a blue and white checked dress belted at her waist and shiny black Ferragamo heels. Jack immediately thought of Miss Ellie Ewing Dallas, circa 1978.

"Amanda Merriwether? I'm Jack Blunt with *The Arizona Republic*. We spoke on the phone," he said offering his hand.

"Yes, I've been expecting you. Won't you come in? I'm thrilled that you're here to interview me about the books I've written. It's true what they say, 'any publicity is good publicity,'" she said, stepping aside to draw him in.

Massive wood beams traversed the vaulted ceiling above them; opulent furniture rested on an enormous Persian rug that graced the travertine floor.

"Sit down please. Tea?" she asked while she poured from a silver set. "Would you care for a splash of cognac in it? I always imbibe this time of day. I don't mind drinking alone but sometimes it's nice to have an accomplice."

"Yes, I would," he replied. "This is quite a spread you have here."

"Thank you. The ranch was my late husband's passion. He bred Arabians and I wrote my novels."

"Wrote? Are you no longer writing?" he asked.

"Forgive my poor choice of words. Of course I'm still writing. I'm working on a novel right now. It's all about corruption within the Girl Scouts of America. Don't tell me those little ladies in uniform don't have ulterior motives. Have you seen the price of those cookies? My protagonist risks her grammar school reputation to become the whistle blower that brings the organization down to its knee socks."

"Sounds compelling," he replied while scribbling in his notebook. "Tell me, where do you get your ideas from?"

She stared off into the expanse of the room and thought for a moment while her eyes settled on the Elvis on velvet that occupied the opposite wall. "I am an artist, my medium, words. I see potential everywhere I look. There's nothing that can't be fictionalized. Take anything, an electrical outlet, needle nose pliers, jellybeans, ham, there's always a story to tell. It's really not that difficult, darling," she sniffed before turning to him with a broad smile. She reached for the Soleri bell on the coffee table and gave it a brisk rattle.

Jack could hear the sound of heels clicking across the travertine before he saw the petite woman with short cropped gray hair enter the room. She had on a monochrome dress with an elaborately embroidered apron cinched around her waist and a faded tattoo of a red rose on her outer wrist. She smelled of yeast and Ivory soap. She wore loyalty upon her face like a beagle, her brown eyes radiating admiration beneath the arched halo of wrinkles across her forehead.

"Hortence, will you please bring out some fresh bread and butter for me and my guest. This is Mr. Blunt. He's here to write a story about me for the newspaper. Isn't that wonderful?" she gushed. "Oh and freshen up these cognacs before you go. I have so much I want to share with our visitor. Open the windows. I see from the garden there's a lovely breeze."

"Yes ma'am," Hortence replied before lifting the crystal decanter and filling first Amanda's cup and then Jack's.

"She bakes the best bread you'll ever sink your teeth into. It's to die for," she said sipping her drink. "Now, where was I? Oh yes, my fifth novel, *Shaken Not Stirred.*"

Jack pieced together a psychological profile in his mind of the braggart who chatted away before him. Diagnosis: extreme narcissist. Hollywood was full of them and he had certainly entertained his fair share.

"Amanda, could we talk about Rosiland Bradshaw?" he asked, intent on her demeanor. "I understand she was the research assistant for all of your novels published to date. Have you found it difficult to carry on without her?"

"Whatever do you mean by that?" she replied, staring blankly through him, her smile evaporating faster than a June rain in the desert.

"Well, it's been eight years since she died and you haven't published anything. Coincidence?" He raised his cup and braced for her response.

Her nostrils flared like a thoroughbred as she rose from her chair, her hands smoothing down the front of her dress, her posture impeccable. She paused in front of the mirror to trifle with her hair before continuing on toward the Alder credenza that held the hardcover copies of her life's work.

"Here they are, my babies. Oh, the pain and agony of creation. Each one a labor of love like no other," she said while her manicured fingertips caressed the fabric covers. "Here it is. My favorite, *The Butcher Wore Lace*. They say you're not supposed to have favorites among your offspring, but every mother knows that's a lie." She cradled the book to her chest and returned to her chair. "Now, where were we?"

Jack pressed on. "A large amount of cash was found in Rosiland's home along with this obscure poem," he said placing the note on the table. "I think she wrote all of those books for you, and the cash was hush money."

"Are you here, by chance under false pretenses? I didn't check your credentials when I welcomed you in. This is supposed to be about me and my accomplishments, not Rosiland Bradshaw. I wrote every one of those bestselling novels all by myself and nobody will ever prove otherwise," she said, her face flushing with anger.

"When you realized you couldn't keep her quiet any longer you set out to get rid of her."

"That's absurd. Her death was ruled accidental." She rose from her seat still cradling the book.

"At the time, yes. But when her husband found the poem and the money he began to wonder. So he hired me to investigate. It says right here, 'cash and crust arrive in tandem.' That's you bearing gifts, money and bread baked by your maid, Hortence. Laced with poison to knock Rosalind out, which it did, later in the bathtub."

Amanda lifted the front cover of the book and pulled out a gun that was nestled inside where the pages had been sliced away to make room for the weapon. She trained the barrel on him, shaking her head as she advanced in his direction. She stopped only feet from him, her hands steady.

"That's a lie. I never did any such thing," she said. "You'll never prove it. I tried to play nice but you're hell bent on spewing your lies. I guess I'll have to kill you too."

At that moment a dove flew into the pristine pane of glass with a clamorous thud distracting Amanda. Jack pounced forward, slapping the gun from her hand. She cried out in shock as her legs crumbled out from under her.

He bent down and grabbed the gun, pointing it at her prostrate frame. "Amanda, Why? What did you think would happen after you killed her?"

Her head hung low, a deep gravelly laugh emerged from her.

"I thought I could pick up where she left off and write the books myself and nobody would be the wiser. It's no use. It was all an illusion. She was ready to tattle and it would have destroyed me. She was so damn good. She didn't seem to mind me taking the credit in the beginning. Then as my fame escalated, so too did her desire for recognition. It was a desperate secret that proved too great a weight to live under," she said her voice cracking like ice as her body heaved.

She was a pitiful sight, despite the elegant trappings. A plagiarizing thief turned killer who would eventually have to pull herself up from the depths to which she had descended and face the music she had composed. A host of emotions enveloped Jack as he stood over her. He thought about the victim, her fate, and Harley as he reveled in the fact that justice would be served for them both.

AMY SCHUSTER is a native of Phoenix. She loves to read, write and people watch, not necessarily in that order. She's hoping to find a literary agent for her first completed novel LOOSE ENDS. She lives in Scottsdale with her husband and their four children.

DEATH BY DESIGN
JUDY STARBUCK

Arizona Biltmore, July 1928

I looked around at the prickly desert that would soon support a major tourist hotel for wealthy vacationers. The skeleton of the massive building known as the Arizona Biltmore had been erected, but it felt eerie in this desolate expanse of land eight miles northeast of downtown Phoenix. My fellow architecture school classmate, Nora Love, and I had just gotten off the Californian at the new Phoenix Union Railway Station early this morning and hired a Ford touring car to bring us here.

The temperature had to be over one hundred degrees and the musty smell of wet sand and creosote permeated the air. My dress clung to me and the stylish cloche hat became an oven. My brain felt like it would melt at any moment. The breeze did nothing to cool me. Rather it stirred up the dust. I started sneezing.

"This place gives me the heebie-jeebies," I told Nora. "We've traveled so far to see something that looks like brittle bones in a wasteland."

Nora was busy looking over the construction workers. "Oh horsefeathers, Frankie. Where's your sense of adventure? This is what architecture is all about. We're smack dab in the middle of a historic project. At any time, Frank Lloyd Wright might appear. We ought to look for the project manager. What's his name? Willy something? Isn't he expecting us?"

By then we had created quite a stir. I took it that women rarely came to the site in dresses, especially women with modern short hemlines. The clanging and banging sounds piped down, and wolf whistles came from several directions.

A beefy red-faced man marched toward us with a scowl on his face and a decided limp to his gait. "Ladies, is there something I can do for you?"

I spoke up. "Yes, sir. Are you Willy Cameron?"

He nodded.

"I'm Frankie Flannery and this is Nora Love. We're second year architecture students from California. I wrote months ago asking permission to observe the process of making the concrete tile blocks. We know the blocks are being produced here. They're Mr. Wright's latest creation and we're so excited to see them. When we didn't hear back we decided to use our summer break and come anyway."

He glowered. "No one is allowed around the tile manufacturing plant. We have security surrounding the place." He pointed to an open-air concrete structure where the mind-numbing sound of mixers whirring and hammers pounding came from. "I suggest you turn around and head back to wherever they wear such spiffy duds." He sized up Nora from stem to stern. She had a chassis that turned a tough guy to mush.

I didn't intend to be given the bum's rush and interrupted his ogling. "Well, sir, you see, Frank Lloyd Wright is my inspiration. My mama named me after him, even though I surprised her and turned out to be a girl. She brought me up using the same type of Froebel blocks Mr. Wright used to learn the elements of construction. Like his mother, mine played Beethoven for me to get the patterns of design in my head."

"You're just beating your gums. What your mama shoulda told you was women who come to a work site all dolled up like that don't belong there." He widened his stance, put his hands on his hips. "That will be all, ladies. You'd better get your ride back here or start walking."

Nora piped up. "We brought work clothes and will change now if you show us where." She pulled out overalls and man shirts from her valise and stood in the vamp pose she used on men to get her way. "Could we just camp out in one of your tents tonight and figure out what to do in the morning?"

Willy took off his hat and wiped his forehead with a bandana. He had a luxurious head of black hair and his face sized up nicely, too. I felt sure Nora took note. "There's plenty of lonely men out here. Not to mention the snakes, scorpions, and insects that come out on summer nights. Once you hear the howl of a coyote, you'll be begging to go back to wherever you came from."

With that I was ready to set off walking. But not Nora. Batting her eyelashes and sticking her chest out even farther, she said, "I'm sure we'll be fine for just one night. You wouldn't let two girls be in danger, would you?"

Geez, she really laid it on. And he took the bait.

His expression softened. "Let me see what I can do. No promises." He walked off toward the tents where a rugged fellow stood with a gun stuffed into a holster on his belt. After much discussion, Willy returned. "Okay, but just for one night. I talked to Milt Patterson. He's our security man. Just know we can't protect you from the varmints, human or otherwise." He was so taken with Nora he probably forgot I was there, too.

I looked around the lot at workers staring at us and shivered despite the heat. I looked up at Willy. "Will there be a way for us to get back to town tomorrow?"

Nora turned to me with a sneer. "Now hush, Frankie. We'll worry about tomorrow, tomorrow." She patted his cheek. "This is nifty. We'll have a chance to see first hand what you big strong men do."

Willy pointed to a man standing a short way from them. "Milt will show you to your tents. Come along. There's a communal washroom. Meals are served at the canteen."

"Thank you," Nora said. "You won't be sorry."

I hoped we wouldn't be either.

Milt Patterson approached, a grin on his ruddy face. He was tall with blond hair, sky blue eyes, and broad shoulders. I would probably have to sit on Nora to keep her away from him.

"You two must have sweet-talked our hard-boiled supervisor. He doesn't give in too easily. We have a couple of empty tents. Want to share one or have your own?"

"Share," I said. "Definitely."

"I'd like one of my own," Nora said.

"Nora, we'd be safer together."

"I'll take my chances." She gave Milt a grin.

I rolled my eyes and turned to Milt. "Do you think Mr. Wright will come out here today?"

My professor had told us he was in Chandler working on the San Marcos in the Desert, and that he was also hired to oversee the closely guarded secret of molding desert materials into plain concrete to form decorative tiles. He had designed four homes in California, all with different patterned tiles, and I had admired them the many times I visited to make sketches. Here at the Biltmore the tiles were set in the shape of palm fronds.

"He's due on site sometime tomorrow," Milt said. "Well ladies, let me show you the layout." He pointed. "Over there is the future hotel. Beyond the canteen is the tile plant and crew office."

After the tour, he left us on our own. Nora and I got settled in our individual tents and changed into work clothes. I stepped out with my sketchpad to survey the site and began to appreciate the tawny look of the landscape, with hues of ochre, copper and brown. Orange orchards were visible in the distance. Newly planted eucalyptus saplings, saguaro cactus, and palms graced the site. Brilliant fuchsia bougainvillea added a welcome touch of color.

When Nora came out, her shirt was form fitting and she had left the top two buttons undone. I, on the other hand, could have passed as a teenage boy. My black bob was tucked neatly under a brimmed cap, and very little skin met the light of day. I didn't intend to be prey for the predators, including the human ones. Nora must have had something else in mind.

I had to shout over the din of the mixers banging in my eardrums. "What is going on with you, Nora? I thought you were here to watch the construction, not make yourself a target. And why aren't we sharing a tent?"

Her eyes lost their shine. Instead a cold veneer of steel caused me to wince. "Frankie, you're such a killjoy. While I'm here I plan to have some fun." She did an abrupt turn and headed toward the tile-making facility. Exactly where Willy had warned us was off-limits.

Now what? In the afternoon heat and humidity it was nearly unbearable to be out of the shade, and equally unbearable to be cooped up inside the tent. I thought I might as well check things out, too, because I was going to leave this godforsaken place after Mr. Wright's visit if I had to swim the distance in the Arizona Canal that fronted the property. I walked away from the construction to do a couple of sketches of the resort.

As I walked the oleander-edged trail, I saw a Mexican man exchanging money with Willy who then handed him a large brown canvas bag. I ducked into a broken-down shed and could barely subdue my discomfort from the thorny brambles that lined the shelter. Bottles clinked as Willy sampled the product then carried the purchase away. So, in addition to his position as project manager, he was apparently also the proprietor of the

Biltmore speakeasy.

I nearly stopped breathing as Willy passed in front of me and walked off into the noise and dust. Since I was curious by nature, I extricated myself and followed him at a distance. He stashed the hooch in a rickety outhouse then locked the door. Although interested, I wanted to stay away from trouble and walked back to the shady spot where I continued to sketch.

Sitting against a palm tree, I worked to create a new structure in my own style. Lost in concentration, the sound of footsteps from behind startled me. I turned to see Milt Patterson, looking at me with a smile on his face.

"What do you have there?" He looked over my shoulder. "Wow, those sketches are really good. I'm a frustrated architect myself. I had one year of school before the finances dried up. I took this security job so I could be around a project like the Biltmore. Maybe someday I'll get back to it."

I handed my work to him. "I'm just playing around with ideas."

After looking it over, he said, "You know your stuff. Why don't you let me show some of your drawings to Mr. Wright when he comes? It wouldn't hurt and maybe he'll take a shine to them."

"You'd do that for me?" I wasn't used to getting this kind of attention. "That would be super. I don't want to put you out or anything."

"I'll see what I can do." With that, Milt went on his way with my sketches in hand.

I had gone back to my tent and rested on my cot. The noise had stopped, so I figured this must be the dinner hour. Rich smells of barbeque and freshly baked bread reminded me that I hadn't eaten since morning. I needed a dollar for the canteen and pulled my wallet from a hidden compartment at the bottom of my valise. The money was gone. I searched every inch of the tent. Someone had gone through my belongings and I knew just who the thief was. Nora! This wasn't the first time I'd lost money with her around. I had called her on it back at school and she made it sound like a huge, horrible misunderstanding.

I found her seated at a table with Willy and Milt. A meal of brisket of beef in gravy, red flannel hash colored by beets and bacon, biscuits as huge as my fist and a slab of apple pie surrounded her.

I slid in beside her on the bench and bumped her elbow. "I need some money for dinner," and raised my voice so the men could hear. "Someone went through my things and stole all my money."

Nora gave me a sympathetic look. "What a shame, Frankie." What a liar she was. "You know, I don't have much." She reached in her pocket and pulled out a few coins and handed them to me. "This will buy you a dinner. I'm sure you've just misplaced your money. You can pay me back when it turns up."

Milt leaned toward me. "You don't want to miss a meal around here. Shorty is the king of the site. We do our best to keep our boys healthy and happy. His menus are an attraction for the workers. Wait until you have his chicken and cornbread."

I smiled at Milt. "I'm looking forward to a few more meals here before I leave." Then I gave Nora a hard look as she played up her generosity, knowing she had taken every last cent of mine. I already had sensed that the reason she traveled with me was so I could bankroll her. But I wanted to make the trip so badly and no one else was interested in coming clear from Los Angeles.

I tried hard to keep an upbeat tone of voice. "Nora, I'm sure the money will turn up, but until then I'm going to have to ask you for some more to tide me over until I do find it."

Nora pulled out a couple of dollars and handed it over. "This is all I can spare right now." I gave her an insincere thank you and went to fill my plate.

After dinner Nora walked off toward the tile factory with Willy. He didn't seem like such a tyrant when she sat next to him, but she knew her way around men.

While she went in the other direction, I used the chance to go through her tent. I knew I would find my missing funds there. Holding my breath, I was ready with an excuse for rifling through her things if she showed up. My heartbeat picked up as time lapsed.

I checked the pumps she wore on the train coming over, the ones I let her borrow. The ones that cost me a whole five dollars and now were ruined. She had wedged them into the back corner of the tent under her cot. Bills were hidden under the inner soles, only a few dollars short. Very clever! Now I knew where we stood and I could play that game too.

I slipped out of Nora's tent and noticed a large vehicle pull up, loaded with women dolled up in fancy apparel. They sashayed across the lot wearing skimpy dresses in greens, reds and yellows, strings of pearls swinging across their ample chests.

Milt walked up beside me. "It's payday. They're hookers who come every Friday to capitalize on the funds. Willy likes to take care of the boys."

I stammered, "Well, gee whiz, I'm not here to pass judgment. I just want to learn about architecture."

Milt started to leave, but then turned back to me. "A heads up, Frankie. Nora's a double-crosser. She's saying you're a Dumb Dora who thinks you're another Frank Lloyd Wright, and you cling to her because you have no other friends."

"She can talk all she wants. As soon as I meet Mr. Wright, I'll be on my way." I gave him a wide grin and patted my pants pocket. "I found my missing funds in her tent. I have money. She doesn't."

"Well, I hope you don't leave too soon. Maybe you could teach me some of the things you learned at your architecture school."

My heart beat a little at the thought of spending time with him. "I don't see how I can stay. You're not set up for women and to be honest, this heat wears me down. You've been so kind to me, Milt. I'll be happy to share some things with you tomorrow morning."

"I hope you change your mind about leaving. You're the real deal."

I held out my hand to him and he gave it a squeeze. Oh my, I may never wash my hand again.

The day had been exhausting: the travel, the heat and humidity, and the knowledge that I had a thief as my traveling partner. But exciting, too. I settled into my tent to think things over when the wind kicked up. The canvas sides of the tent flapped like a sail. The air smelled like dirty rain, and soon the sky emptied, pummeling my refuge. Thunder roared and lightning illuminated my space, but I was too busy thinking about Milt to be bothered.

A harrowing thirty minutes later, the pounding storm stopped. I opened the flap of my tent to look out. The late night sky had darkened and the temperature had dropped. I decided to take a short walk to cool down. Staying out of sight as much as possible, I eased close to the tile production plant and heard angry voices.

There was a bright work-light hanging from a pole nearby and I clearly saw Nora come around the corner followed by Willy. I ducked behind a wide post. The sharpness of their tones allowed me to catch most of the conversation.

She was the first to speak. "Listen, Willy, I can make you a site manager for a wealthy architect in California. You would make a lot more than you do now. Just show me how the blocks are made and you can share the profits. My man will pay almost anything for the formula."

Willy shook his head. "I can tell you a little about it, but that's all. How much will he pay me for that?"

"Depends on what you have to say."

"The precast concrete blocks have interlocking grooves that join their ends. Horizontal and vertical steel rods called rebar, held together by grouting cement, reinforce the cast concrete and increase the tensile strength. Cross struts of steel tie together the inner and outer shells, holding air in-between and making the walls waterproof and insulated."

"How much do the tiles weigh?" Nora asked.

"Between thirty-five and fifty pounds apiece. Light enough that a worker can position them by hand and weave them into the building."

"You mean a pretty strong worker."

He nodded. "We have plenty of them around."

"Sorry, that's not enough information for me to get you anything. I need to take a peek at the work. No one will ever know. I won't stay long."

"Under no circumstances can you go in. Your benefactor doesn't have enough money for me to jeopardize my job. You'll just have to come up with your own way to manufacture tiles." Willy turned to walk away.

She grabbed his shirt and pulled him back. "Imagine the money and fame, Willy."

He turned to face her and raised his voice. "Why would you want to steal ideas from Mr. Wright anyway? For the money? You should be creating your own style, not cheating off others."

"You don't know how hard I tried to work with Mr. Wright. He rejected me in California last year. Why else do you think I'd come here with someone as pathetic as that wannabe, Frankie? She's under the delusion the two of them share the same genius, just because she shares his name. She's my meal ticket and I plan to make my case with him again."

I scowled at her description of me. *Pathetic?*

Willy laughed. "At least Frankie shows Mr. Wright the respect he deserves. Don't come cattin' around my men anymore. I want you on the train back to California in the morning."

Nora glared at him. "I bet the police would like to know that you're selling hooch to the workers."

"Hah. The cops are my customers, too."

She spun around and walked toward the door leading into the factory. "Fine. I'll bet your wife would like to know what happened between us last night."

"Stop right there." Willy jerked her away from the door. "Go back to your tent and don't leave there 'til morning. I'll make sure you're out of here by noon if I have to take you to the station myself."

Nora gave him a push. "You'll be sorry." He laughed. Then she pushed him harder.

Willy's eyes narrowed as he shoved her. She fell hard into the pit beside a stack of completed tile blocks. Her head struck one and knocked her cold. He rocked the stack of tiles back and forth until they toppled over, crushing her. "Can you see them now, you little bitch?"

I screamed, running from my hiding place to see if I could help Nora. Willy turned and came after me, a look of fury on his face.

I yelled, "Help. Somebody, help," then took off running. Scrambling on loose ground, I stumbled over a piece of loose rebar and fell to my hands and knees. I picked it up and tried to regain my footing, impeded by the chunks of concrete littering the yard. I couldn't see anyone around in the crew offices and didn't know which way to run. Willy grabbed my shoulder. With no knowledge of fighting, I did the only thing I could and swung the rebar, connecting with the side of his head. He reeled and lost his footing. I swung it again and smashed his knee. He howled in pain then dropped to the ground.

Faces peeked out from the tents. The hookers must have understood the call of a woman in distress. More bare than covered, three of them ran toward us and pummeled Willy with their fists and feet. They joined in with my screams and soon more and more people ran to restrain him. By now five other women held his arms and legs, while others rushed over to tend to Nora.

By the time Milt got there, the ladies had the situation under control. He slapped handcuffs on Willy and we all waited together until the police and medical help arrived. I stood to the side with the women as the doctor examined Nora. He shook his head. "There's nothing we can do to help her."

I thanked my new friends for coming to my rescue, and spent the next few hours answering questions about what I'd witnessed. The horrifying experience had worn me down, and shock left me shivering uncontrollably.

Milt came over and put a gentle hand on my shoulder. "I'm sorry you had to go through all that, Frankie. You held up and told the authorities what they needed to know."

As I walked toward my tent, I smiled. *Guess I'm not so pathetic after all.*

The next day, Mr. Wright arrived in his Cherokee red Cord convertible. After touring the site, he summoned me. "Well hello, Miss Frank Lloyd Flannery. I'm pleased to meet my namesake." Milt stood nearby, a grin on his face as Mr. Wright said, "It seems you were a hero last night. I'm sorry to hear about your traveling partner, and shocked to learn about Willy Cameron. The boys have been instructed to make you feel comfortable until you leave."

I looked at him with sincerity. "Thank you for your kindness, Mr. Wright. This has been a tough experience, but I'm very grateful I had an opportunity to meet you."

"Milt here showed me some of your sketches. You're a talented young lady. I'd like to have you contact me when you receive your certification. Perhaps you can join the fellowship in Wisconsin and help me complete my next project, Taliesin West in Scottsdale."

"Gee, Mr. Wright, that would be swell. My mama will be overjoyed. She raised me for this very moment."

I shook Mr. Wright's hand and walked over to Milt. A breeze kicked up and the heat didn't seem to be bothering me so much. Maybe I shouldn't be in such a hurry to leave.

† † †

JUDY STARBUCK is a Scottsdale teacher, handwriting analyst, award winning poet and mystery writer. Her publishing credits include: seven short stories, several newspaper articles, newsletter and blog posts. She is involved in adoption search and support groups, is an Arizona-certified Confidential Intermediary, and an active member of Sisters in Crime. She and her husband live in Scottsdale, Arizona.

A SEASON FOR DEATH
JUDITH STARKSTON

"Muumuu," she said and glanced at her husband.

"Huh?" He gave her a funny look and returned his attention to the road.

"Muumuu," she repeated loudly.

"Yah, sure, dear."

She looked at her hands lying in her lap and began to work her wedding ring round and round her finger. They were on the way to the grocery store. She was trying to tell him what they needed. *What did they need?* She twisted the gold band. She didn't want to sit in the car. *Where was he taking her?* She wanted— She turned the ring over and over as though it held the answer to—to what?

Jim swung the car into a parking spot, relieved to find a place close to the entrance. Sometimes he didn't think he could find the patience to cope with Lizzie anymore. At times the desire to escape was so overwhelming he felt it would rip out of his chest like the creepy alien in that movie.

He came around to Lizzie's side. He stood for a moment, took a deep breath, then opened the door for her. She stared straight ahead as he leaned down and took her elbow, edging her out of the car.

She started scrambling out, as if embarrassed to be caught in a daze, brushing away his arm and pushing herself up so quickly she bumped her hip on the door and cried out. "Why did you knock me? Get away from me!"

Jim looked around the parking lot. No one heard her. Sometimes people approached him when she acted this way in public places. Once someone accused him of abusing her. He put his arm around his wife's shoulder and guided her toward the entrance. She smiled up at him and for a moment he saw his darling the way she used to be. He kissed her cheek.

She rolled the cart, looking at the boxes lined up on the shelves. "What do we need?"

"Cornflakes."

She looked at the shelves. "What do we need?"

"Cornflakes. Corn-flakes."

He made that upset sigh. He didn't used to be so rude. She just asked a simple question.

"What do we need?"

"Cornflakes. Repeat after me—cornflakes. God damn coooorn-flakes." With a thud that made her jump, a box with the green and red rooster landed in the cart.

† † †

The February sun felt good on Jim's back—the best time of year to be outside in the desert. He didn't mind the Phoenix summers as much as most people and gardened right through them, though both his regular tennis games with Sam and the gardening moved into the early morning when the sun had barely risen. Today, blessings be, he could stay outside all afternoon. Glorious. He knelt to pull a weed and then laughed as his yellow lab, Hector, wormed his head under his arm to lick his face.

It had taken a while for Jim to get used to so much free time when State Farm forced him into early retirement—laid off was the truth of it, though they didn't call it that so he couldn't sue the company for age discrimination. Eventually he relaxed and found he had fun with Lizzie, reading and planting a garden in their new patio home. "Patio home"—that was as much a euphemism of failure as "early retirement." What was it about their tiny box of a house that made the four-foot slab of cement patio the distinctive feature? The phrase was as laughable as the "estates" down the road that were just pathetic tract houses. He loved their big house at the base of South Mountain, but that had to go when his salary went.

Across the yard, Lizzie worked at deadheading the coreopsis, clipping each shriveled bloom. Most of what he and Lizzie did together when he first retired was gone now—no more stimulating discussions of books, but she could still garden.

She looked over at her husband, happy in his garden. Out here she didn't have to pretend she knew what he was talking about. She understood what to do for the plants, same as she had since her brother taught her as a girl. The wind dropped those yellow puffs down on her from the tree in the neighbor's yard. *What is that tree called? Something dangerous.* She could feel the stuff in her lungs. *Something with an "a" maybe, allergy? That seems right.* She liked it out here in the yard even if she found it hard to breathe.

Jim went into the garage and rooted around in the cupboard until he found some snail bait. *Been a while since the vegetable garden was overrun by snails. Desert's a tough place on slimy, wet critters.* Fine with him, but there was one kind that occasionally reappeared, a tiny, black-shelled snail. He grabbed a roll of chicken wire to put around the vegetable garden. He didn't want Hector snuffling about and making himself sick. The bait smelled nasty to him, definitely something lethal, but dogs ate the stupidest things.

He set the bait on the patio table and glanced over at Lizzie. With relief he saw she pruned back the dead stalks of Russian lavender with her usual expertise. She was fine at home, at least for now. Her doctor told him he would have to consider a self-contained Alzheimer's unit soon both for her safety and his sanity. He'd agreed only to a "care provider." Carmen came three times a week so he could play tennis and let off some steam. She was a reliable woman. She and Lizzie got on well together, and he could afford her.

But as for the special care unit—no way. For all she drove him nuts with the repeated questions and flashes of temper, he couldn't imagine locking Lizzie up in one of those places. They felt so saccharine and artificial, with bent over old people singing "olde timey" songs and bouncing beach balls back and forth as their exercise program. That wasn't his Elizabeth. She'd had a biting sense of humor and could point out the fallacies in any politician's drivel, and for exercise she went climbing with him and Hector on the desert mountain trails. He couldn't see her among the benignly mindless even if they could afford the facility.

He'd researched the cost—it would bankrupt him. That is exactly what the state bureaucrat he'd contacted advised him to do. Pay the costs until he had no savings left and then the state would cover it, providing he chose a state-approved home. Those were not the nice ones.

"What am I supposed to do after that?" he'd asked. *"I'm not dead. What am I supposed to live on?"* The bureaucrat didn't have an answer for that.

He'd care for Lizzie even if he had to keep track of her by tying a rope from him to her like he had when he was housetraining Hector.

As if reading his thoughts, Hector loped up and leaned in against Jim's legs. He rubbed that spot behind his dog's ear and Hector sighed in contentment.

"I feel like a Virginia ham." Lizzie's words startled Jim. What now?

Hector turned his head sideways and pulled back his ears as if to say, "What nutty thing is she up to now?"

Hector licked his hand and Jim patted his dog's head. "My old predictable buddy. We never know what she'll do next. Do we, Hector?"

Lizzie spoke up again. "You know how people cut little pieces away from a Virginia ham, one little chip of salty, dry ham at a time? My mother used to have one on the Christmas buffet each year. That's me—a Virginia ham. Someone keeps chipping away another piece of my brain each day. I can feel it. That's how it's going to go 'til there's nothing left. I want to finish myself off before then."

"Oh, honey. Don't say that." He glanced over at the big globe mallow bush just starting to burst into orange blooms. It was good to hear her make sense, even if it was depressing as hell. She'd said a million times she wanted to die before she lost her mind. He didn't like to hear her say that. Now her mind seemed pretty lost, and she was still here.

She returned to pruning.

He rolled out the chicken wire. It sprang back and cut his forearm. "Damn it!" He stomped on one end and bent it around the other way, then threaded a short piece of rebar through the holes so he could make it stand up. He slammed the rebar into the ground and walked the chicken wire around the area infested with snails. As he threaded the second rebar he glanced across the yard at Lizzie. She was turned away from him, but something about her posture seemed odd. He quickly pounded in the rebar so he could let go of the chicken wire, then went to her.

Her face was bluish, and she struggled to breathe. Yellow acacia flowers coated her hair and sweater.

"How could I be so damned stupid?" He looked over at the neighbor's yard. He hadn't even noticed the acacia had started blooming. He never should have brought her out in the yard with those things casting pollen all over. He pulled her up to take her inside. "Your allergies. Where's your inhaler?" He tried to walk her along, but she couldn't get her breath and he couldn't drag her. He hadn't realized how easily she could suffocate from her reactions. This was worse than it had ever been. He lowered her to the ground and raced inside, frantically searching for her inhaler.

She'd had allergies for years—red, bumpy rashes and a runny nose, but it had never been bad. There wasn't any of this asthma disaster, not until she had a penicillin reaction a few years back. Her immunologist said she'd be a "firecracker" from then on. These days a little contact with a globe mallow or any of those desert plants with toxins in their leaves and she blew up with hives, and the acacia pollen inflamed her lungs and made her especially weak when they bloomed. The penicillin reaction had gone straight to her lungs and any airborne allergen triggered the asthma. *Where was that inhaler?* He found it on her bedside table and ran to Lizzie.

The inhaler worked its magic enough to get her inside. He pulled off her sweater, coated in yellow powder, and wiped her hair. She patted his arm and smiled weakly—it seemed like she was telling him not to blame himself. It was so like his Lizzie, his old Lizzie.

He stretched out on the bed next to her, holding her and listening to her breathe.

She needed to get up. What was she supposed to be doing? Something important. She slipped off the bed, careful not to wake Jim. He looked tired.

She walked into the family room. The dog stood by the sliding glass door. She opened it and followed him outside. He peed on a bush. She watched a bird flutter in front of some blue flowers. *What are those called?* She smelled them, felt their softness against her cheek. The dog was sniffing at something on the table. She remembered. *I like giving the dog treats.*

Jim jumped up from the bed. Where was Lizzie? It drove him nuts trying to keep track of her. He shook his head. She didn't cause any harm. He just had to check on her, that's all. *Calm down, or you'll make yourself crazy.* He walked out into the family room. Lizzie was sitting on the couch. *See?* he told himself.

Outside the sliding glass door Hector lay on the patio, taking his sunbath. Lizzie must have let him out. He peered out the window. Hector's legs stuck out at odd angles. He pushed open the door and ran to him. The dog's mouth was drawn back in a rictus of agony. *What the hell?*

He glanced across the patio through the window. From his angle the box of snail bait, still on the table where he left it, appeared silhouetted against Lizzie on the couch. He bent down to Hector and felt for a heartbeat. *Where do you feel for a dog's pulse? How do you perform CPR on a dog?* He put his head on Hector's chest, shook him, looked at his nose to see if it was moving. Blood dribbled out, but Hector wasn't breathing. Hector was dead. Jim buried his face against his dog's fur and rubbed the velvety spot behind his ear over and over.

He picked a shady spot under the palo verde, scraped away the gravel and started digging, alternating with shovel and pick ax in the caliche desert soil. He caught himself stopping and looking around for Hector to make sure he didn't hit him with the ax. *Damn it,* he was digging Hector's grave and even then he couldn't get it that his buddy wasn't there. He pulled out a Kleenex and blew hard. He should go check on Lizzie, but he didn't.

She drank her coffee. He read the newspaper. A section of the paper lay beside her cup. In the morning she could read. She liked his eyes when she talked about something in the paper. But not today. He wouldn't look at her. He had never been so mean.

She stood up and looked out the window. *What's that bare spot under the tree? The garden is all dug up there.* She turned to her husband. "You should scold Hector. He's been burying his bones over there." She pointed through the window. "Look what a mess he made. Dirt all over. He's a bad dog." Her husband stared at her and then got up. She heard the front door slam.

What's wrong with him?

What did she need to do? Something important. What was she supposed to do? She walked into their bedroom. Her desk. Her work must be on her desk. She sat down and opened the top drawer.

She saw her name on a piece of paper. "Elizabeth, read this." *Elizabeth, read this? That's me. I'm Elizabeth.* She remembered. Elizabeth. She read the paper aloud. "Instructions on how to kill yourself after your mind goes and you don't want to live anymore." She remembered now. She had written it to herself. In case she forgot what to do. She didn't like it when she forgot things. She folded the paper and tucked it into the sleeve of her sweater. She would keep it close so she wouldn't forget again.

Jim walked through the bedroom to the closet door. Lizzie stood in the middle of the bedroom doing nothing. He shrugged—whatever entertained her was fine with him. Carmen would be here soon. He had to change into his tennis clothes. He and Sam, his doubles partner, had been training for months for today's match. The "Senior Olympics." Whatever. At seventy-two, he'd buy the senior part, but Olympics seemed a bit pretentious. That didn't make him any less determined to win. He and Sam had competitive streaks a mile wide. They loved beating the pants off other doubles teams. Besides, he really had to get out of this house. Now.

His cell phone rang. It was Carmen. He put it on speaker while he pulled on his clothes.

"Mr. Jim, my tire—I was driving to your house and it goes crazy. I call my husband already and he says he is coming to fix as soon as he can, but—"

"But you're going to be late?"

"Yes, Mr. Jim."

Jim looked around the room, making himself count to ten before speaking. He glanced at Lizzie lying on the bed. The congestion her allergies caused made her snore. She napped in the middle of the day pretty often. She'd likely sleep a long time. God knows how a disease of the mind could tire out her body so much.

"Look, I'll stay here as long as I can, but I can't be late. Lizzie's asleep. She'll be okay. You have your key, right? You say your husband is on his way?"

"Yes…"

Jim ignored the hesitation in her voice. He was not going to miss this match, and he wasn't going to stay in this house. He flipped shut his phone.

He realized it would actually be a while before Carmen would get there. He tied his shoes, listening to Lizzie's shallow, rough breathing. The acacias and other desert blooming trees had inflamed her lungs, not much room to breathe. Weird, how if she said that, she could mean it literally: "Give me room to breathe!"

His Lizzie would laugh if she could still catch a joke. He didn't feel like laughing at anything. He'd be so much happier if he could just wrap his arms around his dog and tell him how lousy he felt.

Carmen had used the phrase "as soon as he could," plus time to fix the flat. It would take a while. He glanced at his watch. He didn't need to meet Sam quite yet. He paced the room, staring at Lizzie.

† † †

Jim and his partner, Sam, came in second overall, the silver medalists. Good enough. Damn good, actually. He looked down at his phone. Six missed calls—Carmen. He pressed the redial button.

Sam slapped him on the back. "Hey, buddy. Congratulations to us! Let's catch a beer to celebrate."

Jim shook his head and pointed to the phone by his ear. "Carmen? Sorry I missed your calls. Everything okay?"

As Jim listened, his heart rate accelerated and he felt short of breath. He stared at his phone a second before shutting it and turning to Sam. "Something's wrong with Lizzie. Carmen found her on the ground. The paramedics took her to the hospital."

† † †

"I'm sorry, sir, but I'm going to have to ask you some questions." Maybe it was the shock of Lizzie's death and all the waiting getting to Jim, but the detective didn't look sorry.

"I don't understand."

"The doctors had some concerns about the circumstances of your wife's death." The detective took out a note pad. "She had Alzheimer's?" Jim nodded. "Can you tell me about this afternoon? The nine-one-one call came in from a Carmen Rodriguez."

Jim described who Carmen was and the phone conversation he'd had with her. He said his friend Sam had rushed him to the hospital, and a doctor in ER told them his wife had died. The paramedics hadn't been able to revive her. He spent several hours shuffling from one waiting room to another until finally Sam had to go, saying he'd check with him later.

Jim had made arrangements with a mortuary. The mortuary was all set, but the hospital wouldn't release her body.

The detective waved his hand dismissively. "Yes, sir, but I'm interested in what happened before Mrs. Rodriguez called you."

"Before? With my wife? I...I wasn't there. Carmen was. I was playing tennis with Sam." He wished Sam were still here.

"When did Mrs. Rodriguez arrive at your house?"

"I'm not sure. I left before she got there."

"You left? Was that typical? You said you'd hired her as a care provider—but your wife was fine to leave alone?"

"No—I never leave her alone anymore. This was the first time in months. Lately I've had to keep close watch on her or she gets herself into trouble. I shouldn't have left her."

"Why did you leave her this time?"

"Carmen called and said she had a flat tire, but her husband was on the way to fix it. I didn't want to cancel at the last minute—Sam and I were playing in a Senior Olympics match—people went to a lot of trouble organizing it. So I left before Carmen arrived. Lizzie was asleep. I assumed Carmen would be there in a few minutes."

"Your wife was asleep when you left?"

"She sleeps a lot during the day—the Alzheimer's. I just thought she'd sleep until Carmen got there. I never dreamed..."

"Did you know your wife was allergic to globe mallow?"

Jim felt unnerved by the question. "Yes, she developed it over the past few years. Actually to a lot of plants."

"But especially to globe mallows?"

Jim nodded.

"Do you know where she might have gotten globe mallow?"

To Jim the detective's tone sounded like an accusation. He wondered what to say. "I don't know. I guess it could have been in our back yard. I pulled them all out when she complained they bothered her. But they grow back all the time. A desert native—tough plant. Seems like the seeds keep sprouting forever after you rip it out."

The detective was distracted by the approach of his colleague. Jim stared at the piece of paper the man was holding, Lizzie's distinctive stationary with her initials swirling in red at the top. "You have Lizzie's letter."

"You know about this?" the new detective asked.

Jim nodded. "Lizzie wrote it a couple years ago. She hated the idea of losing her mind, but I didn't think she'd ever actually go through with that plan. I just thought it was a kind of therapy for her, a way to assert her dignity or something." He looked from one detective to the other. "She kept it in her desk. I guess I'd sort of forgotten. How come you have the letter?"

"One of the nurses found it caught in the sleeve of her sweater. Seems like she did exactly what she said she would. You must have remembered this letter when you heard how your wife had died, didn't you?"

Jim stared at him. The bunches of mallow she'd been lying on, even pushed into her mouth? Just like she described in her letter. He pictured the toxic bristles lining every branch and leaf. And the acacia were blooming—she'd told herself to wait for the time of year when the acacia weakened her lungs. Yes, he remembered the letter, but he only nodded dumbly.

The detectives looked intently at him, studying him. One started to ask something but stopped. They looked at each other. Jim felt too exhausted to think of anything to say.

Finally the second detective held up the letter. "Grim way to die, don't you think?"

Jim shuddered. He tried to picture Lizzie before the acacia and globe mallow. He needed something to replace this last image of her.

The detectives stood silently, waiting. Then one of them said, "It sounds like your wife's Alzheimer's was fairly advanced. Do you think she was able to kill herself in this way without any help? If she had written these directions back when she was more coherent, someone might have thought they were being kind to help her."

Jim frowned. "Well, I'm sure Carmen wouldn't have helped her, so I guess Lizzie managed... I shouldn't have left her alone. It's my fault." His stomach didn't feel right.

"You're sure she was asleep when you left?"

Jim nodded. He reached for one of the plastic chairs lining the walls and fell into it. The detectives apologized for keeping him so long with their questions. Finally they left, after giving him a business card to contact them "if you have anything further to tell us."

The first thing Jim did when the taxi dropped him off at home was dig up the rest of that damn plant. He swept up all the leaves and threw the whole thing into the garbage.

A breeze lifted the palo verde's branches. The colorful blooms of Lizzie's perennial bed swayed solemnly.

He sat down next to Hector's grave and wept.

JUDITH STARKSTON writes historical fiction and mysteries set in the Bronze Age environs of Troy and the Hittite Empire, as well as the occasional contemporary short story. Her website www.judithstarkston.com includes book reviews and history. She is a classicist (B.A. University of California, Santa Cruz, M.A. Cornell University) who taught high school English, Latin and humanities. She and her husband have two grown children and live in Phoenix, AZ.

SPEED DATING
KATE JOY STEELE

The moon was so high, so bright the desert could only hold secrets small enough to fit in the shadows, pitchy black in the milky light. Cactus spines glowed silver. The desert gleamed, cold and surreal.

I had to get out of the moonlight and the cold wind. My white cotton dress wasn't much protection, and with the billowy skirt flapping around me like a flag against the backdrop of silent, immobile boulders and cacti, I could not hide my presence much longer. At least I wore flat shoes.

I stumbled into a steep-sided, dry ditch where I managed to hollow out a spot just above the dry streambed, squeeze in and gather the damn skirt around me to hide it from sight. I made myself breathe slowly in spite of the creepers, night traipsers, and slitherers hiding down there with me, praying none of them bit or stung me.

I was tempted to shut my eyes, believe again that if I couldn't see the monster he couldn't see me. But this monster was real, unlike the one my big sister said would get me if I got out of bed one more time. *How did I get myself into this fix?* My brain whirled ifs: *if* I had paid attention to my instincts instead of giving Gunnar Hunter my phone number. *If* I Googled his name before meeting him for dinner. *If* I paid attention to the flash of warning when the way he said his name sounded as if he were telling a sly secret.

Damn! Speed dating at my age?

The slit of sky I could see was still dark, but the full moon would set about the same time the sun rose, so dawn was close. My watch glowed four-thirty. I'd been running and hiding for six hours.

The impression of footsteps muffled by sand jerked my brain to a mid-whirl stop. I held my breath and listened. The animal prowling noises stopped. We were all mute, poised for attack or retreat, waiting for the intruder to pass.

His boots scraped a rock above my hiding place. Air whooshed around the pebbles he plunked into the ditch. He must have stood up there, probably just a few feet away, as the stones bounced once, twice, three times, then thudded softly onto the sand.

I hunkered farther into my hole in the dirt bank. *Does he know I'm here? Is he just messing with me?*

"I'm gonna getcha," he said, over and over. His sing-song voice, ominous and gleeful at the same time, made me cringe.

Could he recognize the trail left by my panicky darting about? Could he see the spill of dirt I had dug out? Tears ran down my face. I cry when I'm sad, pissed off, frustrated. Sometimes, I don't know why I cry. But these were tears of absolute terror. I clamped my hand over my mouth to muffle my blubbering.

I don't know how long he stayed up there, but eventually the skittering and insect-songs started again. My legs were cramped, and my back and neck ached fiercely from the scrunched position. I flexed my legs carefully, trying not to make any noise or move any rocks or dirt. My knee popped, sounding like a gunshot. *What if he's still up there and heard that?* I felt frozen in place, but knew how urgently I needed to get away, find water and help.

My sense of urgency was bordering on panic after another half hour. I pushed myself out of the hollow and rolled up onto my hands and knees in one clumsy thrust. I crouched and listened, then peeked over the ditch bank, trying not to expose too much of my head—my silvery hair and pale skin would give me away for sure.

I listened hard again, sniffed the air for his musky aftershave. I didn't smell anything but cool, dusty desert. I looked around carefully. No monster. I gathered up my voluminous skirt and duck-walked down the ditch.

I stood upright when the shelter of the ditch petered out. *What now? Which way?* Panic scrambled my brain again. Forcing myself to focus and breathe, I tried to picture the Arizona map in my mind: the highway was west—I hoped. To get there, I would have to keep the rising sun squarely at my back and my shadow straight in front of me, watch where I stepped and look around for him, all at the same time. *Okay, Hannah. Just do it.*

My soft-soled Mary Janes didn't keep the sharp rocks from bruising and cutting my feet. I stumbled along, using a three-thumbed saguaro on the crest of a high ridge as my landmark to keep myself from walking in circles. I stopped frequently to scan for the monster: I rubbed my eyelids gently to keep the moisture in my eyes moving around. If I had to take out my contacts, distance dead-reckoning would be impossible.

The day burned hotter and hotter. I pulled the back of my skirt up over my head to shade my eyes. I stumbled about every third step. My skin was getting clammy, and my pulse hammered in my ears. Confusion, heatstroke, and even imminent death were distinct possibilities.

When I finally reached the bottom of the ridge, I was too tired to climb it to get my bearings. I sat down on the hot ground to rest. Nothing to see through my swollen, gritty eyes but shimmering mirages and more desert. I touched my blistered face and tried to remember how water tastes. I closed my eyes and put my head on my knees, just for a minute.

A snuffling sound jerked me awake. A coyote pup shied away and stood back, watching me warily.

I laughed, sounding like a hysterical crow to myself.

The pup came closer. I put my hand out. The coyote sniffed it and didn't back away. I was shaking from heat exhaustion and anxiety, but it didn't occur to me to be afraid when the coyote came closer and offered its head to be petted.

The pup jumped up and walked away slowly, turning after a few steps to look back at me.

I knew it was nuts, but I followed. The coyote led me along a distinct trail, staying a few steps ahead of me. Each time I stopped to look around for Gunnar Hunter or any other predator, the pup seemed more and more anxious, running ahead a little, then coming back to me as if to say, "Hurry up! Come on!"

I tried to move faster, but fell again and again, tasting the hot, creosote-scented dust, scraping my already raw skin. Each time I faltered, the pup gently licked my face until I got up and moved again.

We traveled that way until late afternoon. My field of vision narrowed to the ground in front of my feet and the pup's tail or nose, whichever was turned to me. Everything else had receded into a gray blur that throbbed with my headache and the blood pulsing from my wounds.

I tripped, went down hard. The pup whined. I thought it was licking my face again until I felt water trickle softly down my throat.

"There, there, don't drink too fast … that's it … just sip."

The pup yipped anxiously.

The gentle female voice said, "You brought another stray, eh, girl?"

The pup whined softly and nosed my shoulder.

I could only croak, "No…no…not a stray…helped me…"

I woke up naked, lying on a sleeping bag spread in the shade of a stand of riverine palo verde trees. The woman sat on a campstool, watching me, the pup at her feet.

"So what were you doing so far out in the desert, alone, dressed like that?" she asked. "Here, let me help you sit up, and you can try another sip of water. You hungry?"

She lifted me easily to a sitting position and gave me a cup of cool, fresh, pure water. I gulped it but my throat was still so raw I could only squawk a little. I nodded. The pup nuzzled my hand.

"You're badly sunburned, so I put you there to cool off." She pointed at a smooth depression in a red boulder submerged in the shallow creek. "This has been an oasis and healing place for thousands of years. When you've had a little more to drink and some food, I'll help you back into the water to keep you more comfortable. I was afraid you'd go into shock if your body cooled too fast."

I nodded again. I couldn't do anything else. My eyelids slid shut.

I didn't know how long I'd soaked when I finally opened my eyes, but my skin was still red and warm, blisters competing for space with the bruises and swollen, angry scratches and scrapes. I was a mess. "How...how..." I whispered.

"On second thought, don't try to talk too much. Plenty of time for that later. Drink up." She handed me another cup of water. "I'm Abby, and this is Sedona." She scratched the pup's ears. "We'll take care of you."

I held the water in my mouth, so grateful for the taste and feel of it I started to cry, not caring that my tears stung my raw face.

Abby peeled the foil seal off a plastic cup. "Here's some banana pudding," she said. "It shouldn't hurt your throat and the sugar will boost your energy."

I hate bananas, but the memory of that pudding is still absolutely wonderful.

"Okay, back into the creek with you," she said. Before I could think about getting up, she knelt beside me, lifted me into her arms, carried me to the rock, then settled me in the shallow depression. The water felt shockingly cold against my burning skin. "You'll get used to the temperature in a few minutes, so just rest. I'll go find something for you to wear. Don't worry, Sedona will stay with you."

She smiled and signaled to the coyote. The pup stretched out on the bank, paws nearly touching the water, watching intently, not taking her yellow eyes off me as her mistress left.

I tried stretching but my muscles cramped painfully. I was in no shape to run or protect myself if he found me. I needed a plan. I closed my eyes to think.

Soft footsteps popped my eyes open.

Sedona whined, looking around, then wagged her tail.

"You look better," Abby said. "Ready to come out of the water?"

I nodded, tried to get my legs under me, but failed miserably. She stepped into the shallow creek and picked me up again. My brain was working well enough to marvel at her strength. A tall woman, maybe six feet, lean and brown, she carried me easily and set me down gently on the sleeping bag, then handed me a soft T-shirt and pajama pants.

"This is the best I can do for clothes for you right now."

"Thank you," I whispered. "Thank you so much. Why are you here?"

"I love the wild, the quiet. Sedona likes it, too. Glad she found you." Abby had a lovely smile, soft brown eyes, and a lilting accent I didn't recognize. "And you are?"

"Hannah. Hannah Miles." The monster popped into my mind. Alert and wary again, I hastily looked everywhere I could see. "Have you seen anyone else? Umm…a…a man?"

"The one you're running from?"

"Umm, yeah. I met him at a conference," I lied. The heat from my blush scalded my face. "He seemed okay, and we live two states apart, so…"

"So he was safe enough to see if you're ready for a romance," she said.

"Yes." I blushed again.

"But he lied to you."

"Yes." I felt stupid for the zillionth time since last night.

She smiled and shook her head. "An old story, that. Some men…women, too, I suppose…are always ready to exploit anyone they can. Not all of them have the killer instinct, but they always leave wounds."

"He showed up on my doorstep with flowers and candy. It was just corny enough to make me let my guard down."

"Then he said he just wanted to be near you," she said, looking sad.

"Right. We went to galleries, wine tastings, worked our way through six pages of the restaurant guide in a week. The last evening he took me home, kissed me at my front door, said he had to fly back home, but he'd like to see me the next night, if that would be okay. Looking hopeful and shy at the same time."

"Ah. Shrewd enough not to rush you. Patient."

"Yes, and cunning as any skulking hound. Arrogant, too. Likes to taunt his prey." I told her about his "getcha, getcha" sing-song serenade.

Abby looked at me, her face set in an expression I couldn't read. "Is this sleazebag tall, good-looking, sixtyish, graying temples? Fancy cowboy boots?"

"Yes." I peered all around me again, expecting him to pop

from behind a boulder or drop out of a palo verde any second. "Have you seen him?"

"Saw and heard him," Abby said, "but didn't meet him."

My heart nearly stopped. "You...he's...around here?" I was so panicked my voice squeaked.

Abby nodded. "Sedona and I were up on the ridge." She pointed toward the trail Hannah had followed. "Looking for medicinal plants. He was on a hiking trail below us, strutting along, singing that 'getcha' song, waving his arms like a drum major leading his own parade band."

"Umm...when was that? Where did he go—?"

"Early this morning. He was going south. Looked like he only had a day pack, so even if he was looking for you, he was nowhere near the trail you and Sedona took. Who is he, Hannah? Why do you think he wants to hurt you?"

"He...he said his name is Gunnar Hunter, that he's a retired real estate developer, lives on the Texas Gulf Coast. I didn't really meet him at a conference." I blushed again. "Two of my friends and I went to a speed dating thing, just for fun. He seemed like the pick of the lot. I fell for him like a silly teenager."

"Where were you when you ran from him?"

"I don't know. He invited me to a party, supposedly at his friend's ranch. We left the freeway near Green Valley and he drove east on the old highway, then farther east on side roads. We'd been driving for two hours when he said he was lost. I took out my cell—I have a GPS app because I'm hopeless with directions—and he grabbed my phone and threw it out the window. Then he said, 'We're going to do some research for the true crime book I'm writing. You'll star in the hide and seek chapter. You hide, I seek, I find, I have fun, I go home and finish my bestseller and think about the movie rights.'"

"So you ran?" Abby said.

"Duh, but not soon enough. I thought he had to be joking ... not very funny, but surely not serious! Then he opened the trunk of his car, grabbed a gym bag, unzipped it, pulled out a knife and held it up for me to see, smirking the whole time. He said, 'I think hide and seek in the desert will be as much fun as hide and seek in the swamps. Gators hide bodies. Desert animals strip them, so I won't have to dig a grave out here, either.' He took out a coil of rope and started toward me, so I jumped into the car and locked it, but he had the keys. Opened the door and grabbed me—"

"How did you get away from him?" Abby asked.

"I kicked him in the crotch, ran down into an arroyo and hid. I waited until dark to move. Thought I'd be safe then, but the full moon came out, so I hid in a ditch."

"Hmm. You came west and north. He was following a trail that goes south, then east. Maybe he wasn't hunting you," Abby said.

"Or he was going back to where I ran away from him—"

"But he isn't important right now." Abby pulled a bag closer to her, took out a jar and began to dab a soothing, lavender-scented gel on my scratches and burns. "Getting you to a hospital is. I called my friend, Molly Riordan—she's a Cochise County deputy. She should be here soon. We'll take you to Sierra Vista and arrange for you to get home from there." She took a roll of gauze out of the bag.

"Okay." I watched her wrap my arm. "But why are you out here?"

"I'm training as a shaman because so many of my patients value ancient traditions. Sometimes, I just need to be alone. Working in refugee camps stains my soul. My first shaman mentor brought me here."

"Is Sedona a coyote? I've read that coyotes can't be tamed."

She smiled. "My friend rescued Sedona before her eyes were open. She thinks she's a person."

Moments after Abby finished bandaging me and helping me dress, I heard an engine, then saw the dusty rooster tail the vehicle raised crossing the desert. A white SUV with a gold star insignia and the words COCHISE COUNTY ARIZONA, SHERIFF'S OFFICE on the door rounded the bend and stopped.

A stocky, tanned woman wearing a deputy's uniform climbed down. "Hi, Abby! I got here as soon as I could."

"So this Gunnar Hunter said that he's never had to dig a grave?" Deputy Riordan asked after I explained my stupidity to her. "What kind of car was he driving?"

"A red Mustang, Arizona plates."

"Can you describe the rope and the knife or the bag?"

"It was rough yellowish fiber, not nylon, about as thick as my thumb. The dagger had notches on both edges. The bag was smallish, green canvas, with an REI logo. Sorry, that's all I had time to see."

"You're doing fine," Riordan said. "When the ER docs have checked you out, I'll get your detailed description of the guy and have you look at some photos."

We had lapsed into silence and ridden for some time when the radio crackled and a brusque voice said, "Hey, Riordan. Got something. Can you take a little side trip on your way in?"

"What and where?" the deputy answered.

"Hiker found what looks to be a body. Ready for the GPS coordinates?"

"Just a second." Deputy Riordan turned to me. "You feel up to this, Hannah?"

"Umm…sure, I think so."

"Okay, give me the coordinates," she said into the radio. Abby, who was sitting in the front passenger seat, entered them into the GPS system and the target location appeared on the navigation screen.

Twenty minutes later, Riordan parked the SUV on a flat spot near the edge of a deep, rocky canyon. A tall man waved in our direction. She asked me, "Is that the man who was after you?"

"No."

"You two wait here, please." She climbed out of the SUV.

Abby and I watched her approach the man, then rolled down our windows to listen.

"Sure glad to see you, Deputy," the man said. "I saw buzzards circling, so I stopped. Looks like a body down there. I was gonna check, then I figured I might spoil evidence or something."

"You did the right thing, sir. I'm going to have a look. I've got climbing equipment in my vehicle." She left him and strode over to us. "Abby," the deputy whispered, "watch this guy.

Something's not right here."

Molly got her gear out of the back. She called dispatch and spoke loudly and distinctly, her eyes on the man: "Deputy Riordan here. I need backup with climbing gear and an ambulance to these coordinates. Notify the coroner, too."

As soon as Molly eased herself over the edge, the man strolled over to the SUV and introduced himself as Billy Hargis. He spoke casually, but kept his eyes moving between Molly's secured line, the road, and us. After a bit of small talk, he said, "Uh, I think I'll go see how the deputy's doing," and sauntered over to the edge and looked down.

Abby whispered, "I don't see any buzzards, do you?"

"No, but maybe Billy scared them away," I said.

"Out here, there are mostly turkey vultures, not buzzards. Vultures are aggressive and one lone human wouldn't keep them from circling and diving to get at carrion." Abby kept her eyes on Billy. He didn't fidget, but seemed extra alert, as if poised to run.

Twenty minutes later, deputy Riordan scrambled back over the edge and took off her climbing gear. "The gentleman is dead," she said. "Now will be a good time for you to tell me about finding him." She took a notebook and pen out of her pocket and looked at Billy expectantly.

"Uh, well...I saw buzzards circling and I...uh...looked down there and called nine-one-one," he said. "Did he have ID on him? What killed him?"

"ID, yes. Cause of death is up to the coroner," the deputy said. "I'd like to see your ID and get your contact information."

Billy patted his pockets sheepishly. "I'm sorry, ma'am, but I leave my wallet in my truck when I hike."

"That's fine. Just give me the particulars."

"I live at one-twenty-two Ocotillo Road—"

"I'll need for you to wait here with us, sir," she said.

"Why? I can come to the sheriff's office—"

The radio crackled. Riordan returned to the SUV. "Abby," she whispered, "stay with Hannah if he runs, okay?"

"How did you know he was lying?" Abby said.

"Climbing chalk on his pockets," Molly said. "And the real

Billy Hargis is seventy-five, lives on Black Creek Road and reported his truck stolen two days ago."

"So who's the dead man?" I asked.

"His ID says 'Gunnar Hunter.'"

"Umm…what killed him?" I whispered.

"Too much animal damage to be sure, but I think I saw a snake bite," she said, "and knife wounds. The coroner will have to determine exact cause of death."

"So, who's the guy who said he's Billy?" I asked.

"His name is Rob Seeker. A bounty hunter, but he went completely off the rails about five years ago. We've had complaints that he's assaulted hikers who happened onto one of his campsites."

"So…this bounty hunter…Rob…stalked and murdered Gunnar Hunter before Hunter could do the same thing to me?"

"The evidence looks that way," Molly said.

"Why would he call nine-one-one and wait at the scene of his crime?"

"Your Gunnar Hunter was really James Elliott Clay. Murdered his wife in Florida, suspected in the disappearance of his girlfriend in Louisiana. He's an infamous fugitive with a big bounty. Maybe Rob Seeker thought he'd collect the reward."

"But why did Seeker say he's Billy Hargis?" Abby said.

"No idea, unless he thought we'd check the plates on the truck for some reason," Molly said.

If James Elliot Clay really was writing about his own crimes, "Gunnar Hunter" would have been a fitting *nom de plume.*

I haven't done any more speed dating, and I'm practicing obeying my instincts and paying much closer attention to those vague warning flashes when a man's smile hints at secrets.

Next weekend I'm meeting Molly and Abby and Sedona in Sierra Vista, and we're going to the oasis to camp and hike.

This time, I'm taking a compass.

† † †

KATE JOY STEELE is a retired business consultant writing fiction after a career of business-related writing, editing, and teaching. She lives on Whidbey Island, Washington, with her husband, Paul Palugyay.

Praise For Sisters in Crime Desert Sleuths Chapter 2011 Anthology

SOWEST SO WILD

Suspense Magazine's Best Anthology of 2011 Finalist

"Arizona proves hot, dry, and deadly in this anthology. There's something for everyone to enjoy here, in tales of murder ranging from the humorous to the macabre."
~**MEG GARDINER**, Edgar Award winning author of
The Nightmare Thief

"An old time sheriff only had six bullets loaded into his gun to take care of the bad guys—with *SoWest So Wild*, twenty different authors take aim and each one hits the bulls-eye. You'll never look at the Wild West the same way again."
~**TONI L.P. KELNER**, co-editor of the *New York Times* bestselling anthology *Death's Excellent Vacation*

"The Southwest never was a peaceful place, and twenty authors manage to put their fingers on a pulse that still throbs with heat and passion. Don't think that unusual characters and violence in the Wild West ever died. The Desert Sleuths Chapter Sisters in Crime prove otherwise in this collection filled with criminal mischief, *SoWest So Wild*."
~**LESA HOLSTINE**, Lesa's Book Critiques

"An eclectic collection of stories dealing with murder and mayhem, from the intriguing and suspenseful to the shocking. This anthology contains tales that will surely whet short story readers' appetites."
~**R.L. COFFIELD**, Moonlight Mesa Associates, Inc. – Award-Winning western book publisher

To order *SoWest So Wild*, please visit the Sisters in Crime Desert Sleuths Chapter website: www.DesertSleuths.com.

Praise For Sisters in Crime Desert Sleuths Chapter Previous Anthologies

How NOT to Survive a Vacation

"Smart, fresh and fast-paced with twist endings worthy of master storytellers."
    ~SOPHIE LITTLEFIELD, author of *A Bad Day for Sorry*

"Like a macabre travel brochure, these chilling mystery stories take you on a grisly tour of choice vacation spots, except instead of Mai Tais, they serve murder."
    ~REBECCA CANTRELL, award-winning author of
    A Night of Long Knives

"A fabulous anthology of murder and mayhem from ship to shore and mountain to desert. The collection will leave you double checking with your travel agent…and begging for more!"
    ~KELLI STANLEY, award-winning author of
    City of Dragons

How NOT to Survive the Holidays

"Stuff your stocking with this string of holiday sparkles, ranging from the chilling to the decidedly wacky."
    ~RHYS BOWEN, Agatha and Anthony award-winning author of the *Molly Murphy* and *Royal Spyness* mysteries.

"The holidays will never be the same! This collection of twisted, talented authors make sure of that."
    ~SHEILA LOWE author of the *Forensic Handwriting* mysteries

"There's no place like home for the holidays. That is, unless somebody in the family wants to kill you…It seems there's a lot of skullduggery going on during the Christmas season."
    ~DONIS CASEY, author of the award-winning *Alafair Tucker* mysteries